MAXIMUM RIDE
FOREVER

Also by James Patterson

MAXIMUM RIDE SERIES

The Angel Experiment
School's Out Forever
Saving the World and Other Extreme Sports
The Final Warning
Max
Fang
Angel
Nevermore

A list of more titles by James Patterson is
printed at the back of this book

MAXIMUM RIDE
FOREVER

JAMES PATTERSON

For Captain Jack, who got this enterprise flying

1 3 5 7 9 10 8 6 4 2

Young Arrow
20 Vauxhall Bridge Road
London SW1V 2SA

Young Arrow is part of the Penguin Random House group of companies
whose addresses can be found at global.penguinrandomhouse.com.

Penguin
Random House
UK

First published by Young Arrow in 2015

www.randomhouse.co.uk

A CIP catalogue record for this book is
available from the British Library.

Hardback ISBN 9780099567479
Trade paperback ISBN 9780099567486

Printed and bound by Clays Ltd, St Ives Plc

Penguin Random House is committed to a sustainable
future for our business, our readers and our planet.
This book is made from Forest Stewardship Council®
certified paper

To the Reader

THE IDEA FOR the Maximum Ride series comes from earlier books of mine called *When the Wind Blows* and *The Lake House*, which also feature a character named Max who escapes from a quite despicable School. Most of the similarities end there. Max and the other kids in the Maximum Ride books are not the same Max and kids featured in those two books. Nor do Frannie and Kit play any part in the series. I hope you enjoy the ride anyway.

Prologue

One

Hey, you!

This is important. What you're holding in your hands is the only written record of the new history of the world. Don't freak out—I know I'm making it sound like a textbook, and believe me, I hated school more than anyone. But this much I can promise: It's not like any textbook you've read before. See, this chunk of pages tells the story of the apocalypse and all that came after—some pretty heavy stuff, for sure, and I don't blame you for being nervous. We all know that history tends to repeat itself, though, so for your sake and the sake of the future, I hope you'll read it . . . when you're ready.

Max

Two

I KNOW WHY you're here, and I know what you want.

You want to know what *really* happened.

You want the truth.

I get it. I've wanted the same thing my whole life.

But now I'm convinced the only real truth is the one you find out for yourself. *Not* what some grown-up or CNN tells you. The problem is, the truth isn't always kittens and rainbows. It can be harsh. It can be extremely hard to believe. In fact, the truth can be the very last thing you *want* to believe.

But if you're like me, you'd rather put on your big-girl pants than dwell on things—and truths—beyond your control.

Like the fact that I was a test-tube baby whose DNA was grafted with a bird's, so rather than your typical childhood filled with cartoons and tricycles, I spent my most adorable years in a dog crate, poked and prodded by men in white coats.

Cowardly jerks.

And how my flock and I escaped and spent our entire lives after that being hunted down by Erasers—human-wolf mutants with truly eye-watering dogbreath.

While rolling with the punches (and bites and kicks), I had a mountain of personal crap to deal with, too. I was betrayed by my own father, who also turned my half brother, Ari, into an Eraser to kill me. Family fun!

Then Fang left us—left *me*, heartbroken—to start a new flock with my freaking *clone*. I won't lie—that one stung.

And I can't forget the crazies. . . . There are a lot of bad people out there who want to do a *lot* of bad things. From the suicidal Doomsday cult to the population-cleansing nutcases, we've fought them all.

And the icing on the cake? Something happened—a meteor? A nuclear bomb? We might never know—that caused all hell to break loose . . . and destroyed the world.

Yep.

But you want to know what *really* happened after the apocalypse. Fair enough. The story belongs to all of us, especially *you*. Our history is your future.

Disclaimer: This is a story of perseverance and hope, but it's also one of grief. I've seen things—terrible things—that no one should even know exist. I've witnessed the world's darkest days and humanity's ugliest moments. I've watched cities collapse, friends die. This is the hardest story I've ever had to tell.

Still think you can handle it?

Let's go back, then. Our journey starts on an island somewhere in the South Pacific, not long after the sky first caught fire. You'll want to make sure your seat is in a locked, upright position, and prepare for some turbulence.

After all, we're talking about the end of the world.

Book One
APOCALYPSE

1

BREATHE, MAX. FORCE the air in and out.

The air was heavy, and the rotten-egg stench burned the inside of my nose, but I focused on inhaling and exhaling as I ran. The earth shook violently and my feet slid over loose rocks as I raced down the slope. Red-hot coals pelted the earth around us as volcanic ash set our hair on fire and ate tiny, stinging holes in our clothes.

"Our backpacks!" I yelled, stumbling to a stop. I couldn't believe I'd forgotten them. "They're all we have left. Tools, knives—the crossbow!"

"We left them in the field!" Nudge cried.

I shaded my eyes and looked up—the air was thick with spewing magma, ash, and glowing rock belched up from deep beneath the earth. "I'm going for them," I decided. As the leader of the flock, responsible for everyone's survival, I didn't have much choice. "You guys get to that rock outcropping by the southern beach. It's the only protection we'll find."

"You have five minutes, tops," warned Gazzy, our nine-year-old explosives expert. "This whole part of the island's gonna blow."

"Right," I said, but I was already sprinting up the hill through the hailstorm of fiery pebbles. I might have flown faster, but I couldn't risk singeing my flight feathers right now. I grabbed the backpacks and raced back.

The ground shuddered again—a churning quake this time that felt like it was shifting my organs around. I lost my balance and catapulted forward, the provisions we needed torn from my arms as I face-planted hard.

Sprawled in the dirt, I focused through the dizziness just in time to see a smoking boulder the size of a refrigerator bouncing toward my head. I tucked my chin and rolled, saying a silent prayer.

Then I heard the sound—*BOOM!* It was like a rocket had been set off inside my brain. I may have blacked out, I don't know.

Shaking my head, I opened my eyes and gasped. The boulder had obliterated the space where I had just been lying, but beyond that, the top of the volcano was now shooting off a thousand-foot column of liquid fire and smoke.

I gaped, mesmerized, as bright orange lava oozed over the cliff we'd called home for the last three months.

Then the sky started to rain blazing rocks, *big* ones, and I snapped back to attention.

Craaaaap.

I leaped to my feet, frantically grabbing backpacks and scooping up the scattered tools that were all we had left. The ground around me was being covered with hot ash, and as I reached for Gazzy's pack, it went up in flames. I snatched my burned hand back, swearing as the nerves convulsed with pain.

"Max, hurry!" My ears were ringing, but Angel's voice was clear inside my head. Ordinarily, I would be annoyed at being bossed around by a mind-reading seven-year-old, but the terror behind her words made my throat dry up.

I looked back at the volcano. Considering the size of the boulders it was hurling out of its crater, conditions could be even deadlier farther down the mountain.

What was I *thinking*, leaving my family? Forget the tools—I had to run!

My mouth filled with the taste of deadly sulfurous gas, and as it tore at my lungs I wheezed, choking on my own phlegm while glowing bombs fell all around me. I stumbled through the ash and rubble, tripping again and again, but I kept going.

I had to get back to my flock.

Another hundred yards and I would be at the meeting place. Pumping my legs, I took the turn onto the rock outcropping at top speed...

And sailed toward a river of boiling lava.

2

WHOAAA—

I windmilled my arms as momentum propelled me out into midair, with nothing but red-hot death below. As gravity took hold and I felt myself starting to drop, my avian survival instinct kicked in automatically. A pair of huge speckled wings snapped out from my back and caught the air, swooping me aloft on a hot, acrid updraft. I quickly wheeled back to the outcropping and closed my highly flammable wings.

"Wow!" Total's voice reached me over the sounds of the eruption, and then I saw his small, black Scottie-like head peer out from a shallow cave beneath the boulders. He came and stood next to me, his paws stepping gingerly on the hot ground. His small black wings were tucked neatly along his back. Did I mention that everyone in my mutant flock had wings? Yup, even our talking dog.

"I thought you were a goner," he said, nose wrinkling from the horrible smell.

"Your faith in me is touching, Total." I tried to steady my voice, but it sounded hollow and shaky.

Gazzy came out and nodded up at the volcano with seriously misplaced admiration. "She's a feisty one. This is just the start of it." With his love of fire and explosions, this eruption was the best thing that had ever happened to him.

"The lava's, what? Fifty feet wide?" I backed up as the edge of the outcropping began to get swallowed up by the tar-like river—a thick black goo with brilliant flashes of orange where molten stone glowed with heat. "We'll fly across, find a safer place on the northern side."

Gazzy nodded. "Right now we can. But see that molten mudslide rolling toward us? It's about two thousand degrees Fahrenheit. If we don't get to high ground fast, we're cooked."

It already felt like my clothes were melting onto my body—clearly Gazzy knew what he was talking about.

"Let's move!" I yelled.

Fang was already grabbing up the backpacks. Always calm and always competent, he was the steady rock to my whirling tornado. I rushed to join him, trying not to wince as my burned hand throbbed. We didn't have much, but what we had we couldn't replace: Besides our few weapons, we had some clothing stripped from the dead, cans of food that had washed up on shore, medicinal herbs plucked from now-extinct trees.

"Okay," I panted. "Have we got everything?"

Nudge shook her head, her lovely face smudged with soot. "But if the lava reaches the lake..."

Then the water supply we've stored there will be obliterated.

"I'll go back for the jugs," Dylan and I said at the same time.

"The sulfur levels just tripled!" Iggy shouted. "Smells like acid rain!"

"I'll go," Dylan repeated firmly.

Fang was my true love, but Dylan had literally been *created* to be a perfect partner for me: It would be against his nature not to protect me if he could. It was both endearing and maddening, because, *hello?* I'm not so much a damsel in distress as I am an ass-kicking mutant bird kid.

Now Dylan touched my burned hand so tenderly that for a second I forgot about being tough and was just grateful for his help during the chaos. He nodded at the other kids. "They need you here. Just work on getting everyone to the northern beaches, and I'll be back in a minute."

I frowned. "Yeah. But be careful, okay?"

"You're not actually worried about me, are you, Max?" His turquoise eyes twinkled playfully.

"No," I said, making an *ew* face at him.

He laughed. "I'll catch up."

I turned, smiling and shaking my head, and of course there was Fang, standing behind me silent as a shadow. He cocked an eyebrow and I flushed. I opened my mouth to say something, but he was already reaching past me for the backpack Dylan had left.

"Hover chain?" Fang asked brusquely. He knew me better than anyone, so he knew when to leave things alone. When I nodded, he unfurled his huge black wings, then leaned down and picked up Akila. A big, beautiful malamute, she was the only non-mutant among us—and the love of Total's life. Trying not to breathe the poisonous air, Fang leaped up and took off across the steaming river of molten rock.

"Okay, Iggy," I ordered. "You're up next! Nudge, get ready. Total, wings out. Gazzy and Angel, I'll be right behind you. Let's go, go, go!"

When I was sure my flock was airborne, I shook out my wings and followed, pushing down hard with each stroke as I struggled through the swirling ash. Burning and smoking debris pelted me from above, and waves of lava roiled below. The air was so toxic I could actually feel my lungs shriveling.

It was a short, hard flight. There was a fierce swirling wind from above that pushed us down almost as hard as we pushed up against it. The lava below us burned a deep red-orange, and as it took in more oxygen, it crackled loudly and started to spit. It took all my strength to stay aloft as my flight feathers curled up in embers. I blinked away tears, trying to spot my flock through the sizzling smoke and steam. The skin on my ankles started to blister—I was literally being slow-roasted, and I prayed that the others had made it across.

You are in a cool place. You are in Alaska. It's freezing. Cool air in your lungs... I saw Fang emerge from the steam, a dark figure carrying a large dog. Everyone else was across now, but I veered back over the river of lava to do one final sweep, make sure we had everything....

My neck snapped sideways as a red-hot rock smacked into my head, and before I knew it I was careening down again toward the smoking, burping mouth of hell. I managed a strangled scream and then felt my whole body jerk as a hand yanked me upward.

"Gotcha." Fang smirked at me with that crooked smile of his and held me in his arms. "What do you say we get outta here?" Even with the chaos swirling around us, my heart skipped a beat at that smile.

Our feet sank into the far bank *just* before the mudslide surged into the river. It sent lava shooting up hundreds of feet like a fizzy explosion of orange soda, but we were already out of its reach. And even though my feathers were smoking and my eyebrows were singed and I was gagging on ash, I was grinning as I ran.

We made it. We've all—

"Wait." I skidded to a stop and turned around.

"What is it?" Fang asked, still tugging at my hand.

The hot air pressed in and sweat dripped down my face, but cold horror gripped my stomach like a fist.

"Where's Dylan?"

3

HOURS LATER, THE swirling wind had turned into a pouring rainstorm. I squinted into the rain and billowing steam, scanning the horizon, searching for the silhouette of a kid with a fifteen-foot wingspan.

I began pacing back and forth across the rocky ledge on the northern side of the island, which was our go-to meeting place. All I saw was the volcano in the distance, still belching its plume of black smoke into the sky.

Just three months ago, this island had been a tropical paradise, a safe haven for dozens of mutant kids like us. That was before some kind of huge meteor had crashed into Earth and killed most everyone on it, as far as we knew. Then the resulting tsunamis arrived to flood our paradise, including the underground caves where the dwellings were.

Where my mom and half sister were.

We'd tried to leave, but the meteor's impact had devastated everything within immediate flying distance. The neighboring islands? As black and crispy as toasted marshmallows. And part of me couldn't just leave without some hope that my mom and Ella had somehow survived the floods. But now, with this erupting volcano as a strong motivator, we had to go whether I wanted to or not.

Dylan's coming. He's on his way. He's fine.

I was pretty beat up, with serious burns on my arms and legs, singed feathers, and a lump the size of a goose egg growing out of my temple. I clenched my teeth and tried to focus on the pain, but even that didn't distract me.

"Max, listen to me. You have to get in here," Nudge pleaded from the mouth of a cave, where Fang was building a barricade. "It's like a hurricane out there. You'll get blown off the cliff!"

Unlike the now-toppled place where we'd made our home before the eruption, our new perch was high and safe from mudslides and lava. But from gale-force winds and acid rain? Not so much.

I'd already lost my footing more than once, but I shook my head. "Everything looks different from before. He probably just got turned around."

Nudge's curls got soaked immediately and stuck to her tan cheeks as she stepped out to survey the landscape. She frowned. "He would've found shelter by now, though. Dylan knows the rules."

The members of my flock had survived because we looked out for the group first. If you went off on your own, you took your chances—there was no room for risk.

But this was different. Dylan would never, ever run away from me. That I knew.

"Come inside the cave," Nudge urged, bending down to put her chin on my shoulder. We're all tall and thin for our ages, but this past year twelve-year-old Nudge had shot past me and was now almost six feet tall—as tall as Fang. "We'll crack one of the cans for dinner and—"

"Dylan!" I yelled suddenly, thinking I spotted movement on the horizon.

But it was just the charred trunk of a tree blowing around, and the only answer I got was the howl of the wind.

Nudge sighed, patted my back, and ducked back into the cave.

Gritty pellets of water whipped against my face. Who was I kidding? No one could fly in this weather. Well, almost no one.

Maybe I could just—

"No, you couldn't. You're not going anywhere," a voice said from behind me.

I let out a breath. "Angel, just because you *can* read minds doesn't mean you have *permission* to root around inside my head."

Angel crossed her arms and studied me with a stern look, or at least as stern as a golden-haired, blue-eyed seven-year-old *can* look. We'd pretty much resolved our differences since she tried to overthrow me as leader of the flock, but she still had her moments. Right now, dirty-faced, wild-haired, and firm-chinned, the flock's youngest member looked like a short, blonde dictator.

I narrowed my eyes. *And who's going to stop me? You know we need to find Dylan. We don't abandon our own.*

"Fang!" Angel shouted in response, her eyes never leaving mine.

Well. She's not the only one with a firm chin around here. Without hesitation I turned on my heel and jumped off the edge. But before I could even unfurl my wings, I saw a flash of black out of the corner of my eye, and felt the breath knocked out of me as Fang's body slammed into mine.

Together, we crashed back to the rocky ground, tumbling dangerously close to the edge. I kicked Fang's shin, and pebbles skittered over the cliff. Fang wrapped his arms around mine, but I *do not react well* to being pinned. Bucking and writhing, I desperately tried to throw him off. Suddenly all that mattered was breaking free to go after Dylan.

"Max, calm down!" Fang snapped, and I pulled a fist free and punched him hard. "Whoa! What's wrong with you?"

By now the others had come out to see what the commotion was.

"We. Need. To. Find. Dylan," I ground out through clenched teeth. "Get off me!"

Cautiously Fang let me go, then jumped back out of my kicking range. He knows me so well.

"Max, we can't go right now. It's a toxic stew out there," the Gasman explained. He should know. He'd earned his name when he was little, thanks to the toxic stew of odors he always produced. "I'm talking melt-your-face-off."

"I can get through it. *Dylan's* out there," I spat. "Doesn't anyone care about him?"

Gazzy chewed his lip and glanced away, and Nudge looked concerned. Of course they cared. Mr. Perfect had caused some strife in our flock at first, but he was one of us now, and even Fang looked grim as the reality of the situation set in.

"He's not stupid," Fang said. "He's probably found high ground until the storm passes and the lava hardens. If he's not back in the morning, we'll go look."

"I have to find him *now*!" It came out as a hysterical plea, which was such a shock that I stopped struggling. I'm not usually a sniveling weenie, but this was one of the most powerful calls to action I'd ever felt: I had to find Dylan.

Not we. *I.*

Fang blinked and sat back on his heels, looking at me strangely. "Tomorrow," he repeated, and stood to go back to his barricade.

Slowly, acceptance replaced my unreasonable urge. Finally I nodded and tried to swallow my fear. As I stood up, sopping wet and filthy with ash, I asked myself a question—the question I had seen mirrored in Fang's dark, brooding eyes:

Would I have reacted the same way for him, or for any of my flock?

Or does Dylan make me feel . . . something more?

4

WE SET OUT the next morning toward the lake where Dylan had gone for water. By then, the heat was unbeliev- able. It seeped up through the uneven mounds of already- hardening lava under our feet, and the ash cloud above us held it in like a blanket. Of course, heat rises, so flying was out of the question. The least-boiling place was on the ground. We were being slow-cooked like bird-kid stew, and I was the bitter onion, so mad at Dylan I could spit.

Most of us were doing okay regulating our body temperature—mutant genes, et cetera, et cetera—but poor Akila was looking a little rough. Her tongue hung out of the side of her mouth, but there was none of her signature drool, and she was panting super loud.

"Are you all right, my darling?" Total asked, trotting

alongside her. Akila whined, and he jumped to lick her face a few times. That was just about the most real, doglike thing I'd ever seen Total do, and I'll be honest, it kind of freaked me out.

"Once Dylan stops being an *idiot* and shows up with the water jugs, everything will be *fine*," I said loudly. Despite our inborn sense of direction, I had no idea where we were—all landmarks were gone. Even the forest of tree stumps had disappeared under the rivers of gray deposits.

Finally we stumbled on the lake, but it wasn't the blue thermal pool we remembered. A thick gray film covered the surface, broken only by the hundreds or thousands of silvery dead fish bobbing through it. The cloud of black flies hovering over them was even thicker than the ash.

"Well, might as well eat 'em before they rot." Gazzy grabbed a silvery floater, brushed off the ash as best he could, and bit into the side. Then he looked up in surprise, his face as dirty and gray as the water. "Hey! It's cooked!"

One by one we grabbed a cooked fish right out of the still-warm water, brushed off the ash, and ate our fill. One downside of our avian genes was a lightning-fast metabolism that meant we were nearly always hungry.

A little farther on, we saw it: Our precious stockpile of water was untouched, the jugs covered with ash but intact. We weren't going to die of thirst—at least not yet.

Luck loves Maximum Ride, I thought, cupping my hands so Akila could drink. But then my heart plummeted. If the jugs hadn't been moved, it could only mean one thing:

Dylan hadn't even made it this far.

For hours we stayed close to the shore where the ash was less dense, and took turns flying through the debris to search the cliffs. But the volcano was still pumping black smoke, and the air was getting harder to breathe.

I was bent over after one of these missions, hacking up some blood and wondering if my fast-healing ability included my guts, when I spotted a charred gray knob poking out of the rubble.

"Another cave bone," I sighed. "Looks kind of femur-y." That's how we had known the island's underwater tunnels had collapsed after the apocalyptic meteor: The corpses had started washing up on shore. We were still finding them, almost three months later. I didn't know if any of the bones had belonged to my mother or my half sister. How would I be able to tell?

"Not necessarily." Fang's lips pressed together.

I held it up: Though charred, it was totally a human femur.

Gazzy shook his head. "It's burned. We don't know how old it is. The lava would've done that if it had been a cave corpse or someone more recently, like..."

Yesterday.

I was having trouble swallowing, trouble breathing.

"Let's go back to the cave," Nudge said gently. "We can try another path—"

I whirled around. "Angel, try to tap into Dylan's thoughts. He's got to be somewhere. He's just hiding. Or looking for us. I'm sure he's nearby."

Angel looked away.

"Ig? Can't you smell him or something?"

Iggy leaned heavily against a rock. Flakes of ash fell from his white-blond hair when he shook his head. Though his eyes were unseeing, they were full of pity.

"It's not him," I insisted, kicking ash back over the bones.

"It's like Dylan's cognitive connection just stopped," Angel said finally. "Like with your mom and Ella—"

"We never found their bodies." My jaw tightened. "We don't know what happened to them. Just like we don't know what happened . . . here."

It was getting harder to say his name.

"Everything is dead, Max." Angel's tone was firm. "Everything except us."

"*No.*" I wanted to shake her.

"Guys."

I looked down the beach. At first I couldn't make out what Fang was holding, it was so black and warped. Then he turned it over, and I saw a tiny flash of color.

That spot of bright green—a shade Dylan loved, that none of us had seen since the last of the trees had died—was enough to buckle my knees, and enough to force out the awful, wounded sob that had been building in my chest all day.

Because that burned-to-cinders object Fang cradled in his hand was one of Dylan's size-twelve sneakers.

5

I WATCHED THE shadow of our V moving across the water hundreds of feet below—one dog in a harness, one bird kid short on the right side—and clutched the charred sneaker tighter to my chest as my wings carried me. We couldn't give Dylan a twelve-gun salute, or even a funeral. At least we could give him one last flight.

I banked left, and the flock fell into line behind me, following like an extension of my own body. Ahead of us, sunlight peeked through the eerie rainbow of color that had illuminated the sky since D-day. Below us, the water still churned with the rough waves left over from the tsunami, and a chain of volcanoes rose from the depths of the ocean. Their combined cloud of ash was racing to cover everything, from the pink cliffs of the islands to the white feathers of Angel's wings.

I'd thought flying would make me feel better, like it always had. Wind rustling my hair and muting my thoughts as I soared into the open. No sounds, no obstacles—just the ocean before us and sky all around. Freedom.

Growing up in a cage makes you really appreciate open spaces.

But it had been a while since I'd seen the world this way, and taken stock of all we'd lost. Cities. *People*. The grief felt like a cold, hard knot in the center of me, pulling me down, down into all that gray water.

I felt a hand on my left shoulder and sensed Fang's dark figure just outside my peripheral vision. "You okay?" I nodded and slowed down, realizing we'd been flying for probably half a day.

I'd just wanted to get ahead of the cloud, to lay Dylan to rest under a clear sky. But the ash was moving too fast.

I held the shoe out and the kids hovered in a circle. It was just a shoe, just a piece of half-melted rubber. I took a breath.

You have to do it. Do it for the flock.

"Good-bye, Dylan," I whispered.

"Good-bye," my flock echoed.

Then I opened my fingers. Just like that.

As I watched the sneaker plummet, I remembered Dylan falling from the roof when I'd taught him to fly, barely a year ago. The feeling of his body beside mine that night we took refuge in the desert. The tree house he had made just for me. His last words: "I'll catch up." Wasn't he always trying to catch up with me? I drew a shaky breath.

No.

I dove hard, reaching toward the chunk of blackened rubber. But I was too late, and I watched the waves swallow up all that remained of Dylan.

I flipped and shot back into the sky, angry tears streaming down my face. He was just one more person who had fallen beyond my reach. Like my mom and Ella.

I'd refused to believe it. Even when Angel stopped hearing their thoughts from the underground caves, and even when the months had passed without any sign of life other than us, I couldn't accept that we were all alone.

Their bodies could still be there, somewhere.

"Let's turn back," I shouted over my shoulder.

Fang looked alarmed. "You want to go back to the island?"

"It's our home." My words were thick, threatening another waterfall. *Their* home.

He flew up next to my ear. "Max, it's a wasteland," he said urgently. "And even if we *could* somehow breathe the air, we'll never make it back before nightfall."

"It doesn't—"

"*Them's the rules, Max.*" Angel's voice in my head.

"I felt a pressure change a couple of miles back—I'm pretty sure we passed land to the west," Iggy offered from my other side. Despite his blindness—or because of it— his other senses were sharper than razors. "It might be worth checking out."

We'd passed other islands before, but most were tiny— no shelter, no fresh water. When we reached the one Iggy had felt, it was different. Bigger. We couldn't even see where it ended. Actually, we couldn't see much: Three active volcanoes just off the coast were spewing towers of lava and ash. It made us feel right at home. Not.

It was a big detour to get around them, but once we were closer to the huge island we saw square cliffs in the distance, spaced like jack-o'-lantern teeth. And near the water's edge, a blur of something big and white and triangular.

Like sails billowing in the wind.

"Is that a ship?" My heart sped up.

Are there people here? Alive?

"No, it's..." Nudge hesitated. "I think it's the Sydney Opera House."

I spun around to stare at her. "How do you know what that even looks like?"

"Because I know things," she replied curtly. "More than you think I do." And then, "Haven't you ever seen *Finding Nemo*?"

I cackled. "That is not seriously what you're basing—"

"Actually, I think *I'd* recognize the pinnacle of modern architecture," Total said, "and that is *not*..."

I tuned him out, really studying the shoreline. I saw

the skeletal remains of a bridge in the surrounding harbor, and the white blur started to look more like a building than a boat. But it didn't make sense—Sydney, Australia, was a huge city.

I worked my wings harder, squinting through the ash to see inland. "That would mean those weird cliffs—" Angel nodded, following my thought.

They're skyscrapers.

6

SYDNEY WAS NOT the booming metropolis we had heard of. In fact, it was pretty much uninhabitable.

Huge waves crashed through the city, flowing through angular valleys created by the buildings. Abandoned cars bobbed like bath toys in the current before they were tossed against the salt-crusted, crumbling skyscrapers. The foam sprayed three flights up.

There were no people anywhere. Dead or alive.

"Where do you think everyone went?" Nudge asked.

"Maybe they're all at the opera," I said dryly.

Nudge grinned. "I *told* you I knew what I was talking about."

"Seriously, though, Max. Shelter..."

I looked at Iggy's pale, drawn face, and the circles

24

underneath Angel's eyes. I saw the salt caked on Nudge's parched lips. I heard the sharpness in Gazzy's cough and realized Akila had barely made a sound since we'd left. Despite their jokes, my flock was just about at its breaking point.

I felt the exhaustion settle into my own body. "What are you proposing?"

Fang nodded upward. "I say we break into a penthouse suite."

Nudge squealed, clapping her hands, and it was settled.

If you want to know how seriously bad weather can get, try to fly through it, like, without a plane. The falling volcanic ash mixed with the ocean spray, forming a gritty mud that pelted us. All visible surfaces were coated in a concrete-like sludge, and the buildings looked like enormous crumbling gravestones.

And my little flock? We looked like gargoyles, dragging ourselves up the side of a tall skyscraper. Our wings grew heavier and heavier, coated with what soon felt like stucco, but we moved them up and down, up and down, and clung to the ledges for dear life. At the very top, Nudge's deft fingers brushed against the metal lock and, easy-peasy, we were in.

It was an office, not the luxury apartment I'd been hoping for, but it was dry and surprisingly well preserved. The halls were still lined with glass-framed posters that said things like LET IT FLOW and ATTITUDE MAKES A BIG DIFFERENCE.

I rolled my eyes and knocked that last one off the wall.

Angel curled up under a desk, folding her crusty wings beneath her. Forget mind-reading, that was her true talent: That kid could sleep anywhere.

Me? I was more interested in tracking down some chow. That lava-cooked, acidic fish was the last thing I'd eaten, and my stomach wrenched at the memory. Fang and Gazzy followed me on the search for a kitchenette, ever the eager consumers.

Just as I was shaking the box of aged, crumbled crackers into my mouth and thinking we'd made out pretty well considering, you know, the *apocalypse*, I heard a low, lingering growl.

"Jeez, Gasman." I scrunched up my nose, bracing for the stench to hit, but Gazzy held up his hands: Not me.

Max, get out of there! Angel's voice.

None of us ever question a warning. In a split second I had dropped the cracker box, signaled Gazzy and Fang, and rushed to the door. It was already too late; the doorway was full of snarling creatures trying to get through at the same time—to us.

"What the heck are they?" Gazzy breathed, jumping onto the kitchenette table and assuming a fighting stance. Fang and I both leaped onto the counter, muscles tensed, adrenaline pumping.

"No idea," I murmured. "Not Erasers. Not Flyboys. Not anything I've ever seen."

They were—doglike, but huge, easily three times the

size of a Great Dane, but with a bulldog's heavily muscled build and a mastiff's powerful, snapping jaws. Their long-fanged mouths were already slavering in anticipation of a bird-kid breakfast.

And we were trapped.

7

"YOU'VE GOT TO be freaking kidding me," I snarled.

"Are those hyenas?" Gazzy asked.

"Or just ugly mutant steroid dogs?" Fang said.

The things *were* hideous, their furless pink skin wrinkled and speckled with flaky black spots. Their flat, massive heads were too big for their bodies—which, of course, meant bigger teeth, stronger jaws.

"Are they sort of hyena-ish?" I asked. "Either way, they look rabid, and they're bad news."

With our luck, it made perfect sense that these hell-beasts were the only other creatures that seemed to have survived the apocalypse, and that they somehow were thirty stories up a skyscraper, running loose in the hallways, ready to corner us.

Quickly I took stock. Small, windowless room? Check. Useless weapons, such as plastic cutlery? Check. Villains engineered specifically to destroy us...to be determined.

The first hellhound flattened its ears and bared its teeth, a low growl building in its throat. Even with me standing on the countertop, their heads came up nearly to my waist. And they were vicious. This was Cujo meets Marmaduke meets the Hound of the Baskervilles.

"How many?" Fang asked quickly. I barely heard him over the high-pitched whining, low growling, and eager, hungry barking.

"Um, somewhere between five and...like, twenty," I said as more flat, slick heads pushed in through the doorway.

"What are they waiting for?" Gazzy asked. "Maybe we can intimidate them." With a roar of his own, he snapped open his ten-foot wings, sending bits of crud flying. And this seemed to be what the animals were waiting for. Their attack instinct kicked in and they sprang to life, crashing through the doorway at us, teeth bared. Their growls became a frenzied, barking hysteria that was deafening in the tiny room.

I fended them off okay at first, with roundhouse kicks and evasive pivots. But then a particularly ugly beast with pink eyes reared up on its hind legs and dug its front claws into my chest, and the full weight of a two-hundred-pound animal made me stagger sideways.

I barely heard a sharp hiss from Fang as one of them

sank its incisors deep into his shoulder, but I couldn't spare a glance—I had a huge snapping muzzle inches from my face. Its tongue slobbered over its teeth in desperation, and its pink eyes bulged, crazed with hunger. *They were starving.*

For a second, I felt a wave of pity for them. But just for a second. In a choice between me and something else, I always choose me. So I gripped Pinky's lower jaw with my hands and head-butted the mutt right between the eyes.

It skidded like an ungainly bowling pin into the giants behind it, but they weren't down for long and when they sprang to their feet, there was a new hatred in their eyes.

"Hang on, Max! We're coming!"

I snapped my head around to see Nudge and Akila pushing their way through the entrance. Nudge was wielding a desk chair in one hand and a marble statuette in the other. I'd never seen Akila look so fierce—she was snarling, her teeth bared, and seemed so much more doglike than she had, say, at her wedding. But even though Akila was fairly big, she was dwarfed by these monsters.

"Nudge! No!" I yelled. "Find a safe place!"

I gave one vicious kick to my closest attacker and then grabbed for the sink hose behind me. Slamming the water on full blast, I sprayed all around, aiming for eyes, ears, and open mouths. The barking and howling hit a higher pitch.

On the other side of the kitchen, Gazzy fended the animals off as best he could, which was pretty dang good, but he was covered with bites and scratches and looked like he was starting to tire. One vicious hellhound dove for him, huge jaws open like a vise. I quickly sprayed icy water into its ear, and Akila snarled and dove at the creature, tearing into its throat. Her fur was stained with blood, and more blood dripped from her mouth. She looked pure wolf in that instant, and as they leaped, her cry pierced the air.

I lashed out however I could—the sprayer, karate chops to noses, hard kicks to their ribs, and, yes, plastic forks to the ears—anything to hold them back, but they just kept coming.

"Max!" Nudge cried, and I watched, horrified, as one leaped at the side of her face and clamped on with those long yellow teeth, tearing flesh from bone. Fang stabbed at it with a knife and it yelped and jumped back.

Nudge stumbled into the fridge, her eyes wide and dazed. She held her hand over the left side of her face, but blood ran through her fingers and spilled down her shirt.

Fang gave one animal a brutal punch in the face that made it yelp and fall back. My own arms and legs were pretty torn up, and I started to wonder...if there were actually just too many of them.

So I did what you're never supposed to do in a dogfight: I charged.

And then the room exploded.

Well, part of it. Before I got to Nudge's attacker, chunks of plaster shot toward me as one of the walls blew inward.

For just an instant, there was silence as we all stared at the destroyed wall in surprise.

On the other side of the gaping hole, Iggy stood in the hallway, waving dust away from his face. "Go!" he yelled, choking on smoke.

While the beasts were still stunned, Fang grabbed Akila, and I reached for Gazzy's and Nudge's hands. We. Freaking. *Ran.*

Another floor-shaking blast made a few more of the creatures fall back, but there were plenty of them still on our heels as we ran through the mazelike hallways, searching for a way—any way—out of this. Then straight ahead of us we saw a conference room lined with big glass windows, and there was no time to hesitate.

"Abandon ship!" I shouted.

Just as the monsters rounded the corner behind us, I closed my eyes, tucked my head down, and crashed through a window, feeling the shards explode around me.

8

I CAREENED LIKE a broken helicopter down half of those thirty flights, but finally I snapped my wings open and righted myself. My wings were still heavy and full of crud—cleaning them off would be job one. After quickly counting heads—all accounted for—I looked back to see the bloodthirsty animals snapping their jaws at us. Several unfortunates got pushed out the window by their eager packmates, and we swerved out of the way as they twisted through the air, baying as they plunged downward.

"They're more like *cry*-enas now!" Gazzy joked wearily as we headed toward the outer edges of Sydney.

I was so dizzy with relief, I didn't even feel the bite marks on my hands, or the feathers missing from my wings, but all of us looked like we'd been put in a blender on "chop."

I was especially worried about Akila. I eyed the bundled form that Iggy carried in the harness, and saw red splotches growing on the cloth. Nudge, too, was a bloody mess, and she flew with one hand holding the deeply torn flap of skin in place against her cheek.

When we stopped on a hill overlooking the city, we took stock of our injuries. Nudge seemed to be injured the worst, and I ripped off the sleeve of my ratty shirt. "Does it hurt bad?" I asked, tying the flannel under her chin.

"It's f-fine," she lied, her voice quivering as she bit back the pain.

I thought of all the times she'd spent scrapbooking fashion models and tried to make a joke of it. "What girl doesn't want more defined cheekbones, am I right?" She nodded and forced a weak smile. "Zombie chic," I pressed, and she actually giggled.

"Lame, very lame, Max." Nudge shook her head and adjusted the bandage, but her eyes were smiling.

"Does that count as zombie chic?" Angel pointed.

A silence fell over the flock as we took in the grim scene below us.

So that's where all the people are.

Our hill overlooked a subdivision, and while we couldn't see inside any of the houses from our perch, we definitely saw the circular cul-de-sac drives—or the vague shape of them. I only caught a glimpse of cracked asphalt here and there, because the cul-de-sacs were *littered* with...skeletons.

Humans, animals, young, old. The ash was doing its best to bury them—it had already piled in drifts several feet deep in some places—but you could still see thousands of corpses in the mass grave.

"Jeezum," I whispered.

It was a modern Pompeii: Some of the skeletons were curled in fetal balls, with arm bones circling skulls. Others lay side by side holding hands, or clasping their own hands together. Many looked like they'd been crawling away, their jawbones hinged open in a permanent, silent scream.

I felt the vomit rise in my throat.

"What *happened* to them?" I asked helplessly, looking for something, any type of answer that might make this somehow easier to understand. "The volcanoes couldn't have erupted until pretty recently, or this whole place would be one big ash pit. But something killed these people long enough ago so that only bones are left."

Gazzy started hacking again, and Nudge lifted a worried eyebrow. "Ash inhalation from some other volcano?" she suggested. When we'd flown over the open ocean, we'd seen any number of "new" islands being formed. It was like the earth itself was splitting in two, and volcanoes were erupting everywhere.

Gasman shook his head. "What about aftershocks

from wherever that sky fire thing crashed? We got a lot of quakes on our island, and that's hours from here."

"Or starvation?" Iggy countered. "Maybe they didn't have any rats. . . ."

"Everywhere has rats," Angel scoffed. "Besides, they've got loads of snakes, rabbits, dogs, cats, deer, even kangaroos. Tons of protein for the taking."

"Maybe the climate change drove all the animals nuts and they went on a murderous rampage," Gazzy said.

"Or someone—or something—more powerful did. . . ." That was probably Nudge's conspiracy-theorist mind going into overdrive, but I wasn't ruling anything out.

"Could've been mass suicide," I said seriously.

"Stop it. Just stop it, will you?" Total snarled suddenly, and I looked at him in surprise. "These aren't statistics. They were families. Look at them holding each other, protecting each other. They died with dignity. Just like . . . Akila."

Shocked, I looked at the bundled cloth that Iggy had set down carefully when we'd landed. I hadn't even thought to check on her, though I'd noticed Total licking her face and talking quietly to her. *Oh, Akila. Not you, too.*

"Total, no—"

Gently Total nudged her nose with his, and I hurried over to kneel by the still, beautiful dog. Her eyes were closed and I put my hand on her side, praying that I would feel her ribs rising and falling with breath. I didn't.

"Total, no," I whispered again, unable to think of anything else to say. The rest of the flock crowded around. Nudge and Angel had tears rolling down their cheeks, leaving odd, pale lines where they washed away dirt.

"A couple of the Cryenas got her good," Total said, his words muffled. "And the ash—she breathed too much of it. She sacrificed herself. Miserable excuses for canines…" He coughed a bark. "Pure courage. Pure grace. That was my Akila."

Weeping, Angel wrapped her arms around Total's scruffy neck, and then he couldn't keep his composure any longer.

If you've ever heard a dog cry, you know it's absolutely heartbreaking, a wail that cuts to the rawest emotion and shakes it in its teeth. Total howled for Akila, but also for Dylan, for the thousands of people below, for the whole world. And by the time he was finished, every one of us was all cried out.

9

TOTAL CHOSE AKILA'S burial site at an abandoned cottage way out in the middle of nowhere. We had no clue if the soil was full of nuclear radiation or if the air was breeding deadly viruses by the second, but there was no ash cloud in sight right now, and that was good enough for us.

The cottage was run-down and looked like it hadn't been lived in in years, but we found a shovel and a hoe in a lean-to, and Fang kicked in the front door in the hopes there would be stuff inside we could use.

We started digging in the hard, parched earth. From the corner of my eye I saw Akila's swaddled form, and something in me felt like it had split open.

"You okay?" Fang asked. He lifted my hand and ran his thumb over my dirt-caked fingertips. "I can take over."

His touch felt solid. Reassuring. But I just couldn't handle it right now. I just wanted to feel my body working. I wanted to dig. Or scream.

"I'm good." I stepped back stiffly, and Fang let his hand fall.

When the hole was ready, Fang gently placed Akila in it. Total's soft sobs made my heart feel like it was wrapped in barbed wire, but as leader, I knew I had to step up and say a few words.

I cleared my throat. "Here lies our brave friend Akila," I said. "She deserves better than this unmarked grave, and to tell you the truth, she deserved better than us. I wish we'd taken better care of her. But even so, she was a true and loyal friend to us, a loving wife to Total, and a fierce fighter under the worst circumstances."

I had to clear my throat again. My eyes were burning from the hot, dry dust, and I brushed my sleeve over them. Nudge had started crying and was trying to keep the stinging tears out of her injury, which had barely started to scab over.

"I don't know about heaven or anything," I said gruffly. "Though God knows we've seen a thousand kinds of hell. But I know that somewhere, Akila is running free, the sun on her face and the wind in her fur, and she's got plenty to eat and isn't in pain."

That was when I started crying. I barely got out my last words: "Good-bye, Akila." Then I took a handful of gritty dirt and sprinkled it on her cloth. One by one, we each threw a handful of dirt on her, and then Total backed up to the pile of dirt and kicked furiously, filling in the hole faster than we could have with the shovel.

"Good-bye, my love, my princess, my beautiful bride," he sobbed. "Our love will never die."

We were all quiet for a couple of minutes.

"I wish we had flowers to put here," said Angel, wiping her face and leaving a smeared streak.

"Maybe there's something inside we could use as a marker," Fang said, turning to the house. "Like a statue or vase or something. Be right back." He headed inside.

We stood in awkward silence until a distant, bone-chilling howl made us all jump...and set the Gasman off.

"What else is alive out there? Max?"

"I don't know, okay?" I said, suddenly exhausted and frustrated and so, so sad about Akila. "I don't have all the answers. The world looks like it's been completely obliterated. So whatever possibly survived is going to be... pretty...yucky."

"I'm sure rats and cockroaches made it," Iggy muttered.

"And us," said Angel.

Dropping the shovel, I covered my face with my hands. *Breathe. Just breathe.*

This was it: I had finally hit my breaking point.

"Guys?" Fang called from inside the house, oblivious. "Nudge, c'mere, I need you."

"Akila won't mind about the stupid fake headstone!" Nudge answered miserably.

"I think you'll all want to see this." Fang stuck his arm out the window, and I stared dumbly at the object he was holding.

Somehow, in the middle of this torched wasteland, Fang had found a laptop.

10

WE GAWKED AT Fang like he was holding an extra-large double-cheese stuffed-crust pizza.

"It's a laptop," I said, frowning in disappointment. "So what? With no Internet, all we could do is play solitaire. We need either actual food or a marker for Akila's grave."

"It's a tablet, actually," Fang corrected as we came nearer. "It's smaller, see? And it has a touch screen!"

I rolled my eyes at his mocking tone. "Can we eat it?" I flicked the hard casing. "Can we use it to fend off the psycho hounds?" I gestured toward Nudge's bandaged cheek.

"Let me see that." Nudge took the tablet, turning it over in her hands. "I can sense the owner's fingerprints. He was anxious, searching for something."

"I knew it!" Gazzy punched the air victoriously. "I

knew there were still other people alive out there. It's not just us and the Cryenas!"

Fang's eyes flicked to mine, challenging. Nudge did have the power to feel leftover energy, but since we didn't know how old the energy was, it didn't necessarily mean anything. And when you've had the kind of epically bad luck I've had, you learn not to get your hopes up.

Still, it *could* mean something—a record of what happened, or a connection to the rest of the world...?

"It means answers." Angel sat on the cracked kitchen counter, swinging her legs. The way she said it—with that weird authority she had—made it seem real, and there was a collective inhale, a quickening pulse, a feeling that maybe, possibly, we might just have a shot.

I bit my lip and then asked the only question that really mattered: "Does it even *work*?"

Nudge held down the power button for a few moments and then looked up with a frown, like she'd been betrayed. Nothing.

"There's no electricity to charge it, either," Fang said, flicking a dead light switch.

I sighed. "Like I said, just another useless piece of junk some poor sap left behind." Seeing some plastic flowers on the table, I grabbed them and turned to head out to Akila's grave.

"Max, be careful out there," Gazzy said. "We definitely heard some kind of wild animal."

"What if we could charge it another way?" Iggy called

after me. A high-pitched squeal made me cover my ears, and I turned to see him standing in the doorway to the next room, holding up a dusty radio.

"Where did you get that?"

Ig grinned. "Oh, just another useless piece of junk I found lying around." He fidgeted with the dial, but all we heard was the crackle of static. "Looks like the antenna's shot, but it has a charging panel—solar powered."

"Doesn't that mean you need sun?" I squinted out the window doubtfully. The sky was dark with ash.

"She still might have some juice in her." Iggy shrugged. "Worth a shot."

Somehow, of course, Iggy found some doohickey thing-amabob, fiddled with it, and managed to plug the tablet into the radio. We crowded around, seeing our anxious expressions reflected on the touch screen. The tiny red light on the power cord blinked on, and we waited.

And waited.

"It's not working," I huffed, tapping the screen.

"Patience, Max." Total licked away the smudge from my grimy finger. "Just give it a minute."

But after five minutes, the radio started to hum with the effort, and the light was still red.

"It's not going to be enough." I started to pace.

Then, just as the radio took its last, groaning breath, a welcoming note chirped from the speakers, and our reflections faded as the screen glowed to life.

11

NUDGE'S HANDS HOVERED over the keyboard, and the rest of the flock huddled around her. "What should I look up?"

"Whoa, you actually have Internet?" Iggy asked. "I'm guessing this guy probably hasn't paid his wireless bill in a while."

"Five G." Nudge wiggled her magnetic fingers. "I know it makes no sense, but don't question it."

We tried all the major news sites. Over and over, we saw the same thing: a white screen with stark black type that read CONNECTION TO SERVER FAILED. Then Nudge started trying anything she could think of. We squealed when an actual site popped up, but saw that it was a shopping list for a homemade disaster kit. Gazzy found "antidiarrheal medication" particularly hilarious, while my stomach growled loudly over such delicacies listed as "canned fruit and meats."

But no contact with an actual human. No clues.

Nudge was trying yet another website.

"Hey, this one works!" She grinned as the log-in field popped up.

"Seriously?" I smirked at her. "The world ends and you want to check your Fotogram? Here, I'll give you another 'like.'"

"Shh," Nudge said, swatting at my hand. "I just want to see something."

She typed *#apocalypse* into the search field, and the screen lit up with images—pages and pages of disaster pics taken with cell-phone cameras. Most of the scenes were beyond anything we could've imagined, and believe me, we have dark, twisted imaginations.

"Whoa," I managed to croak.

Because what else could you say about a selfie of a woman clutching a Bible as, behind her, a two-hundred-foot tsunami obliterated Los Angeles?

Or a shot of silver fish flopping on marble staircases while the train tunnels in New York's Grand Central Station flooded with water?

We saw the city of Tokyo decimated by earthquakes. The president of France speaking to the press, wearing a hazmat suit. A row of houses in Spain buried by a freak blizzard.

It was as if the world had been tossed in the air and all the puzzle pieces were jumbled.

A sea of blue-masked faces showed us Hong Kong under quarantine. We saw forests burning, buildings burning, and people burning. Dead birds rained from the sky in so many of the pictures, they had their own hashtag: #crispycritters.

This was the end of the planet, chronicled before us.

There were hundreds of thousands of images, but the events were so varied, the effects so utterly weird, that everything started to blur together.

What happened? didn't begin to cover it. It seemed like *everything* had happened, and more.

"Hey, we should check the blog," Fang said suddenly. "I haven't updated it since we took off in Pierpont's jet, but it had a ton of followers..."

Nudge's fingers were already flying across the touch screen as she nodded. "And maybe some of them are still checking in."

12

AFTER FANG'S LAST post, there were a bunch of comments congratulating us on stopping the Doomsday cult, entries worrying about Angel because she had been missing, and a few standard Max-is-my-idol rants (no biggie). *Then* we got to the good stuff—the Fang-girls.

I started reading those comments aloud, of course. "*'Come to Cali, the water's warm! Love,* **TeeniBikeeni**.*'* " I wiggled my eyebrows at Fang. "**Babette99** says she'll give you a tour of Rome if you want to experience love, Italian style. *Ciao*, Babette!"

Fang blushed a deep red. "Okay, we get it, Max. Ha-ha."

"And look! **Brklynb8b** likes vampires—guess your name gave it away, Snaggletooth. Are those the kind of comments you always got? No wonder you used to spend so much time on this thing," I cackled.

"All of these are from January eighth," Gazzy said. "That would've been it—wouldn't it?—the day before..."

The laugh died in my throat as we all stared at the glass screen, realizing these might be some of the last words written in the history of the world.

Total had been flopped morosely on the floor, but now he said, "They don't really seem to do our culture justice, do they?"

But then again, what words could?

"Those aren't all of them." Fang pointed. "Some of the postings are more recent if you keep scrolling. Check out the time stamps here. **JumpinJoanie** wrote '*stay strong, bird kids. 6 jugs of water with the flock's name on em in traverse city michigan.*' That one's from March."

As Nudge scrolled down, it was clear that Fang's blog had turned into some sort of rogue news site since the Event—whatever it was—had happened. The reports were either posted as Anonymous or under Friends of Fang, and they came from kids across the globe, sharing what had happened to them and trying to make some sense of things.

And *boy*, did things not make much sense.

Are Europeans checking this board? Since it went Dark, can someone verify if all of England incinerated, or just London? Thx for any info.

Just London? I stared in stunned silence at those words and let out a choked breath. I don't know what I'd expected, but I wasn't sure I could handle this.

Anybody heard news W of Denver? Updates apprec.

Fires coming from the west as far as Mississippi R. and flooding still seeping from the east. We're heading north to Ohio.

"From what we got on the island, I expected the flooding." Fang looked up at me, his thick brows knitting together. "But what do you think is causing the fires? Was it from another natural disaster—more meteors or volcanoes—or something man-made? Something planned?"

I shook my head uncertainly. "Look at this one. *'Whole fam got sick. I'm the only 1 left.'* Do you think that's the virus my mom told us about—the bioweapon?"

Nudge clicked the link to see the responses.

Make sure you protect yourself. H-men sweeping populated areas now. Especially west coast usa.

Are H-men Erasers? My mom said they're same as Doomsday cult, but I thought the flock got rid of those guys.

"*What!*" I jumped up and jabbed my finger at the screen, disbelieving. "If I have to deal with feral robotic man-wolves along with the dissolution of civilization, I am seriously going to lose it."

We had almost scrolled all the way down to the bottom, and we weren't any closer to the answers. The last comment was by **PAtunnelratt**, and all it said was *We miss you guys.*

It was from four minutes ago.

"Do you see that?" I jerked forward.

"I told you!" Gazzy's eyes lit up. "Quick, Nudge, write them back!"

FangMod: *@PAtunnelratt, it's the flock. Are you still there?*

"Ugh, this connection is so slow!" Nudge groaned as she hit Refresh over and over again.

Fang shrugged. "Well, the world *has* ended."

Finally, it showed one reply, and we all crowded in closer to read it over Nudge's shoulder.

PAtunnelratt: *Awww yeahhh. FLOCK 4EVER!! I knew if anybody could survive it was U guys.*

FangMod: *Where are you?*

PAtunnelratt: *West Penn. In the mountains. Ppl thought Dad was nutz to buy underground silo. Sometimes impulse buys work out I guess. Ha-ha.*

"Ask him about Erasers," I said.

"And Cryenas!" Gazzy added.

"Oh my God, now it's frozen," Nudge groaned. "This *always* happens."

"Sorry!" Fang said dryly. "Next time I miraculously find a working computer in the middle of freaking nowhere, I'll try to make it speedier."

FangMod: *Tunnelratt, are there any other people in your area?*

It finally went through, but Tunnelratt wasn't responding.

"We have less than three percent battery left," Nudge said nervously. She fired off another message.

FangMod: *Have you heard anything about Erasers?*

PAtunnelratt: *No. but I heard of the Remedy.*

"What is the Remedy?" Nudge typed lightning fast into the white box.

But the screen was already fading to gray as the tablet powered down.

13

SEVEN THOUSAND MILES due north, twenty stories underground, in a New World city known as Himmel...

The young man had left the lab without any instructions. All he had was a folded slip of paper with an address. This address. He made a fist with one gloved hand, the leather squeaking, and reached up to knock.

The door opened silently and a colorless servant with downcast eyes gestured him into a grand ballroom. A plain black office chair was the sole piece of furniture in the enormous room, and the white-haired man in a crisp lab coat was the only person.

"A10103!" the man shouted in greeting, his voice echoing around the chamber.

The young man stood in the doorway, unsure what was expected of him. He clasped his hands in front of him and awaited instruction.

The white-haired man in the white coat stood and circled him for several minutes, measuring his height, his biceps, his feet, shining a light into his eyes to check his pupil reflexes. The servant had silently reappeared and wrote down everything the older man muttered.

A10103 stood tall and straight, and when the older man occasionally met his eyes, A10103 made sure to gaze back evenly.

Finally, seemingly satisfied, the older man looked up at the tall, handsome youth standing before him and reached a delicate hand forward. "I'm your designer. You may hear people here refer to me as the Remedy..." His face split into a garish smile that was all shiny pink gums. "But I'm really just a doctor, trying to mend things in my way. I apologize for the formalities, but we've had...violations of code in the past. You never can be too careful." He sighed. "How are you feeling?"

"Quite well, Doctor. Strong."

"Wonderful! And how do you like my...parlor?" The doctor gestured.

A10103 gazed up at the ceiling hundreds of feet high, decorated with gold leaf and intricately painted frescoes. He nodded appreciatively.

The doctor sank back into his office chair. "It's a bit indulgent, perhaps, but I do so value my space, and for the next few years anyway, I'm afraid I won't be able to spend much time aboveground." He sighed deeply. "See how frail we humans are? Worthless creatures, really, so slow to adapt. I swear, I'd take my own life for the good of evolution, but *someone* needs to get things back on track."

A10103 smiled.

"And speaking of getting things back on track, I have a mission for you, my child. I believe you are familiar with the background of Maximum Ride and her so-called flock?"

A10103 nodded, and the doctor raised his eyebrows expectantly at his pupil.

"Six youths..." A10103 began. "Ranging in ages from seven to fifteen and possessing a number of advantageous gifts. Raised in a lab as the fifty-fourth generation of genetically mutated animal-human hybrids, and only the second hybrid form to be viable. With avian-human genetic material—"

"Human-avian," the doctor corrected. "They're only two percent avian—*mostly* human." He looked disgusted. "Those initial models were full of amateur mistakes. You understand the grave risk this flock poses, don't you?"

A10103 hesitated. "Should they...breed...you mean?" he asked.

"Indeed." The doctor shifted in his chair uncomfortably. "For a time we believed they'd be useful, but now that there are over a thousand mutants working out there in this new world, beautiful children like yourself, all scientifically evolved, we see the truth: Those specimens are a *virus*." The man known as the Remedy slammed his fist into his palm, his face flushing. "And I'm a doctor, first and foremost," he sniffed, calming himself. "I've worked tirelessly all my life to heal our sick earth, and with the advances being made in our species, my dream is at last coming to fruition. But in order for our endeavor to succeed, the virus cannot be permitted to spread."

A10103 nodded intelligently. "They must be eliminated."

"Your genetic makeup was altered for just such a highly specialized role. You are one of a group of carefully selected individuals, my horsemen in this last race to achieve paradise, you might say."

"Like in the Bible."

The doctor looked at him disconcertedly. "Excuse me?"

"The four horsemen of the apocalypse," A10103 explained innocently.

"Yes, exactly." The man cocked his head. "My, you're a regular encyclopedia, aren't you?"

A10103 tapped his temple and smiled. "The new upload."

"I'll have to be careful, or soon my little gadgets will be smarter than I am." His creator's lips curved into a thin, tight smile, and A10103 cast his eyes down.

"As the first Horseman, you'll have the most important role, but there are other Horsemen as well, of course. One must always have backups." He chuckled softly. "As you can imagine, I have a very difficult task, keeping all my little projects in check, and this is one I'd *so* like to cross off my list. Despite their genetic disadvantages, Maximum

Ride and her flock have always been rather... *slippery*, so don't fret if you find it difficult to complete your task."

"It won't be a problem, Doctor," A10103 assured him.

"Yes, well, I know it can be a terrible burden to track them all down, so if you should fail..." His mentor met his gaze and flashed that wide, gummy grin of his. "It would be my pleasure to send the next Horseman along after you."

"It *won't* be a problem."

14

A10103 WALKED QUICKLY through the city, searching for the address of his next appointment. There was no wind ruffling his hair, no cars clogging the road. The air held at a steady temperature, and the streets were spotless. With each step he took, the skyscrapers rose up around him. The sun shone, the sky was blue, and the smooth, sleek towers were gleaming symbols of money and power.

Or so you could convince yourself for a while.

They were all just holographs, he knew—changing images of London, Singapore, or sometimes Vienna, projected on the walls of the winding tunnels. A10103 tried to pinpoint the seams in the images as the light shifted around him, but he had to admit, they were pretty convincing.

If it weren't for the sour taste of canned air on his tongue, he might almost believe he was outside.

A10103 at last located his destination and stepped into a cold metal cone, pressing the number written on the slip the doctor had given him.

"Generating relaxing dreamscape," a soothing female voice informed him from the speakers. Moments later, the doors reopened onto a pillowed paradise.

He entered and sank into the soft luxury of silk and down, and gazed up at the 3-D experience in wonder. Brilliant green leaves unfurled around his head, giant flowers hung low from their stems, and the illusion of sun filtered onto his face. And though he couldn't feel any heat from the sun's rays, he could imagine well enough.

Just like he could imagine really being with the girl leaning over him.

She was beautiful, but doll-like, almost like an anime character brought to life. Her chin came to a delicate point, and her lips pursed in a small, perfect bow. Thick locks of brilliant red hair cascaded over her shoulders and huge, jeweled eyes gazed at him tenderly.

A10103 almost screamed when she touched him.

He'd thought she was a hologram, along with the rest of the space. But no, she was real—a real girl tracing her soft fingertips along his jaw. He doubted she was completely human, but she was definitely real.

"What's your name?" he asked her, sitting up. He wasn't really familiar with these types of situations, but that seemed like something you should ask.

She smiled. "What do you wish my name to be?"

He smiled uncertainly, unsure whether she was trying to please him or she really hadn't been given a name, like him. "A10103" was branded on him, but he needed something more personal, at least for himself.

"I'm Horseman," he offered. That would do for the time being—remind him he was a man with a mission, and a rather dark one at that.

She lay next to him on the pillow and gazed at him through long, curling lashes. "I love you, Horseman," she sighed in a voice so sweet it was cloying.

"What?" Horseman laughed uncomfortably and tried to sit up on the impossibly fluffy pillows. "You seem nice and everything, but we just met."

"How can that matter?" She threaded her hands through his. "We are the children of the future. Created for one another. I adore you. You adore me, don't you?" She cocked her head like some exotic bird, studying him in puzzlement.

He understood then. This living doll was a gift from the Remedy, a bonus for his services. She was someone who would love him without question, which was all he'd really ever wanted.

So he'd thought.

Horseman felt an overwhelming empathy for her then, a sadness at the uselessness of her existence, and a deep, gnawing guilt. Because this *girl*, or whatever she was, had been created just for him. Yet he knew beyond certainty that he would never love her back.

And right now, she was compromising his mission.

"I have to go." Horseman sprang out of the pillows and stood up, backing away from her. "I'm sorry. If I make it back from my job, I swear I'll try to fix this."

Her poised, painted face frowned as the metal door opened and the projection faded back into the freight elevator it had been.

"Come back, my love. I can help you find what you need. Just come back..."

15

HORSEMAN STUMBLED ALONG the streets, desperate to get through the winding labyrinth of tunnels, eager to start his mission. He dragged his hand against the tunnel wall and watched the colors project onto his clothing. The projections seemed less charming when you'd seen what was behind the mirage, and the canned air was starting to make him gag.

He knew too much—he understood that. Felt too much. Or more than he was meant to, at least. There was some glitch in him, like with the flock, and that was dangerous. He worried it was starting to become a liability.

The guards posted at every checkpoint resembled heavily armored tanks shaped like men, and their eyes followed him from behind their goggled masks. Horseman knew his movements looked erratic, and he tried to slow his pace, to look professional.

Not that he felt any fear.

Inside the smooth leather of his gloves, he stretched his fingers—his only weapon. Because the Remedy trusted him to get the job done. Not like these goons with their heavy artillery. He had been *crafted* to be superior, after all.

So what was he waiting for?

He ran past the stern-faced guards, but before they could even yell "*Ostanovis!*" Horseman snapped open his wings—giant, powerful things that he controlled as dexterously as his fingers—shot up into the fake skyscrapers, and burst through the ceiling vent.

By the time he heard the rapid *powpowpow* of their AK-47s, Horseman was soaring over land that lacked the rubble of destroyed civilization but was still tainted by layers of the ever-present ash and covered by a dense, acrid blanket of toxic air. His embedded GPS sensors told him he was in a remote part of Russia.

There was nothing on earth like flying. Horseman reveled in the bite of the cold air in his lungs—even if it happened to be sulfurous—and loved zipping fast enough to make his eyes water—even if the ash caused a stinging pain. You couldn't do this in the tunnels, that was for sure.

He wondered what other things had been programmed in the later generations. He had more wing power, sure, better vision. He had been made stronger, bigger, and his tracking skills rivaled those of any bird of prey.

But was his smile his own? Was his joy? Did everyone feel this...utter *elation* when they were in the air? Did the flock? They did, he was sure.

One more thing he was fairly sure about: He hadn't been programmed to ask these kinds of questions, which was why he'd do well to keep his mouth shut.

In fact, he'd better study up on what exactly was expected of the first Horseman if he was going to be successful on this mission. The information appeared behind his eyes as if on a screen—images of art and scholarly assessments feeding into his thoughts—and the Horseman couldn't help grinning as he got to the interpretations.

He thought of the brooding doctor, his creator. Had his master understood the multiple meanings when he'd named A10103 his first Horseman? Did he know that the white horse could stand for both righteousness *and* evil?

It was going to be fun finding out.

16

YOU'D THINK DISCOVERING there were other people alive out there would leave us hopeful, revitalized, and closer than ever, right? Well, then you wouldn't be taking into account what happens when a bunch of raging egos try to make decisions. Instead, it led to the worst knock-down, drag-out argument the flock had ever had.

"So, I guess we go to Pennsylvania first," Iggy said. We were rummaging through the claustrophobic little cabin, taking stock of the supplies. "From what that Tunnelratt kid said, it sounds like there are more survivors there."

"The survivors aren't the issue," Fang said. He was still holding the tablet, trying to get the thing turned back on. "The killers are. Why not try to find these H-men dudes first? Find out if they're just random bots, or connected to something bigger." He was all action, which was how I usually operated, too. "I think we should head to the coasts and—"

"We're going to Russia," Angel said out of the blue. She pulled her head out of a lower cupboard she had cleared out, and now sat among some rusted, battered pots and pans that wouldn't even be of use to whack someone with.

"That's stupid." Gazzy dismissed his little sister as he stood on a chair to reach the upper shelf of a closet. "Ooh, tea tree oil. Gotta be flammable. Why would we go to Russia? You saw those comments. People said all of Europe might be wrecked."

"It isn't," Angel said authoritatively. "And if you want to know the truth about what happened, you'll follow me."

"Let me guess. *I'm the big-shot psychic and I know everything.*'" Gazzy mimicked Angel's voice perfectly, and Nudge giggled, then winced in pain. "Okay, Ange, don't hold out on us. Go on, tell us what *mysterious* future awaits us in Russia." He wiggled his fingers and made his eyebrows jump.

Gazzy had always been protective of Angel, but clearly some tension had been building between them. Angel was definitely not smiling. She crossed her arms over her chest but didn't answer.

"That's what I thought." Gazzy snickered as he jumped off the chair with his find.

She stared at him evenly. "I know it's hard when some of us are developing even more extraordinary powers and you're still trying to control your *hilarious* toxic farts, but don't you think you should grow up, *Gasman*?"

Gazzy looked at Angel in surprise. They were standing toe to toe now, blue-eyed mirrors of each other, and I was getting a little nervous—a threatened Angel is an unpredictable Angel. I looked at Iggy. He'd always been so good at neutralizing tension, but his jaw was set tight as he let it build and build.

"*I'm* the one who needs to grow up?" Gazzy said. His cheeks were flushed with anger. "First you were just loooving being Max's precious little baby, and now you pull this 'I'm the Chosen One' crap every time you don't get your way."

"I know what I'm talking about!" Angel stamped her foot.

"Oh, are we going to have a tantrum now?" Gazzy taunted.

"Okayyy," I said, and blew out a frustrated breath. "Let's just all take a step back here. Ange, honey, I know you haven't been sleeping. Maybe you just need some rest."

"We're all going to Russia!" Angel shouted.

"I'm going to the US!" her brother raged back.

"*I'm* not going anywhere," Nudge said. "Whatever's out there..." She glanced toward the door and touched a hand to her cheek, where the blood had soaked through the cloth again. "It's not any better than where we were."

"We don't know that, Nudge," Fang said. "If we catch these guys, things might get a lot better."

"Maybe Nudge is right," I said. "Maybe we should go back to the island for a while."

"What?" Fang jerked his head around.

"What?!" Gazzy repeated.

Fang took me aside, keeping his voice low. "Max, how can you say that, especially now that we have a clue about what happened? You don't think we owe it to those people to help them?"

I shifted uncomfortably. There is no purer form of humiliation than when someone you love and respect suggests you might be a self-involved jerk.

"Of course I want to help people," I said quietly. "But we know there are people sick in Asia, too, and that's a lot closer. And we know Pierpont stocked the vaccine in the caves on our island. Maybe we should try to find a way in again."

Fang sighed and looked away.

I touched his arm. "I just think we need to figure things out before we make any crazy decisions."

"I couldn't agree more," Total said.

"Yeah, because the decisions she's made have always been spot-on, right?" Iggy muttered.

I narrowed my eyes. "What's *that* supposed to—"

"It means that maybe if you hadn't insisted we stay on the island after the apocalypse, Dylan and Akila might still be here."

"Watch it, Ig," Fang warned.

But the words already hung between us like bullets aimed at my heart. I knew they were true.

"I..." I was remembering the bloodied sheet in the grave and thinking of the green sneaker as it had slipped out of my fingers. I couldn't breathe.

"It was the best thing for us then," Fang insisted. "We were protected. We didn't know what else was out there."

There were other things, too, deeper reasons I hadn't left the island—things I couldn't say aloud. When you fail at saving the world, it's difficult to imagine facing the ruins of what's left. When you blame yourself so completely, it's hard to look for who might be responsible. And when someone claims your mom and sister are dead, it's almost impossible to believe it without proof.

I know you were grieving, the voice said inside my head. *I know you couldn't accept the loss. But you stopped making decisions for the flock. You put us all at risk.*

I glared at Angel. "Get out of my mind."

"They're *dead*, Max," Angel said gently.

"We don't know that!" My hands clenched as I struggled to hold on to that belief. "Dylan could still be there. My mom might be alive. Ella might—"

"They're gone!" Iggy shouted, and for the first time I saw the real anguish he felt at losing my half sister, the girl he'd totally fallen for. "Why can't you just accept that, Max, so we can all move on?"

Because. I can't. I won't.

He nodded toward where Angel and Gazzy stood. "I'm going."

"Okay then." Angel clasped her hands together as everyone glared at one another. "We'll head out in the morning. Max and Nudge can stay behind and the rest of us will go."

"Except me." Fang stepped closer to me and threaded his hand behind my back. "I'm staying with Max."

17

ANGEL'S EYES WIDENED. "That's not allowed."

"What?" I said, still reeling from Iggy's attack. "You mean because the flock isn't supposed to ever break up again?"

"No, not because of that," Angel said, and grabbed Fang's arm. "I said he has to leave. Every second you stay here, you're a bigger threat to the world's survival."

Fang shook his head. "I love you, Ange, and I get that you're still sore about this Save the World crusade. But news flash: We lost." He kicked a warped can across the room, and the clang echoed in the small space. "The world already ended, and I sure didn't have anything to do with it."

I felt a pang. Fang could separate himself from it—no one had told *him* he could stop it—but my conscience still said *my fault, my fault, my fault.*

"You're a threat to Max, too," Angel continued in her patient parent voice. "We each have a role. I'm supposed to lead..."

"And I'm supposed to die, right?" I felt how tense Fang was next to me, how the air itself seemed to pulse. "Are we back to this again?"

Angel shrugged her slight shoulders, but her gaze never wavered. "You can't continue being selfish, Fang," she said, and his eyes hardened.

"Angel, come on," I cut in. "I think we've all had enough right now."

But Fang held up his hand. "No, it's fine. Doesn't faze me anymore. She's been saying this for, what, two years? At first it was kind of spooky, but at this point, she's just the girl who cried wolf. And as for her leading..." He stared down at her, meeting her eyes with a look of pity. "That only seems to happen when you weasel your way into people's heads and make their decisions for them, doesn't it, sweetie? No one *wants* to follow you, Angel."

He let that hang in the air for a second. Angel glanced at Gazzy, and her brother wouldn't meet her eyes.

Angel's nostrils flared, but she held her composure. "I know you can't understand. I've had to make sacrifices. To spare you all the burden—"

"Sacrifices." Fang nodded, pursing his lips. "Seeing the future and doing nothing. Not a word until the freaking sky actually caught on fire. *Sacrificing* all those innocent lives. You're a real martyr, aren't you?"

"You think I want this?" she shrieked, her eyes brimming with tears. "I tried to warn you. I tried to prepare you. But I guess I'll have to show you!"

Her eyes turned a milky white, and I sucked in a breath. We all looked alarmed as Fang's expression started to change. He stared straight ahead at Angel, but it was like he was watching a movie. I saw the sweat pricking above his lip, the color draining from his face.

Suddenly the pressure changed in the room, pressing agonizingly in on my skull, making my eardrums pop. Fang's nose started to bleed. Nudge, Iggy, and Gazzy each sank to their knees, holding their heads and moaning.

"Angel, stop it now! That's enough!" I shouted.

Fang jerked his head sharply from side to side, winced painfully, and then collapsed.

I sank to my knees next to him, pinching his nose to stop the blood. He didn't seem to see me. His eyes were haunted, and he was muttering. When I took his hand in mine, I felt it trembling.

"What did you do?" I demanded. "What did you do to him?"

When I looked up at Angel, her white wings seemed to fill the room, and despite her young face, her expression seemed as old as time. She wasn't a little kid at all. Maybe she never had been.

"I showed him the truth," she said softly. "I'm sorry, Fang, but you can't change it. *It's your fate.*"

18

"FANG!" I SHOUTED, trudging along the path he'd cut through the high brown grass sloping up behind the cottage. "Fang, answer me!"

I found him farther up the hill in a clearing hidden by brambles and dead-looking eucalyptus. He held a thick branch with both hands like a baseball bat and was hitting one of the trees again and again.

I leaned against another tree, studying him. His expression was as unreadable as ever, but his flushed skin suggested the fury boiling just beneath the surface. "Are you really going to let Angel do this to you?" I said after a few seconds.

In response, Fang continued swinging. Strips of bleached bark fluttered to the ground each time he connected with the tree, the *CRACK! CRACK! CRACK!* echoing against the hollow trunk. When his makeshift club broke in half, Fang's face went as still and closed as marble.

"Hey!" I protested as he started smashing what was left of the stick against the ground. I grabbed his arms from behind, pulling against the momentum of straining muscles. "Come on, stop it."

He finally chucked the stick and whirled around. "Angel's right," he choked. His eyes were haunted, his pupils still dilated. "I'm a danger to you and everyone. It's the reason I left before, and I never should have come back."

"What?" I said, gaping at him in disbelief. "What on earth did Angel tell you?"

Angrily he shook his head.

"Fang, this is me! We can tell each other everything!" *Can't we?*

I waited and after a full minute realized he *wasn't going to tell me.* He actually was not going to let me know what Angel had showed him. I gave him another minute to apologize and realize what a douchebag he was being.

"She's right," he repeated instead. "I can't be a coward. I can't put everyone I care about at risk."

Underneath the distress on his face, I saw the rational, calculating Fang I'd always known, and that's when I started to get scared.

He was serious.

"So, what?" I said scathingly, trying to keep my voice from shaking. "You're just going to run? You think that's less cowardly?"

"Not run." Fang's jaw was set with conviction. "I'm going to do whatever I can with the time I have left to figure out what happened, to find out who's responsible, to stop this thing. I'll go to California, find some of those cleanup crews..."

"You mean you'll go to California to meet up with BikiniBimbo456, or whatever her name was," I spat.

It was petty, I admit, but give me a pass, okay? I was feeling pretty bitter at that moment.

"You know that's not it." He walked over to me and tried to take my hands. When I crossed my arms, he settled for lifting my chin so I was forced to look at him. "You know you're it for me. The only one. The forever one."

I wasn't willing to budge yet, though those were the most amazing words I'd ever heard from him. "Am I?"

Fang sighed. "Maximum Ride, you're the most stubborn person I've ever met, and sometimes it seems like your sole purpose in life is to make mine harder, but I swear, I love you more than I thought I could love anyone or anything."

"Then stay," I whispered, clenching my eyes shut just as they started to well up.

I felt Fang's hands on the sides of my face, his thumbs wiping away my tears. I felt the heat coming off his body, heard the catch of his breath. And when our lips finally came together, our kisses were urgent, our bodies hungry. As he moved his hands through my tangled hair, I looked up at him. Inhaled. And said, "Yes."

We sank to the ground, the dried leaves crinkling under us, and time fell away for a while.

I couldn't tell if our voices rose in pleasure or pain, couldn't tell if my heart was breaking or bursting open with joy. I only knew I didn't want to pull away from him for a single second, and it was only when we both gasped for a breath that I realized Fang's eyes were squeezed shut and his lashes were wet.

"I'm sorry," he whispered hoarsely. It was the most vulnerable I'd ever seen him.

"It's okay." I pulled him closer, cradling his head tenderly. When he kissed me again, I tasted the salt on his lips, but I still found it sweet. "It's going to be all right."

19

FANG AWOKE WITH a start, shivering violently. His shirt was soaked with sweat, clammy against his skin, but the air had grown chillier overnight, and the ground beneath him felt like a block of ice.

He stared out between the brambles at the ash covering the hills like a strange dark snowfall—quiet and eerily beautiful. He concentrated on slowing his breath, trying to shake the vision that had echoed in his dreams, waking him up every hour.

Angel had put it there, playing on a loop, and the fall was like a punch to the gut each time. It was cruel, but he understood why she had done it: He never would have left Max otherwise.

Not ever.

Fang felt her next to him on the bed of dried leaves, and was so relieved in that moment that his breath left his chest in a long, aching sigh. His body curled around Max in a spoon, the way they slept every night. In sleep, her mouth was open like she was about to say something—to ask him again not to go—and he wanted so badly to tighten his arms around her, to kiss her chapped lips one more time.

That longing was the sharpest, most acute pain he'd ever felt, and he had to bite his tongue until it bled to keep himself in check—he could not wake her.

Instead, Fang wound a strand of Max's tangled hair around his fingers, breathing it in, saying good-bye. But it didn't smell like Max anymore. It, like everything else in his world, smelled like ash.

Carefully he rolled away from her, picked his way through the brambles, and crept past the sleeping house, as silent as only he knew how to be.

He wasn't sure if dawn had broken or not—ash blotted out the sun. Fang spread out his large black wings to their full span. He stretched the muscles, felt the power there. How could they fail him? He wasn't sure—Angel hadn't shown him that part.

So this was what it felt like. To be told you had terminal cancer. To be given a death sentence by a stone-faced judge. To know the plane was going down.

He couldn't see his life as it had been, or the things he still needed to do. All he could focus on was that ground, coming up to meet him. Fast.

Fang doubled over as the vomit rose in his throat.

He staggered to a puddle of water, and his reflection shook him even more. His olive skin was ashen, his cheekbones sharper than ever. Fang had always excelled at being a shadow. Was he now becoming a ghost?

His hand smashed through the image as he splashed the polluted water on his face. Then he stood up and kicked ash over his vomit, disgusted with himself. The awful canned pasta they'd found in the cabin had been the best meal he'd had in weeks, and he couldn't even keep it down.

Fang ran his fingers through his mop of wet hair and blew out a long breath. He was better than this. He had to be. He had to accept certain things as fact, now.

If he loved Max, he had to let her go.

He was going to die.

Okay.

Fang wasn't going to cower from it—that wasn't his style—but he wasn't just going to wait for death, either. Instead of trying to shake the vision Angel had shown him, he began to focus on understanding it.

"This is your fate."

In his mind's eye, he saw the flakes gathering in his hair. He could feel them on his face, melting on his eyelashes. It wasn't ash, like he'd first thought; it was snow. Angel hadn't told him when this horrible *thing* would happen, but it was close to the end of May now, which meant winter was over in the Northern Hemisphere, where he was headed.

Maybe he had another year to live. Maybe he had several. Maybe he even had enough time to catch this Remedy maniac.

He'd start with the H-men, like his gut had first told him to. He'd start with California.

20

FANG FELT THE heaviness in his body as he flew away from the cabin and tried to focus on his breathing. It was impossible to shake the sense that each wing stroke carried him closer to his end, but he was determined to hold back his panic.

Breathe in. Breathe out. Keep going.

But when he inhaled deeply, he smelled something strange. The air carried smoke from the ash cloud and salt from the distant ocean, but there was something else, too—something sour and stinking.

Like death itself.

Fang dropped low over leafless trees and abandoned houses, scanning the valley for what he expected would be another mass grave.

Instead of the stillness of death, though, he detected movement. Even from above, he instantly recognized the hulking backs and long, thick necks hanging low.

Cryenas.

And they were swarming toward the small cabin he'd just left.

Fang wrenched his right wing downward sharply, starting to make a U-turn to warn the flock, but then paused. He hovered over the slinking shapes, considering.

Two, four... only ten of them. Fang chuckled darkly. Ten to one wasn't exactly stellar odds, but he would deal with these monsters himself. It would be his parting gift to the flock.

After all, it wasn't like the Cryenas were going to *kill him.* Not unless Angel was very wrong.

Fang brought his knees to his chest and then kicked sharply up at the sky, surrendering to his bird instincts. His wings folded tight against his back, his hands cut downward as he gained speed, and he zeroed in on his prey with calm precision as the ground rushed toward him.

The second before he smashed into the earth, Fang pulled up his head and grinned. "Gotcha."

With all the momentum of his dive, he plowed into the leader of the pack, sending it knocking into the other Cryenas like a perfectly spun bowling ball.

It was almost cartoonish the way the stunned creatures were flung outward on impact, and Fang might've laughed, but he was pinned under one of them, and his mouth was full of dirt.

Fang reached his arms around the Cryena that was crushing him. The hairless skin moved over powerful muscles as the animal squirmed in his grasp, and Fang was disgusted to feel rough, scabby sores beneath his fingers. He hurled the creature off him and jumped to his feet.

The other Cryenas were already moving in on him now. Their tongues hung out of their mouths, already salivating as they started to circle him, herding him. Up close, the foul smell was overwhelming.

"You guys reek." Fang hid his nose in the crook of his arm.

These Cryenas were in much rougher shape than the ones they'd seen in Sydney. Some of their spots seemed to be actually melting off, and their skin looked thin and grayish, almost as if they were rotting from the inside out.

Fang knew he'd have a much better shot striking from above, so he shook out his wings and leaped into the air, taunting his pursuers as he zigzagged just above their heads. They loped around him, trotting closer and moving away.

"Come on, you cowards!"

Each time he struck one on its humped back or flat head, four more would hurl themselves at him, nipping at him and whining as Fang rose again.

Blood was seeping from a dozen bites on his legs, but there was freedom in the pain. It meant he was still alive, still feeling, and he felt invincible.

Whatever they did to him, however hard they fought, in the end, he would win.

Then one jumped higher than the rest, and Fang stifled a scream as the skin on his left forearm was torn away. The pain was shocking, stunning, and as Fang dipped for just a moment, they pulled him down.

Their target felled, pack mentality kicked in, and the Cryenas swarmed all at once. Claws dug at his chest, teeth sank into his shoulder, and wet muzzles nuzzled in, ready to feast on his insides. The weight of all the bodies pushed in and in and in on him, and Fang would have gagged from the smell if his chest wasn't being crushed.

You will not die today, Fang repeated to himself. *Angel showed you where you would die, and it's far from here. A world away from Max.*

A tense grunt escaped him at the thought, and all the hurt and frustration and bitterness he felt rushed to the surface. Just *knowing* his fate was more painful than the most gruesome death he could imagine.

Maybe he should let these monsters just kill him now.

But then a strange light caught Fang's eye—something slowly blinking green behind one of the Cryena's ears. Frowning, Fang let his eyes trail to the scabs he felt at its sides.

And in the place where the tawny skin had torn, Fang saw the dull shine of metal poking through. And he understood: They were robots.

Someone sent them here. Someone is tracking the flock.

21

FANG LET OUT a violent roar of fury.

After all they had been through the last few months—tsunamis, volcanoes, and living on the edge of starvation—*they were still being hunted.*

So Fang reacted like a hunted animal, one that had been cornered and threatened and beaten down too many times, an animal that just needed a way out.

He went completely ballistic.

He seized the head of the biggest beast, wrenching it toward him. Other Cryenas scrambled away, but many jaws still lunged at him, refusing to abandon their meal.

Fang's fingernails tore at spotted flesh, his arms found strength to break bones, a couple of well-placed kicks cracked their thick necks sideways, and his teeth gnashed at anything that would bleed. Fang had finally snapped, and he would not back down.

It was only when he paused for a few ragged breaths that he saw that most of the Cryenas were dead or had run away, and he had torn the pack leader almost completely apart.

Fang toed the body cautiously. It was clearly dead, but a high frenzied howl was coming from the fallen Cryena.

Fang grimaced as he peeled back synthetic skin that clearly hadn't been made for these harsh elements. Real animal or not, dissecting this creature that had been clawing hungrily at him moments before felt grotesque.

But Fang needed every puzzle piece he could find that would lead him toward justice. He didn't have time for squeamishness. He had to know.

The Cryena's insides were a complex labyrinth of lab-grown bones and tendons, with added wires, sensors, and metal upgrades. It wasn't like anything he had seen before—even the Flyboys had been more mechanical and better designed.

The creature's howl went on and on. It seemed to echo his own anguish, and Fang wanted more than anything to make it stop.

He'd learned all he could here, so he used a rock to crush the robotic skull. The green light stopped blinking as the scene finally settled into silence.

There would be more Cryenas, he was pretty certain of that. Worse things, too, probably. But not yet. Not today.

He had given the flock a parting gift, given them the thing he himself wanted most in the world: a little more time.

Fang gazed up toward the cottage. He saw the shadowy outline of Total's solid little body, his tail wagging.

The Scottie dog barked, and Fang raised a hand in farewell.

22

I FELT THE cold at my back when I woke, and sensed the emptiness there even before I turned.

Fang was gone.

Footprints in the film of ash led away from our secluded spot. Away from me.

I flung myself up, stumbling between the eucalyptus trees. I got tangled in the grasses and whacked my shin on a low stump, but I finally made it back to the house.

"Fang?" I couldn't help calling, but I knew it was pointless.

The front door banged on its hinges as I burst inside, tracking ash behind me. Iggy and Gazzy turned from where they knelt next to the coffee table.

"Is Fang here?" I asked.

"Haven't seen him," the Gasman said.

He couldn't have left. He would've told me, right? He couldn't be *gone* gone. Especially when Iggy and Gazzy didn't even seem to care.

My gaze traveled to the coffee table, where they had their backpacks and their various bits and pieces of explosives and weapons spread out.

"What are you..." I started to ask, but then I understood: *They don't care if Fang's gone because they're getting ready to leave, too. For real.*

I'd thought we'd talk over the fight in the morning, make up and tease one another—like the old days. But their tense shoulders and distant expressions said otherwise.

Uh-uh, my denial-loving brain insisted. *This is not happening!*

I picked up a couch cushion and threw it at the table like a Frisbee. Bottles and fuses went tumbling every which way.

"You guys are idiots!" I glowered at the boys. "You're really going to just leave? What about our promise to stick together?"

Gazzy stared at the stained carpet guiltily. "What other choice do we have?"

"Just...trust the flock." I pounded my fist into my palm. Part of me was imagining Fang's face there. "*Trust* that we can do this together, like we always have. Is that so hard?"

"Trust the flock? Or *you*?" Iggy asked.

"We just want answers, Max," Gazzy said. "And that doesn't really seem like a priority for you."

Iggy stood up. "We want to learn who's still alive, but you're too worried about who's dead."

Like my mom. I didn't know what to say. Instead, I stormed out of the cabin, hoping to see Fang soaring back toward us, like he'd just gone out for a morning zip around the block. But no...things don't work the way they used to in the pre-apocalyptic world. No Hollywood endings here.

I spotted Nudge and Total in the garden over by Akila's grave. "Has anyone seen Fang?" I called out.

Nudge shook her head miserably. She looked like she'd been crying all night.

Iggy and Gazzy came out of the cabin wearing their backpacks.

"You're really going, then?" I said angrily as they strode past. "That's it?"

"Maybe you should start trusting *us* for a change," Iggy said. "You ready, Gasman?"

Gazzy glanced up at the roof. Angel was balancing on top of the lightning rod, swaying with the wind. She didn't make a move to come down.

"Let's see if America is still the land of the free." Gazzy arranged the pack straps on his shoulders, and both he and Iggy snapped open their wings.

Nudge walked over to join me. As we watched the boys take off, I shoved clenched fists deep into my pockets. Silent tears ran down Nudge's face, and when Total put his paws against her legs, she bent down and held him tight.

Before I could even process the fact that I might never again see these kids I'd known since they were hatchlings, Total pulled away from Nudge and touched my hand with his wet nose.

"Fang left at dawn," he said quietly. "I think he wanted me to tell you."

"He—" I squeaked, but the words felt strangled in my throat. After...last night? I thought that had cemented things between us. Now it looked like it had done the opposite.

I'd known the truth, deep in my bones, even if I hadn't wanted to believe it at first. Now it was real, verified: He wasn't coming back, despite everything. Despite me. He was *gone* gone. Total's sad eyes confirmed it.

Fang really was gone.

Forever.

23

I STARTED TO hyperventilate.

"You know that boy adores you, Max," Total said.

"Stop it," I said, covering my ears and squeezing my eyes shut tight.

Tears threatened to overflow, but I couldn't give in to them, not yet. I was too furious—at Iggy and Gazzy for leaving, at Fang for not even bothering to say good-bye, at Angel for starting this whole thing.

I stomped across the yard and glared up at our little towheaded mystic. Angel was crouched like a gargoyle, her lips pursed into a pout.

"Are you happy with yourself?" I snarled. "We could've figured out a plan. A place to go together. Instead, you broke up the whole flock!"

She looked down at me sadly, unblinkingly, for a long time. Finally, she stepped off the lightning rod and fluttered down to the ground. "I should get going, too," she said.

With those words, the reality finally hit home: I was going to lose her—again. As hard as I'd tried to keep us together through the years, she was leaving, along with everyone else—my mom, Ella, Dylan, Akila, Fang, Gazzy, Iggy . . .

The anger disappeared, and I reached out and clutched her to me in a fierce hug. What else could I do?

"Please," I whispered. "You can't go."

Angel wrapped her arms around my neck and I pressed my face into her ashy, once-fluffy locks, remembering how I use to smooth her hair from her face when she was little, how I'd promised I would protect her. I imagined Angel out in that awful new world alone, without her flock. Without me.

I'm not your baby anymore, Max, her voice said in my head. *I never really was.*

She wriggled out of my grasp and turned to Nudge and Total. "Take care of each other, okay?"

Nudge nodded and hugged her tearfully, and Total licked her face, leaving odd clean streaks. Angel unfurled her wings, her primary feathers still tipped with crud from the ash and rain. But before she took off, she turned back to me.

"One day you'll understand," she said, her face an

infuriating picture of Zen confidence. "You might even thank me."

"I seriously doubt that," I muttered.

I guess we can't all be enlightened. Angel grinned. *See you in Russia.*

Moments later, I watched the little kid I'd raised and loved and butted heads with fly away from me. I watched her curls bouncing as she pushed off, waiting to see if she'd turn her head again, but she never did.

Instead, Angel's white wings rose through the ash, and soon she was a speck I couldn't tell apart from the rest of the sky.

24

I STOOD NEXT to the mound where we'd buried Akila, staring up at the churning sky and biting hard on the insides of my cheeks as I tried to keep from screaming.

They've left. They've really left.

Sure, we'd had our ups and downs. The boys had splintered off briefly before. Fang had gone off on his own more than once. Iggy had joined a cult. Nudge once wanted to cut off her wings. Gazzy almost blew up his sister, and Angel had always had a bit of a God complex.

But this was the first time that the flock had really, truly, broken up, and it was the worst possible timing. After the world ends, you really need someone you can count on, you know?

No problem. Just leave it to Numero Uno to pick up the pieces. As usual.

I went back into the house, past Nudge and Total, who were sitting dejectedly at the kitchen table.

"I used to think you couldn't trust adults," I announced, banging open the cupboards to search for anything we could use. "But really, you can't trust anyone. Not kids, not mutants."

My fingers trembled with rage. I swiped my arm across the shelf and Total whistled as dishes clattered to the floor. I flung jars of rotten Vegemite at the wall and stabbed a dull, useless knife into the counter. Nudge gasped.

"Nothing, nothing, *nothing*!" I bellowed.

I collapsed onto the couch and raked my hands back through my snarled hair, trying to get a grip on myself. "How am I going to do this alone? There's no one left."

"Gee, thanks, Maximum," Total said pointedly, and strode out, his black nose pointed in the air.

"Come on," I called. "I didn't mean—"

"That we don't count?" Nudge said coolly from the kitchen, where she was opening other cupboards. "Even though we're the only ones who stayed with you?" Her cheek was healing, but there was still a huge, jaw-shaped wound, and it made her expression hard to read.

I sighed. "Of course you count, Nudge. Let's just go back to the island, all right? Like we said."

"There're no *boys* left is what you meant," she continued bitterly, cocking her head. "No Dylan. No Fang. No more cute guys to obsess over you."

I pressed my lips together and stared at her. "What?"

But Nudge was on a roll. "Poor, poor Max," she said, finding some ancient cans of tuna and an old jar of hearts of palm. Who *eats* that? "How are you going to survive with no one to fight over your attention?"

"Nudge," I said, getting up, "you know I've never been the princess. Always been the dragon-slayer. Look at me: If I wanted guys falling all over me, don't you think I would wash up once in a while?"

Nudge frowned but followed me through the cottage as I gathered our meager belongings, layering clothes and tucking a rusty hammer and an old water bottle into my tattered pack. It wouldn't last much longer.

"It's just always about you," Nudge said, but with less heat.

That stopped me in my tracks. I turned and took both her shoulders, looking up into the face that might never regain its startling, budding beauty. "Sweetie," I said softly. "It's always about us, the flock. It's always, always, *always* about the flock. I don't know how to do it any other way."

Nudge gave a shuddering breath, then nodded and rested her untorn cheek on my shoulder. We hugged for a long time, until a neglected Total weaseled his way between our legs, pushing like a little bulldozer until we made room for him.

With a watery smile, I patted his head and nodded at Nudge.

"Pack up," I said. "It's time to go."

We would survive. We always had. We just had less to lose now.

25

THE JOURNEY BACK to our island seemed to take twice as long as we remembered. Ever wonder why birds fly in a V? Because each bird deflects a little of the wind for the birds behind it. It's all about teamwork, folks. Of course, with just Nudge and Total, my team was really more of a trio.

Despite Total's protests about the fabulousness of his wings, he's still a little guy and flying long distance is hard for him. Nudge and I took turns letting him piggyback. By the time we saw the outline of familiar cliffs in the distance, I was more exhausted than I'd ever been, and the only thought in my head was *The flock is over. The flock is over. The flock is over.*

"Just a little farther," I said, as much to convince myself as Nudge and Total.

But our island was still a desolate disaster. Black smoke hung thick over everything, and by half a mile out, Nudge sounded like she was coughing glass, and tears streamed down my face as tiny flecks of burning material flew into my eyes.

The air was so toxic that flying inland just wasn't possible. Instead, we flew along the outer edge of the island, heading upwind for the far north side, away from the volcano, where the smoke wasn't quite so thick.

"I'm so tired," Nudge complained, moving her wings in slow arcs to conserve energy. "Max, what are we gonna do?"

"We'll find a place to land," I assured her, though it was hard to keep the doubt out of my voice.

My flock of three hovered in silence for a few moments, contemplating the ash cloud and the sea of lava that now coated everything.

"Max . . . I'm not questioning your judgment, but our former home doesn't exactly look livable at the moment." Total gave my neck a brief lick, as if to soften his words.

Total had always been a little high-maintenance, but I had to admit he had a point. Food alone was already starting to feel urgent, and anything that had survived the initial explosion and tsunami was now almost certainly overcooked barbecue.

We were in dire straits indeed.

"Wait—there's something moving down there." I pointed. "Look."

As we dipped lower, I saw that it wasn't just something alive. It was some*one*. *Human.*

"Hey!" I screamed at the boy. *"Hey!"*

If you know me, you know I'm normally a big believer in Stranger Danger. My friends wouldn't exactly describe me as a people person, since I generally loathe most of the people I come in contact with. (To be fair, a lot of them have tried to kill me.)

But the population of the world had been sliced drastically, I'd just lost most of my family, and I really just wanted a little sympathetic company, okay?

So I kept shouting and waving like a maniac, barely noticing when one of the figures moved away from the others and bent down to position something on the shore.

And when I saw the spark, my first thought was about how these people could be useful to us, since they had a lighter.

But then there was a whizzing sound in the air, and the small spark suddenly got very large as it rocketed up at us. Suddenly, it all clicked into place for me.

"Bank!" I yelled, yanking Nudge's arm right as the firework exploded with a pop of dazzling red.

26

"OOF," I SAID as my body bounced and then sank against the woven rope net held taut by dozens of hands.

They saved us! was my first thought.

They shot us! was my second.

Remembering the rocket, I wiggled my fingers, making sure I hadn't lost any digits. Other than a ringing in my ears that was going to lead to a whopping migraine, I was in one piece.

I peered at my attackers through the rope. Some of them had webbed toes, and others had legs that were fused together to the knees, so that they sort of hopped.

Mutants.

They turned their heads as someone approached, and I saw that all of them had little slits behind their ears, opening and closing as they sucked in air. Gills. Just like ours.

"Release them," a male voice ordered, and they all let go at once.

Nudge, Total, and I tumbled into one another on the ground. "Hey, easy!" I said, and looked up at the mutants' apparent leader. "And you are...?"

"Rizal." He was short and muscular with brown, deeply tanned skin and hair that hung down into his eyes. From the way the other kids were looking at him, he was clearly in charge.

"So, Rizal." I shook the netting free from my shoulders and stood up, matching his even gaze. "Do you mind telling me why you shot a rocket at us and trapped us in nets?"

"That was a defense mechanism Jonny Diamond has been working on for months." Rizal nodded to a skinny kid with glasses. "He calls it the Jeweled Star."

"I don't care what it's called," I said. "Why did you shoot us out of the sky?"

"It was a warning. To stay away from our island."

Say what?

My eyes narrowed. "Um, I'm pretty sure this is *our* island," I said, suddenly feeling very territorial about this unlivable piece of volcanic rock.

"Hang on." Nudge cut in. "I know some of these kids. Hey, Angela!" She waved. "And Barry!" The fish kids didn't wave back, but Nudge didn't seem to mind. "We all swam together at the waterfall the first day Nino Pierpont brought us here! Remember? We thought everyone else had died! Where have you been the last three months?"

"So you were part of the original people?" I asked. "I guess we all belong here, then."

"Not anymore," Rizal said. "We're an exclusive community now."

The two kids flanking him leveled the sharp-arrowed ends of their spearguns at us, and others used the nets to bind our hands.

What did I tell you? You can't trust anyone.

27

I STARED AT the bare feet with their webbed toes approaching us. I was already cranky from the night we'd spent tied up in an oversized lobster cage—just *ask* me how much I love cages—and the new day wasn't looking much better.

Now that I'd lost my freedom, I was starting to see how shortsighted my argument for taking things slow really was. I wanted to know who was behind this, and I wanted to know *now*.

"Who's in charge?" I shouted at the fish kids as they passed by. "What happened the day the sky caught fire? Are the caves still accessible?"

None of the fish kids would so much as look at us, though, and every one of them was heavily armed this time, with spearguns strapped over their shoulders and knives hugging their ankles and thighs.

"The full battalion, eh?" I observed dryly. "If I didn't know better, I'd think you were afraid of us."

"Overgrown guppies," Total growled through his teeth. They'd wrapped seaweed around his snout to make a makeshift muzzle, but if there's anyone you can't shut up, it's Total.

Then Rizal himself stood in front of us and pulled a large hunting knife from his belt. He tested the blade with his thumb, and I scowled.

"It's a little cowardly to kill somebody when they're tied up, don't you think?"

Silently, Rizal released the door of the cage and then cut through the rope that bound our wrists. I rubbed my raw skin, not taking my eyes from the knife. If Rizal made a move, I wasn't going down without a fight.

"Our weapons are for hunting," he said evenly, and dumped a basket of fish at our feet. "And no one gives us orders. We rule ourselves."

I hadn't understood how starved I'd been until then, and Nudge, Total, and I all lunged for the basket. When I held a silvery body in shaking hands, I told myself it was just like sushi. Like a sushi kit. The sushi was just still inside, that's all. As the mutant kids looked on with expressionless faces, I hungrily tore into the fish's side, ignoring scales and fine bones and just chomping away. I ate it like an ear of corn, turning it around, nibbling off every bit of flesh, and then throwing the head and tail into a pile. Then I grabbed another one.

By the end of our messy feast, we all had shining scales flecking our hair and skin, bloody mouths, and unnamable gore lodged so deeply under our nails that it would probably never come out. I felt a thousand percent better.

After Total let out a delicate burp, Rizal finally spoke. "We've decided you can stay in our community," he said. He walked back and forth in front of us with his spear slung over his shoulder. "Once we are there, you will not swim in the open water. You will not be permitted to hunt. You will not leave the caves."

I looked up from my pile of fish bones. *So the caves are intact.*

"I am an excellent paddler!" Total protested. "And the girls both have gills. . . ."

Rizal dismissed the suggestion. "If you don't follow the rules, you'll be killed."

"Wow, love the hospitality." I wiped the blood from my lips and accepted that my hair would smell like fish guts for the rest of my life. "You rule yourselves, but you kill any dissenters. Is that what happened to everyone else?"

"We didn't murder the other mutants. When the sea first flooded the caves, there was no way out. The bird kids, the bug kids—everyone drowned all around us."

"What about the humans?" I asked, trying to temper my hope. Maybe Angel couldn't sense anyone's thoughts on this part of the island after the first few days, including the fish kids and my mom. There was a chance....

Rizal snorted. "Pierpont barricaded himself in the food vault because it was watertight. It was almost a month before the sea receded enough for us to pry open the door."

"He left everyone else to starve?" Nudge gasped.

Rizal nodded in disgust. "We found him curled on the floor. Ironically, he escaped drowning but died of thirst. Every can of soup and fruit had been sucked dry."

"And the others?" Total asked quietly. "Do you know their fates?"

"The girl, you mean? And the veterinarian?"

My half sister, Ella. My mom.

Rizal flicked the dark hair out of his eyes absently, as if nothing at all was riding on his next words. "Same as all the rest," he said, shrugging. "The water came in. We swam. They drowned."

"Oh," I said in a flat voice, and gripped the rock floor for support as I felt my blood draining.

Deep down, I'd known that was the likeliest scenario, but I understood now why Iggy hadn't wanted to stay on the island: Not *really* knowing was so much better than knowing.

Because you could never get that hope back.

28

"DON'T BE AFRAID of Rizal," the kid called Jonny Diamond said. "He can be harsh, but he's just trying to keep us safe."

Everyone was getting ready to go to the caves, but I'd remained rooted to the rock long after the feast, thinking about my family. I thought about how Ella's face lit up when she looked at Iggy, and how she never even got to go to a school dance with him. About how, even though my mom was supersmart and at the top of her field, she was always trying to do mom things for me, like cooking great meals and getting me my own bed with fancy sheets and snuggling me, even when I resisted, because she knew I secretly craved that contact. I remembered how they'd both opened their home to me the very first day we'd met—never mind that I was a stranger, a mutant, and being shot at by stupid teenage boys.

Yet, though I managed to look out for the rest of my flock, I hadn't kept my human family safe when it mattered. And now, though I could still hear Ella's laugh and remember what my mom smelled like (antiseptic, vanilla shampoo, and cinnamon gum), I couldn't quite picture their faces.

Anyway, I'd been meditating on that cheery subject for hours, so I must've looked pretty desolate by the time Jonny came in.

But *scared*? Of Rizal? Doubtful.

"Who says I'm afraid of anything?" I asked, sitting up straighter.

Jonny chuckled and scooped up the pile of fish bones, tossing them back into the sea. "Well, you *should* be scared about the state of the world. If you've survived out there for this long, I figured you'd know that by now."

I eyed the belching volcano in the distance and the swirls of hardened lava just a few feet away. My expression softened.

"Yeah, this whole apocalypse thing is pretty surreal, huh? Did my mom...Did Dr. Martinez know what happened? What caused it?"

Jonny grabbed the rope netting, then sat down next to me on the rock ledge. "I thought she said something about Russia's betrayal..." My eyebrows shot up at the mention of the very place Angel had gone to, but Jonny shook his head uncertainly. "That day was really crazy, though. Pierpont had all this high-tech equipment, but all it told us was that a few small objects had exploded on contact with the earth's atmosphere."

Meteors. That's what Dylan said, too. But they couldn't have been small. They must have been huge, and more than just a few of them, judging by the mess we saw.

"We were all in the caves by then, though, so we couldn't see what was happening outside."

"The sky caught fire," I said, remembering how there'd been a huge black hole ringed in flames.

"But here's the thing: The hits were only reported in the Pacific."

"So?"

"So the local tsunamis would've been caused by the impact, but what about the other reports we heard?" Jonny seemed to catch himself. He focused on the net in his lap, knotting it expertly. "Sorry, you don't want to get me started on all my theories. . . ."

"Hey, I asked, didn't I?" I took a length of rope and mimicked his hand movements. "I'm a big fan of conspiracy theories."

They line up with my real-world experience: that pretty much everyone I meet is out to get me.

Jonny's eyes became animated. "Okay. So, the meteor fragments were in the Pacific," he repeated. "But that first day, we got news blips from all over the world about other sudden disasters—too many global events for coincidence."

He gestured with his speargun on the rock as if marking spots on a map. "I'm talking rumors of nukes being deployed in Africa, several heads of state murdered, a lockdown in the US, a major epidemic in East Asia...There's a lot we don't know, but I'm positive it was all orchestrated by people with a lot of money and power. They wanted to destroy the world, and might not be too happy to find out a bunch of mutant kids survived. I've been telling Rizal we need to make more weapons." He stabbed the spear into the sand and looked up as if scanning for trouble from the sky. "We have to be prepared to fight."

I guessed his theories were more right than wrong. What else did he know? "Right before she died, my mom warned us about a biological weapon called the H8E virus," I told him. "Did you hear about any connection to the Apocalypticas? Or the Doomsday Group? Or H-men? Or the Remedy?"

If anyone knows her genocidal terrorist flash cards by heart, it's me. I certainly have enough experience with them at this point.

"The epidemic started right before the meteor, and together they must have wiped out most of the people in the world. We haven't heard any updates since that very first day, before the tsunami hit and the caves flooded. Which reminds me—we should be heading out in just a few minutes. Let's get you suited up." He stood up and started lugging over the ancient oxygen tank he'd brought in. "Since all the equipment stopped working, we've been totally cut off from the rest of the world." He shrugged. "Rizal says it's better this way—that we have everything we need in the caves, and we shouldn't go looking for trouble."

Sounds familiar.

"What do *you* think?" I asked.

Jonny opened his mouth, but hesitated. "I think trouble's rarely in hiding," he answered finally. "And if someone *planned* something on this scale?" His eyes widened, magnified by his glasses. "Then none of us is safe."

29

"I DON'T NEED that," I said, waving away the oxygen tank Jonny had set in front of me.

He continued sorting tubes. "There should be a bit left in the cylinder. The Aquatics don't really need them, but we keep a couple of spares for emergencies."

"I can breathe underwater," I insisted. "Same as you."

Jonny sat back and looked at me. "For how long?"

"Well, a long time," I said. "And at great depth." I nudged the cylinder with my foot. "So I don't need that. Trust me."

Jonny frowned at my wings. "Those things are going to cause you serious drag."

"At least I don't have freaking *scales* all over my back," I snapped.

Jonny grinned good-naturedly. "Don't take it so personally. There's always someone in the group who's a little vulnerable." He touched the frames of his glasses and grinned. "How many Aquatics do you think need a prescription?"

I pursed my lips, unmoved, and Jonny shrugged.

"Okay, so you don't need it to breathe, fine. But can you do me a favor and bring it with you? That way the tanks will all be at the caves. Otherwise, I'll have to leave it here."

Okay, that made sense. I could do him a favor. I lifted the backpack with its heavy, dinged-up tank. The straps weren't going to fit over my oh-so-disgraceful, draggy wings, so I wore it backward, with the single tank in front of my chest.

Nudge, also carrying an oxygen tank in front, went in right before me. I plopped in last, splashing with my awkward tank, and as I swam after them toward the mouth of the tunnel that would take us to our sanctuary, I tried to work on a little thing called humility.

30

WE SWAM. I kept my wings tightly folded against my back. I'm not a bad swimmer, but the Aquatics had obviously been designed for this: Though clumsy and awkward on land, in the water they became graceful, fluid, powerful swimmers.

The ocean, which only three months ago had been crystalline, a clear, clean aqua, was now a murky, opaque sludge with almost zero visibility. I followed Jonny mostly by the swirling eddies of ash particles, while trying to keep an eye on Nudge. The stupid oxygen tank made it hard to swim, weighing me down, and I considered just ditching it.

"Aiiieeeeee!!!!"

The panicked scream was garbled and muffled, but

unmistakable. My head whipped around but I saw nothing but churned-up sludge. More screams echoed through the water around me, and I glimpsed a couple of the Aquatics speeding past me with terrified expressions. *What's happening? Where is Nudge?*

Was it a ... party? The murky water seemed alive with streamers whipping and writhing in the currents. Could this be some sort of welcoming ceremony? Someone had been surprised and had screamed?

Oh, God, oh, God. My brain had no time to think except to register: *These streamers are alive.*

They were eels or water snakes, and they were freakishly large. Slick ropes of muscle fifteen feet long and as thick as my waist, they made looping *S*s through the water, disappearing and reappearing confusingly so that I lost all sense of direction.

But the most horrible part was their mouths. Their whole *heads*, really, were circular vacuums of death, with rows and rows of teeth spiraling inward toward a gaping hole. The kind of thing you don't want to see on a movie screen, let alone near your leg.

Uh-huh. My leg.

There it was, slimy and quick, with its razor-sharp teeth moving closer and closer to my flesh. Once it attached, I felt a powerful leechy sucking sensation and then the first jolt of pain. I kicked at it, but my splashing just seemed to attract more of them, and I could only hold them off so much longer.

Desperate, I did the only thing I could think of: I slipped off the straps of the oxygen tank and quickly turned its valve. Immediately, pressurized bubbles burst out of it with the power of a fire hose, sending the eels wheeling away from me. I grinned victoriously but then blanched when I realized why the eels weren't returning.

A flash of color in the olive-green water caught my eye. It was striped, like Jonny Diamond's shirt. They'd found a new target: Jonny. I kicked with my legs, aiming my tank, but stopped in horror as I took in the scene:

One had suctioned onto him, and the snakelike body streamed out from his chest. For a second it just seemed like a small inconvenience, an odd extra limb, and Jonny tugged at the tail determinedly.

For a second.

And then Jonny's expression changed.

His mouth opened in a silent scream, a flurry of bloody bubbles escaping from it, and the muscles in his neck tightened into cords of agony. His eyes bulged in disbelief as his legs flailed and his hands scratched and tugged at the creature desperately.

The sucking mouth was burrowing into him.

Aiming my tank, I opened the valve, but only a tiny stream of bubbles came out: I'd used up the last of the oxygen. My mouth pressed tight in shock, I saw Jonny's head go limp, his whole body becoming boneless, like a rag doll's. Instinctively I moved away from him. When I looked back a final time, more toothy mouths had latched

117

on to Jonny's body, burrowing into his chest, thighs, and stomach until he looked like some sort of mutant octopus. Two brilliant red ribbons of blood floated up out of his nostrils.

Something brushed against my arm, and I kicked wildly, a rush of adrenaline making my ears sing. But it was only Nudge, as stricken as I was.

I was freaking out, but I grabbed Nudge's hand and swam hard in what I thought was the direction of the tunnels. All I wanted was to breathe real air, scream, and then cry. When a few inches of space opened above the water, we surfaced, gasping. Behind me, a bloom of crimson stained the turquoise sea.

The splashing had stopped.

31

IN TODAY'S WORLD, heaven pretty much boiled down to actual beds, reliable shelter, and a consistent food source. The caves were something else altogether.

"Look how beautiful it is." Nudge's voice was tired; her face was pale with shock and the effort of swimming through the death tunnel. I tried to quickly count heads, but I could only estimate that we'd lost about six of the Aquatics. More than half of the number that had started with us.

And the weird thing was, not a single person seemed bothered by Jonny's gruesome death or the loss of several of their friends. No one had mentioned it, no one seemed surprised, and no one was crying. Which told me that it was a common occurrence. That they had known about the horrific eel/snake/leech things and had gone anyway. Had made us go in anyway.

Now we were here, in supposed safety. I kept Nudge close to me, not trusting these guys for a second.

The tunnel opened up to a large hall, and Nino Pierpont had gone all out with the decorations. There were pillars and balconies, and the walls were elaborately carved shells. The ceiling hundreds of feet above was a skylight of thick glass, so dull light shone down and speckled the puddles of water, making them shimmer.

In one part of the complex, a lake had formed in a low spot when the ocean had receded after the tsunami. The result was an Olympic-sized natural swimming pool that was cut off from the danger of open water. I watched other Aquatics splashing around, flicking their fins happily.

"Max," Nudge whispered. "Doesn't it remind you of...?"

I nodded. This mutant kid utopia reminded me *exactly* of the paradise we'd first believed our island to be, and that's what made me nervous.

Because we all know how well that turned out.

I found Rizal at the communal table, surrounded by elaborate platters of fish, more fish, soup with fish in it, and then for dessert, like, fish. I slid into the seat across from him. He looked mildly annoyed, but he didn't ask me to leave.

"Let's talk about the huge, kid-eating eels of death," I said conversationally.

Rizal was distracted with his dinner and barely looked up. "Hmm?"

"The giant eely-snake things that turned Jonny Diamond into Swiss cheese?" I prompted.

"Oh, them." Rizal shoved a large spoonful of stew into his mouth. "Lampreys."

"Lampreys aren't that big. So I'm assuming they're weird, gigantic, mutant lampreys. At any rate, no one seems too bothered that those lampreys just reduced your number by six." I stared at him impatiently.

"It happens," he said, chewing. "We tend to lose someone every few days."

"Every few *days*?" I repeated, gaping at him.

Rizal shrugged. "Generally, they only pick off the less advanced."

"*There's always someone in the group who's a little vulnerable*," Jonny had said. That was supposed to be me, and would've been, if I hadn't had the oxygen tank he'd insisted I take.

"Have some sashimi," Rizal said, spearing some hunks with his knife and plopping them in front of me. "The eel is terrific."

My mind flashed back to that horrible image of Jonny—the moment he stopped struggling against the lamprey. Nauseated, I pushed away the plate and left the table.

I needed to think—which meant I needed to fly.

Unfurling my wings, which had been folded up all day, I pushed off and rose up toward the glass ceiling. My feathers twitched as I tried to imagine myself flying in circles around these walls, day after day. I was already feeling claustrophobic.

Cruising high above the chatter, I went over everything Jonny had said earlier that morning. I needed something to make it easier to cope, a moral to take away from this, and my thoughts drifted back to the flock.

Like Iggy, Jonny had needed a resolution. Like Gazzy, he had been building tools to fight, instead of hide. And like Angel, he had been sure there was more to be done.

I'm not saying I was wrong, before—I'd never say *that*—but maybe I could understand a little better why my flock had insisted on leaving.

If there was a reason so many people I cared about had died, if none of us was safe, could I really keep looking away? Didn't I owe it to them to hunt down the truth?

"Rizal says we shouldn't go looking for trouble," Jonny had said, and that was pretty much what I'd told the flock yesterday.

But if I lived by that rule, would I really be Maximum Ride?

32

"NUDGE, WAKE UP."

I didn't know why I was whispering. There were rows and rows of beds built into the coral wall, but Nudge's and mine were the only two that were occupied. I guessed the lampreys had pretty much decimated the Aquatics. What was Rizal thinking?

Total was lying on the floor—since Akila died, he'd been uncharacteristically quiet, spending time on his own, lying around a lot. I knew he was grieving, and I wished I could do more for him.

Looking at the empty beds, I could still feel some lingering sense of the kids who should've been here, the mutants and humans who had believed they were safe. I wondered if Ella had slept in any of these bunks.

"Come on, Nudgelet, let's go," I said more loudly, and shook her shoulder.

"Go?" Nudge mumbled, sinking deeper into the sponge mattress.

"Yeah," I said. "We should be gone before the Fish Sticks return from the morning hunt."

Nudge propped herself up on her elbows, alert now. "You wanna leave? Why?"

"Uh... because we're in mutant-eating-lamprey-infested waters? Did you see how everyone shrugged off Jonny's death yesterday? Rizal is just another crazy leader in a long, long line of crazy leaders we've dealt with. Do you really need another reason? We can't stay here."

Nudge blinked at me, her eyes round with alarm and already brimming. "What do you mean we can't stay?"

From the ground near the door, Total raised his furry eyebrows at me, but he didn't say anything.

Nudge, on the other hand, was incredulous. "You wanted this! The flock split up, everyone left us because you wanted to come back to this island!"

"I know. But that was before..."

Before I knew my family was really dead.

Before I heard Jonny's theories.

Before it seemed like someone could be held accountable.

"That was before we knew the vaccine was wiped out in the tsunami," I said. "Now there's no reason for us to stay. I mean, don't you want to know what happened? Don't you want some answers?"

"No!" Nudge shook her head emphatically. "That's why I didn't leave with Angel. I know more than I ever wanted to know already, and most of it's terrible. I'm tired, Max. Tired of flying around hoping for something better. The Aquatics have a good thing going here—rarities like, you know, food and actual beds." She waved her pillow. "These kids are survivors, just like us, and we're lucky they made us welcome."

"These kids are not like us. These kids are *sociopaths*."

Nudge shrugged. "Maybe their culture is just uncomplicated."

"Staying here won't help you forget about the past," I said gently.

"And leaving won't help you change it," she bit back. "The world ended, Max, and I promise, nobody blames you for not being able to save it. You don't have to go."

I held Nudge's gaze for a long time, weighing her words. "I need to know the truth," I said quietly. "I didn't before. But now I think...I think truth is better than relative safety."

Nudge nodded and hugged her pillow close, and I knew she wouldn't change her mind.

"So—you're going to stay here," I said, just to make sure. Nudge nodded again.

I looked at Total. The Scottie dog stood up, puffed out his wiry chest, and seemed to grow a little taller. "I will miss you, of course, Max. But I will stay here with Nudge. I need...time to heal. Time to reflect."

"Of course you do," I said, picking him up. He snuggled his head into my shoulder, and I tried not to cry. Nothing about my life made sense—I was going on pure instinct, and it was like walking on a tightrope, with the safety net of my flock gone.

When Total looked up, his chocolate eyes were glistening.

"Here," Nudge said, taking an oversized sweatshirt from her bedding. "Rizal said temperatures are dropping—they can sense the extra oxygen in the water."

"It's okay. I don't need—"

Nudge rolled her eyes. "I know. You don't need any help from anyone. I'm trying to give you a farewell gift. Just take it, okay?"

"My Nudgelet." Her spiral curls were fuzzy from sleep, and I kissed the top of her head affectionately. "You take extra good care of yourself, hear? If I come back and find you dead, I personally will haul you out of the grave and kill you again."

My stern lecture earned a watery smile. "You take care, too, Max."

As I walked through the cavernous halls toward the tunnel entrance, it was the first time in a long time I'd been alone, and if I'm being honest, it scared the crap out of me.

But there was one other thing Jonny had said that stuck with me: *There's always someone in the group who's a little vulnerable.* On my own, at least I'd be forced to be strong.

33

I LEFT THE caves at low tide, because the last thing I wanted to do was set foot in that water again.

I flew as long as I could through the tunnel, squeezing my body into the small space between the waves and the ceiling and flapping my wings in stunted little flicks. I was still forced underwater a few times, and I was on such high alert that I almost strangled a rogue piece of seaweed.

When I finally burst out of the tunnel, I was so happy to be free that I wanted to stay in the air forever—I didn't care how polluted it was.

Let me tell you, that feeling got old real fast.

I started off heading north. Angel had promised answers in Russia, and my mom had mentioned it the day the sky caught fire. Like Jonny, I had to trust that there were no coincidences—in this strange new world, my gut was all I had to go on.

Unfortunately, my gut didn't warn me of a tropical storm on the ol' radar. I only saw it when I was almost upon it, because of how ash-filled the sky was, even at ten thousand feet. I immediately swerved west and tried to outfly it, but it was too big.

Storm-force wind, needlelike rain, ash, and debris blasted me from all sides, twisting me around and trying to take me down. I was in the middle of the ocean, so I couldn't land; I couldn't sleep; I couldn't stop flying, even for an instant.

Out of the storm wasn't much better. I flew north for several days, alone with my thoughts and shivering inside my sweatshirt. Rizal had been right—the temperature continued to drop. I was numb and alone, and hunger gnawed me inside out every minute, but two words sustained me: *Find. Truth.* The truth, bobbing just beyond the next wave. The truth, rising with each new hazy day. It became everything.

When I finally saw the uneven blob in the distance that suggested land, I was convinced I was hallucinating. But the strip got bigger, filling the horizon. I had no idea where in the vast Russian countryside Angel would be, but I was sure she'd jailbreak my brain and send a little message via the voice—the kid had no boundaries.

So far, nothing.

As I flew farther inland, a vast, circular valley stretched

out below me, with a gray shelf of rock built up all around it. Hulking objects dotted the yellow land, and when I dove lower to get a better look, I thought I was seeing things in my exhaustion. At first my spirit soared at the realization that those dots were thousands of animals . . .

Until the smell hit me.

Every single creature lay dead. Lions, zebras, giraffes, all in varying stages of decomposition.

Uh, pretty sure there aren't giraffes in Russia, rotting or not.

I saw someone wrapped head to toe in a burgundy fabric, huddling over one of the fresher corpses—some kind of deer. I stood watching nimble fingers snatch bones already picked clean and tuck them into hidden pockets.

Finally, I tucked my wings inside my sweatshirt and cleared my throat, and the figure turned.

The amber-colored eyes were all that was visible beneath the folds of fabric, and they widened at my approach.

"You are not burned!" a woman's voice exclaimed.

"No . . ." I said uneasily.

Was that something she hoped to fix?

"Every person that comes to us from the city is burned." A man I hadn't seen stood up from behind the bulk of a water buffalo. He was also in a full robe.

"Well, I don't know what to tell you. I'm not from the city. Which city, by the way?"

Which country and which continent, for that matter?

The two swaddled figures turned toward each other in silent communication.

"Do you know why all these animals died?" I interrupted.

"Come," the woman said, walking away. "Come with us to our home and we will talk."

Exhausted, starving, and desperate for answers, I followed.

34

"THERE WAS A very bright flash of light, and then heat all around." Azizi was an animated storyteller, and his breath made the candle jump.

Once inside the mud-packed hut, my hosts had pulled their cloaks down around their shoulders, and I saw that Azizi and his sister, Nuru, had albinism. "We have to cover our skin," Nuru explained. "Or the sun cooks it."

They reminded me of Angel and Gazzy, and it wasn't just their fair hair and skin. Nuru was measured and unreadable, while Azizi could be goofy, filling the spaces between his sister's silences.

"A Jeep from one of the travel groups, its windows, *pfft*." Azizi made a fist and shot his fingers out to signify the explosion of glass.

The travel groups were safaris—I learned that I was in eastern Africa, in the Ngorongoro Crater. I'd gotten pretty turned around in that storm.

"And then the animals, they sink to their knees and lie down, one by one," Azizi went on. "They raise their voices and beg for Death to come to them! And Death, he comes."

Nuru was boiling the bones she'd collected earlier for their marrow, and she looked over to where we sat cross-legged on the mat.

"At first it was very good fortune, you can imagine. So much meat that we didn't have to hunt. But now, as you see, the meat rots, and we are very hungry."

"After the animals, every person we see is a burned man," Azizi continued. "Until you."

I leaned closer. "And what did the burn victims say?"

"One man saw a smoking tree rising into the sky, its branches full. Another said it was a pale woman standing tall with a basket on her head. My sister, she says it is God they saw in the sky."

I chewed my lip, thinking. Dead animals, burned men. Another seemingly huge disaster, but what did it have to do with a virus in Asia, or a betrayal in Russia?

"So none of these people were actually in the center? Was everyone else killed? You didn't wonder what happened?"

The siblings looked at each other—that silent understanding I'd seen earlier. Nuru's voice was soft when she spoke. "Yes. We wondered. But we cannot go back to the city."

"Why not?"

Azizi got quiet for the first time all evening. He shrugged the bright purple cloak aside, and when he unwrapped his arm, I saw that his left hand was gone at the wrist.

"In our country, albinos are said to be good fortune. Witch doctors like to lie to the people to line their pockets. So there have been attacks..."

"Someone *cut* your hand off?" I gasped.

"Bad fortune for me," Azizi said, somehow able to laugh about something so horrible.

"We came to the caldera because the Masai tribe thinks we are better luck alive than dead," Nuru said. "Many times, they bring us their cattle blood milk." She held out a cup to me.

I didn't particularly love the idea of the vampire diet, but I wasn't too picky these days. I also didn't want to be rude, so I took a long swig.

"Mmm." The mixture was thick, closer to pudding than milk, and wonderfully warm as it went down my throat. It was salty, with a sharp, coppery tang, but it wasn't half bad.

"Yes, it is nourishing." Nuru nodded as I tipped the clay cup back again. "This is the last of it now, so soon we will die."

I sputtered, choking on the dregs—I couldn't believe I'd just gulped down the last of their stash! "I'll help you find food," I promised, taking Nuru's hand.

"There is nothing." Azizi shook his head sadly. "We

have searched as far as our feet can carry us. There are only bones."

"I can search farther than you. And I can go into the city." I pulled the sweatshirt over my head and shrugged it off my shoulders, stretching my wings long.

Azizi fell backward in the dirt, scrambling away in terror, but Nuru was grinning at me.

"You are a gift to us!" she exclaimed.

I had to smile. In the rest of the world, mutants were old news, but here, I was still a novelty. Here, people still thought I could help.

35

I STRETCHED MY limbs out on the woven rug. I felt the dried grasses poking through my sweatshirt, but I didn't mind.

The earthy scent of the walls filled my nostrils, along with the musk of bodies packed close and old cooking spices—the smells of community.

I'd always thought of myself as so independent, but as I listened to Nuru's and Azizi's slow, steady breathing across the room, I realized just how terribly I'd missed my flock, and I finally felt some comfort.

In the moment before I drifted to sleep, the peaceful snoring stopped. Instead, I heard a ragged, nervous inhale, and my peripheral vision caught the arc of the blade swinging down behind my left shoulder.

My wings exploded outward, and I burst up through the mud roof before the knife could find its mark.

From twenty feet up in the air, still bewildered, I stared down through the wide, crumbling hole I'd torn in the hut. Nuru was on her feet, looking up at me, slack-jawed.

She was holding a machete.

I swooped back through the hole and tore it away from her, then glided out the door with it before my feet had ever touched the ground.

Nuru ran out of the hut, her brother trailing close behind.

I held the weapon in front of my face and plucked a cleanly halved feather off the blade. I exhaled a shaky breath.

So. Close.

When I looked back at Nuru and Azizi, the brother and sister I'd talked and laughed with, my temper exploded. "What were you doing with this thing?" I demanded, gesturing wildly.

"We are sorry," Azizi said quickly, trying to smooth it over. "It is a mistake, you understand, a misunderstanding, that is all. Do not be angry with my sister."

"We were only hungry, you see," Nuru explained.

"You were going to *eat* me?" I asked, incredulous.

"Of course not!" Azizi answered. "We are not cannibals."

"Just your wings," Nuru admitted.

Call me crazy, but I didn't find that very comforting.

"I told you I would help you find food," I said sadly, turning away from the little bit of warmth I'd yearned for.

Obviously hoping my offer was still good, Azizi called, "Come back! We are sorry!"

"No doubt," I answered, but I was already halfway across the desert by then.

36

NOW WHAT?

I had flown long enough for the cannibal creepshow to be far, far behind me, but my strength was giving out. I hadn't seen anybody or anything for miles—no trees, no water, and definitely no food. I landed on a big pile of hard-packed dirt and thought. I was hungry and dehydrated, on the wrong continent, and completely alone. No flock, no Fang, no Dylan, no nobody.

Our island in the Pacific had been destroyed, apparently Australia had been destroyed, and now here I was in eastern Africa, which seemed extra destroyed.

That was a hefty chunk of the world. What in the heck had happened, to cause so much destruction on such a huge scale? Could any one being mastermind such a thing?

It was time to gather the very last dregs of my energy and head to Russia, thousands of miles north-northeast. The very thought made me want to cry. But first I had to—

"Gah!" I yelled, leaping up and flailing my arms and legs like a maniac. I whipped off my sweatshirt, tore off the undershirt beneath that, and scrambled out of my torn and worn-out jeans. Then I did a chaotic, herky-jerky shivering dance all across the dirt.

The mound I had been sitting on was a termite colony. And those little suckers had survived and were swarming all over me like white on rice.

"Gross, gross, gross!" I screamed, since no one was around to hear. I whirled and jumped and shook my hair out and rubbed my arms and legs until I seemed to be mostly termite free.

Then, panting, I looked back at my clothes, which were now a living carpet of pale white bugs. I was in my underwear and sports bra. I would not be going anywhere like this. I had a bit of mirror—I could maybe set the bugs on fire? That mirror was...safely in the front pocket of my jeans.

I stomped a couple of times and shouted every swear word I knew, which took almost ten minutes. Then, seething, I glared at the termites. Would they eat my clothes? I stared at the sweatshirt Nudge had given me until my eyes swam with tears and my vision blurred. Once my vision blurred, those stupid bugs looked just like...rice. I remembered that many animals, including humans, ate termites. The flock and I had eaten bugs before. Not termites, but big crickets, locusts, et cetera.

My stomach felt so hollow you could practically see my spine through it.

Time to suck it up, Maximum.

I lunged for my sweatshirt, grabbed it up, and started scarfing termites.

37

TWO HOURS LATER I felt practically cheerful. That termite mound, once huge, was almost flat. I'd found termite nurseries where I could scoop up handfuls of pupae and wolf them down. Once I'd gotten used to the little feet and antennas tickling my throat, I'd started to appreciate their delicate, nutty flavor.

Now I lay flat on the ground, my belly full, my body surging to life with nourishment. "Yes, the African termite," I murmured sleepily. "A bit tart, piquant, slightly reminiscent of quinoa..."

"Ugh, get up, Max. You can rest later. You're on a mission: You have to find out if whatever happened here is connected to something bigger." Had anything Nuru and Azizi told me been true, or had they deceived me from the beginning?

So before I went to Russia, I journeyed south, figuring

that Tanzania's biggest city, Dar es Salaam, should be within a couple of hours' flight.

And it was. Or at least, what I assumed was Dar es Salaam. Basically what I found was a city of ashes.

A large, circular area had been completely razed, with every single building leveled. I didn't see any people. No corpses, either. Just shadows where everything had been incinerated—buildings, cars, and citizens, all together.

Away from the center, a few buildings were still partially standing—mostly the ones made of concrete. I flew to the top of one of them to get a better view, and I saw that its roof tiles had bubbled and blistered.

On the next block, a high-rise hotel looked like it had buckled at the knees—the lower floors had collapsed into a pile of rubble, with the untouched penthouse now balancing on top of it.

What happened here?

I was almost positive it wasn't a natural disaster. It looked more like pictures of Hiroshima after World War II.

"But who would do this?" I wondered aloud. As far as I knew, Tanzania hadn't been any kind of global threat. "Why *here*?"

"The Remedy does not discriminate."

I whipped around at the sound of the deep voice and almost gasped: A giant of a man stood watching me. I have extra-good hearing—how had he gotten so close?

"Paris, Hong Kong, New York, here... All the world's people must answer for crimes against the earth."

"Who are you?" I asked sharply. And, more important, "Who is the Remedy?"

I remembered the word from the conversation on Fang's blog. We'd thought it was a vaccine, maybe for the H8E virus. But this guy talked about it like it was a person, or some other kind of entity.

"Maximum Ride," the broad-faced man said, ignoring my questions. "You seem to have lost your flock. The Remedy doesn't like loose ends."

"I'm starting to think me and this Remedy dude wouldn't really get along."

The giant may have been freakishly huge, but he couldn't fly. I started to spring, but he was amazingly fast, and he batted me back down to the broken tiles with his massive fist as if I were a fly.

I'm stronger than most grown men, and I've been fighting for my life since I was barely able to walk. I'm lethal, and I know it. Now I fell back on the hand-to-hand combat I'd relied on so many times, dodging and weaving and getting a jab in when I could. But this guy was much stronger than most men, and stronger than me, and my hits didn't seem to faze him.

He gave me a hard left to the head, smashing my cheek and whipping my head sideways. The sudden, awful pain made me want to throw up, and my reflexes slowed.

Swallowing down bile, I lunged across his right side for a kidney jab, but he caught my neck in a headlock. We stumbled around in a strange waltz as I tore at his arm.

The giant flexed his muscles, crushing my windpipe more and more. . . .

A euphoric feeling flooded my system as the blistered roof tiles beneath my feet started to blur and my legs turned to rubber. My vision went swimmy and it suddenly seemed so easy to just give up.

No!

With my last bit of breath, I fumbled for a steak knife I'd tucked into my belt.

I chopped down hard, burying the knife in the giant's thigh. He grunted and his grip slackened a tiny bit, but it was enough. I dropped down, deadweight, and slipped out of his grasp. As he reached to pull out the knife, I seized a shard of broken tile and gouged at his eyes.

It was so, so horrible and gross. But effective.

He shrieked and lurched backward, stumbling blindly close to the edge. His huge ham hands covered his eyes, blood running through his fingers. There was a length of broken, rusty rebar sticking up out of the tiles, and I snatched it up and pointed it at his chest. If he lunged forward, he would impale himself. And I would help him.

"Let's try this again," I snarled. "Who is the Remedy?"

The giant began to laugh, his blood running into his mouth. "You believe you can escape him?" he asked. He laughed and laughed, until I was sure that grating sound would live on in my dreams. "I have failed, but more will follow, and you cannot escape us all. The Horsemen will ride on," the man said, and then leaped to his death.

38

NUDGE'S HANDS BROKE the surface of the cool, dark water as she dove. The cold made her gasp at first, but as she swam her body temperature adjusted and her skin tingled with pleasure.

The lake was Nudge's favorite place in the caves, and she came here in the early mornings while the Aquatics were out hunting. The limestone walls reflected the light through small openings, making the shadowy water glow green. It was eerie and beautiful, like a place where fairies would live. Plus, no huge, kid-eating lampreys. A definite plus.

The other kids didn't know what to make of her, so they kept their distance. She had gills, but no fins or webbed feet. But Nudge was strong, and by swimming lap after lap every day, she was getting stronger.

Her arms cut into the lake again and again with smooth, confident strokes. Her wings were folded tightly behind her. She stayed just below the surface of the water and opened her mouth like she'd seen the Aquatics do, letting in a little water so she could focus on filtering the oxygen through her gills instead of relying on her lungs.

They would call her the Flying Fish by the end of the summer.

She kept her eyes open and watched the fish swimming below her. It was so calm here, undisturbed by all the nightmares that were happening outside the caves. No snapping Cryenas, lampreys, Flyboys, or Erasers. She *hated* Erasers.

Nudge cherished the calm, even if it meant she got lonely. Even if it meant she would never see beyond these walls again.

"Don't you want to know?" The memory of Max's question nagged at her, and Nudge felt the smallest flicker of doubt.

She pushed it down as she always did, and got lost in the rhythm of her strokes until somewhere, as if in a distant world, she heard the barking.

Then a splash sent the whole lake rippling, and Nudge saw leather-booted feet wading toward her. She took in everything at once: Something was off.

The Aquatics don't wear boots.

They don't wade—they swim.

Nudge flipped, kicking hard against the wall, shooting away from those boots like a torpedo.

Her swimming had gotten quick, but he was quicker.

A gloved hand clamped around her foot, yanking her back. She felt the leather against her skin and thought of the scientists who'd tested and poked her—people always wore gloves to do dirty work.

That was when her panic really set in—the understanding of what might happen. What was about to.

No! Nudge's brain railed against the possibility. *I'm stronger than that!*

She twisted in his grasp, thrashing fiercely, but iron hands closed around her throat. A heavy booted foot pushed her down, pinning her against the lake floor.

Don't give up! a panicked part of her said. *You're the Flying Fish, and fish don't drown!*

But even flying fish need to breathe...and the hands were cutting off her gills *and* her windpipe. Her arms and legs felt weightless. The hands felt like an iron vise.

"Don't you want to know?" Max's words throbbed in her head.

As her eyes started to bulge in their sockets, the last thing Nudge saw was the strange look on the young man's face, looking down at her through the rippling water.

Now I know, Max, she thought. *Now I know the truth.*

39

HORSEMAN TRUDGED OUT of the water of the lake. His pants clung to his legs, and he was breathing heavily after the struggle.

He had expected the whole thing to be easier and was surprised at how emotional he felt. That definitely wasn't what the doctor had had in mind when he'd programmed his soldiers.

He waited several minutes, studying the rhythms of the ripples until he was sure his voice would be steady. Then Horseman pressed the call button implanted in his wrist.

A middle-aged face appeared on the screen: the Remedy. "A10103!" he exclaimed.

Horseman nodded with a humble half-smile.

"I must admit I was beginning to worry. I nearly sent a rescue mission to root you out." The doctor grinned wolfishly, and Horseman was grateful for the poor pixelation. "Tell me, how are your ... travels?"

Keep it brief, just stick to the basics, Horseman reminded himself.

"I had a most satisfying morning, Doctor."

"Oh, yes? Report: You haven't killed the whole flock, have you?" The man's bushy eyebrows jumped in feigned delight, but Horseman knew the doctor must have the same information that he did.

"No, sir. My coordinates indicate that the group has split up, so I am tracking them individually. But you'll be pleased to know that Nudge ... official name Monique," he corrected himself, "is dead."

"Well done!" the doctor praised Horseman, but blinked back at him expectantly, waiting for more information.

"Monique did not detect my approach, and my skills far outmatched hers. It was over in seconds." Horseman knew his maker would want to know how strong he was, how impenetrable.

"I see," the doctor said, sounding disappointed that there were no gruesome, salacious details.

"She ... wept in fear," Horseman offered.

"This is why we must press on in our cause." The doctor's voice rose emphatically. "The newer generations are stronger, more perfect. When it comes down to it, these so-called heroes are just accidents, like all of the older generations."

"Yes. Accidents," Horseman agreed. "Which reminds me..."

He looked across the pool of water at the ledge where Nudge's limp body lay. He watched the small dog licking her face and smiled, then positioned his arm so that his master could see the image.

"Should I also destroy the remaining canine?" Horseman asked. "It would be my pleasure."

Book Two

EVOLUTION GONE WRONG

40

RUSSIA WAS OUT—for now, anyway.

The sorry piece of crap known as the Remedy seemed to be taking credit for at least some of the destruction that was happening in the world, and the giant had said there would be more Horsemen serving him—*H-men*, as they were known on Fang's blog.

Okay, I had to think. Nudge was safe back at the caves. Angel was apparently in Russia, and God knew she could take care of herself. The boys were going to Pennsylvania, but at least they were together.

That left just me. And Fang. He'd headed to California, because someone had mentioned looters there—at least, other people. I was here, not really enjoying Africa as much as I would have liked to.

Among the cities the giant had mentioned, Paris was out—I was never going there again. Hong Kong was, I was pretty sure, a lump of rubble on the coast of China. That left New York. The fact that New York and California were on the same continent had nothing to do with my decision.

It was about seventy-five hundred miles to New York, as the bird kid flies, ha-ha. I have a top speed of over three hundred miles an hour, but I'd need a lot more calories to keep it up. So I gave myself two whole days to get there.

Oh, New York...

I almost fell out of the sky when I saw the city, or what was left of it. My mind couldn't make sense of the images it was processing: The eastern coastline was completely flooded.

I don't mean flooded like Sydney, with the waves lapping against the bottom of buildings.

I mean: New York City was *completely underwater.*

The island of Manhattan looked like hundreds of teensy different islands, with only the very tops of skyscrapers rising out of the sea. The water reached dozens of stories up, and still the tide bit at the windows, insisting on destruction.

The Brooklyn Bridge was now an underwater attraction, and as for the Statue of Liberty, only the tip of her torch broke the surface of the water.

There weren't any real torches burning, either. The City That Never Sleeps had gone completely dark.

I didn't know if it had been a tsunami or an earthquake

or a sudden melting of all of the polar ice caps—I just knew what I saw, plain and simple: the end of the world.

But in a city this huge, there had to be some survivors, right? I searched the tops of high-rises for huddled groups of people but saw no one.

Where would all the people have gone? Or had whatever happened, happened too fast? I remembered the wall of water Fang and I had seen on the day the sky caught fire—hundreds of feet high, bulldozing everything.

I'd almost drowned that day. Without wings, most people couldn't even try to fly away like we could. Unless...

The airport.

Given the state of Manhattan, I knew the New York airports would be gone. But inland—how far had the water gone? I flew to New Jersey—or the flooded space where I thought Jersey should be. The Hudson River no longer separated the two states. The river no longer existed at all.

I found my way to Newark Airport, though to this day I wish I hadn't.

The floodwaters reached about twenty-five feet up, lapping at the cabins of the bigger aircraft. Some of the planes were partially burned or otherwise wrecked; others seemed perfectly preserved, waiting in line for the runway. I saw one jet whose entryway was open, and I dipped down to check it out. Maybe there were cookies or crackers or sodas.

The smell alerted me within twenty feet, as it had in Africa. But these weren't animals. These were people. This jet was jam-packed with...corpses. Beating my wings hard, I swerved away, then did a slow cruise around the other planes. No matter the size of the aircraft, I could see that every seat was full, every aisle crammed with people. They'd been desperate, trying to escape any way they could.

Maybe a few had made it into the air—though from what I'd seen of the rest of the world, I couldn't imagine where they'd be headed. But what was left here was grim.

I spotted the control tower globe sitting high above everything like a giant eye. If anything was still moving, I'd see it from up there, so I made straight for a hole in the windows. I thought I could hear voices as I approached, so I burst into the tower room, hardly taking notice of the shattering glass around me.

Could it be...survivors?

The circular room was empty, but the voices continued, cutting in and out with static. Someone *was* alive—I could hear them on the radio.

My heart pounding with hope, I fiddled with the knobs until I got a clear channel, but what I heard was more gruesome than anything I'd witnessed that day.

"The Remedy said to shoot anything that moves," a young voice was saying.

"A clean slate means no survivors," another answered.

I covered my mouth, inhaling sharply. The giant had said the Remedy was striking around the world indiscriminately, but I still didn't know what the scope might be.

What do these kids mean, "No survivors?"

How many other places in the world resemble the destruction of New York?

What could this man's motive possibly be, and why does he call himself the Remedy if all he wants is death?

I surfed through the stations for hours, desperate to find some information I could use, but I didn't find any other signs of life. Finally I flicked off the switch. I couldn't go back out into this awful world, though. Not yet. Not today.

Instead, I curled up on the thin carpet, and I let myself cry.

I wept for the billions of dead, and the thousands more still dying.

I wept for New York. I wept for Sydney. I wept for Dar es Salaam and for Jonny and Rizal on the island. I wept for Ella, and my mom, and Dylan, and Akila.

I wept for my lost flock, for Fang. I wept for myself.

I wept for the whole human race, because for the first time in my life, I really felt like a part of it, and I understood, finally, how much we had lost.

I cried until my throat was raw and my eyes were swollen shut, but even then, I couldn't sleep.

41

FANG HAD NO idea where to start.

He'd made it to the western United States, but that didn't mean he had any idea how to find these so-called H-men. It wasn't like he could just ask, either. LA was underwater, Vegas was a blackened ghost town, and anyone he did happen to see was so panicked and terrified that a productive conversation was impossible.

He'd taken to flying low along the coast, scanning for pockets of people among the destruction. But without friends to talk to, without Max, the days felt empty. And long.

Now that Fang had a death sentence, he felt like he had all the time in the world, and it was excruciating. The last thing he needed right now was an existential crisis, but it turned out that the more time you had, the more questions you started to ask. Like *Why me? Why now?* Until you couldn't think around all the *whys.*

Until your whole existence was one big question mark.

When the heat from one of the prevalent forest fires got too hot for him, Fang rose high above the clouds. He saw a flock of seagulls in the distance ahead, and though such a routine sight should have comforted him, like everything else, it left him questioning.

He hadn't seen a single other bird in weeks, so why were these gulls here? Why, instead of in a typical V, were they flying in a chaotic, swirling flurry? And why were there so many of them?

More and more birds joined the mass, rolling toward him like a snowball, gaining speed and power.

Fang had a brief flash of watching seagulls squabbling viciously over a potato chip at the beach. As hundreds of slate-gray eyes with their pinprick pupils honed in on him, he had a sudden realization: He was the potato chip.

Fang jerked back, but the gulls were already all over him. Dirty gray wings beat in his face, and they screeched and jabbed one another in their frenzy to get at his skin.

They went for the exposed parts of him first—his face, his neck, his hands—but soon dove at anything not covered by fabric. Sharp beaks tore out clumps of hair and gouged his cheeks.

Fang held one arm across his eyes and tried to gain altitude, but the gulls didn't let up. On every inch of skin, exposed nerves sang in protest as the wind found the fresh wounds.

I'm one of you! Fang wanted to scream, but they were pecking at his lips, and he couldn't open his mouth.

The squawking in his ears and the full-body attack made coherent thought impossible, and Fang kept trying to fly upward, unsure of what the gulls' top altitude could be. This meant his wings were fully exposed, and with raucous cries the birds tore into his glossy black feathers. Fang felt the rawness in the spaces between them as whole rows were plucked away.

Looking over his shoulder, he found that his wings didn't look like his own. They looked *alive*, and he couldn't see a single glimpse of black through all the gray and white.

The weight of the seagulls' bodies pulled down on him, and flying was getting tougher and tougher. The gulls pulled his right wing down, and he spun. He tried to force both wings up together, and he veered.

Fang felt the déjà vu sensation he'd had in Angel's vision—his guts rock-heavy, panic mounting, wings useless. He didn't feel invincible like he had with the Cryenas; he felt wracked with panic.

This is it. This is it. This is it, the seagulls seemed to shriek.

But Fang balked. This couldn't be it—not out here, not like this.

He wasn't ready yet.

He coaxed every bit of power he had into his torn-up body and slingshotted himself high into the sky at close to two hundred miles an hour.

The last-ditch effort worked and the birds were sucked off him, but it almost didn't matter at that point.

Fang wasn't sure how much of him was left.

42

I WAS FLYING west over what I thought was Kentucky when I spotted my lunch.

With its long, W-shaped wings, it had looked like a vulture, and my chest tightened at the thought of all the corpses that were piling up everywhere. The world was a scavenger's feast.

But as I got closer and saw the white torpedo-shaped body, I realized it was a seagull. It was weird to see one this far from water, but it was probably starving, like everything else that was still alive.

My stomach grumbled pointedly.

I guess it's a bird-kid-eat-bird world we're living in.

The gull had good evasive maneuvers, but I was better, and it had been ages since the termite-fest in Tanzania.

Afterward, my stomach seized in protest and I wondered if the bird had been ill or full of poisonous chemicals. I felt nauseous and dizzy for miles, concentrating on not puking up the only food I might see for days, and when I finally looked down, I realized I'd gotten completely off track.

I thought I'd been flying over the Midwest, but I didn't recognize the landscape at all. The earth was as parched as a desert, with a deep, endless gash in the ground that I couldn't identify. The snaking shape was like a mini Grand Canyon, so big that it was certainly a landmark I would've recognized.

Then it hit me: It was the Mississippi River. The gull had probably been trying to find water. The thing was, there wasn't any. It was *completely dried up.*

As I continued westward, things got even weirder. The city of St. Louis seemed to have a big barricade around it, and between the windmills of the prairie states, the tall grasses fed whirling tornadoes of fire.

I didn't buy everything Angel had said—I still thought it was better to gather information than follow a bossy kid wherever she commanded, for example. But after seeing the extent of the devastation, I knew she was right about one thing: Something bigger was building.

And if, as I'd overheard on the radio, there were people massacring whoever they found, then having the flock members separated and vulnerable was about the worst idea ever right now.

Which brought me to: I had to find Fang.

43

FANG HAD LOST a lot of blood in the bird attack, and by the time he'd reached the edge of the Rocky Mountains in what was probably Wyoming, he'd been so exhausted and light-headed that all he could do was flop down in a dry creek bed.

Now all his wounds were covered with pus-filled scabs, he was so dehydrated that his lips were cracked and bloody, and he was near starvation. He thought he'd read that you could eat anything that smelled like mint, but the spiny purple flowers he'd found had made him hallucinate for three days.

So when he first heard the voices, he wasn't sure they were real.

"I mean, I signed up for the cleanup crew to kill some

freaks, you know?" a young male voice complained from shockingly nearby. "But everybody's already dead."

Fang had been so weak he hadn't sought out proper shelter. Cursing his carelessness, he flattened himself against the dusty red earth.

He'd spent days trying to track down the H-men and hadn't been able to catch even a whiff of their scent in the crackling desert air. Now that he was in such bad shape, the Remedy's goons were the very last people he wanted to encounter.

That was the way the world worked, though: Life always managed to surprise you with child assassins at just the right moment. And find him they did.

"Well, look what we have here," a stocky boy said with obvious delight when he almost stepped on Fang.

So much for hiding.

"Nice score, Chuck." Another kid with bright yellow hair and a face erupting with acne stumbled into view.

The boys couldn't be more than twelve or thirteen, but they already had the swagger of abusive power. Fang eyed the shotguns slung over their shoulders. They held the guns with casual affection, obviously used to handling them.

"You said the scavengers had picked these trails clean," chubby Chuck said to his companion. He nodded at Fang's wounds. "Looks like they got a taste and decided the meat was too tough."

That's not too far off base, Fang thought.

"Lucky for me, my Benelli doesn't discriminate," the blond one said, his hand caressing the gun.

Fang stared back at them from sunken eye sockets. Were these posturing preteens, who days earlier he could've knocked out cold with a flick of the wrist, really going to be his executioners? Fang actually started laughing at his sorry situation.

"Is something funny?" Chuck demanded, trying to sound tough but verging on a whine. "Keep laughing. We'll shut you up by cutting out your tongue before we kill you."

"Or we could just string you up in a dead tree," the nameless pimpled punk offered. "Leave you for the vultures to polish off."

"Go ahead, please prove your manhood by one-upping each other in acts of cruelty," Fang said dryly. If they didn't use the guns, he might stand a chance. Maybe.

Trying not to wince, Fang struggled to his feet. The boys immediately cocked their weapons, their faces twitching nervously, but neither shot.

"Who do you think you are?" the blond kid demanded, and Fang didn't miss the slight quiver in his voice. He would take full advantage of it.

Fang unfurled his huge wings. With his black feathers framing his scabbed face and haunted eyes, he looked like the Angel of Death, and he knew it. He smiled, and the blond kid stumbled backward, suddenly pale.

"Renny, look at him," Chuck chided, awestruck. "He's obviously a Horseman. Idiot."

Fang kept his poker face. He still had no idea what the H-men looked like, but if he could convince these twerps he was one of them, he'd take it.

"A Horseman?" Renny asked excitedly. "Maaan. Who did you fight?" He glanced at Fang's scars and bruises.

"A whole bunch of...survivors," Fang said, mildly amused. If he played along, maybe he could actually get some information out of these morons.

"Did you cut their heads off?" Chuck asked, his cruel eyes sparkling. "I heard they're like zombies—if you don't cut off the head, they're not dead."

Fang's jaw twitched with fury as he imagined his flock's necks stretched over chopping blocks.

"The weak must be rooted out," Chuck recited. "The earth shall be cleansed so we may evolve."

Pretty sure that's not how evolution works.

Fang stared at these little monsters with black, unblinking eyes. "Who did you say you were with again?"

"We serve the One Light," Renny said. He lowered his gun and sat on the rock across from Fang.

So the Doomsday Group is still alive, still wreaking destruction.

When the flock had run across the cult a year ago, its glassy-eyed members had a mission of global genocide. The flock had done a lot to break the cult up, but obviously not enough.

Since then, apparently someone had taken things to the next level.

"We're hoping the Remedy will turn us into Horsemen one day," the yellow-haired boy continued chattily. "They say you just have to kill fifty survivors. I'm only at seven so far, but Chuck's already up to like twenty."

"Twenty-two," the bigger kid corrected.

Fang had no doubt that number was an exaggeration, but from the naked meanness in Chuck's eyes, Fang was sure he'd killed at least a couple of helpless souls.

Fifty people, Fang thought disgustedly. The Remedy was convincing kids all over the world to kill at least fifty innocent people each.

"That's just a rumor," he said. "The Remedy values intelligence above all in his elite squad." He raised a skeptical eyebrow at Chuck. "Guess that means you boys are out of luck. Sorry."

"I could do anything the Remedy asked me to do," Chuck said hotly, his round cheeks flushing with color.

"Maybe you could train us," Renny suggested eagerly. "Teach us what it takes to be an elite soldier."

"Maybe so," Fang said. "My services aren't free, though. You got any food?"

Renny nodded and fished some jerky from his pocket.

"Okay, then." Fang's dark irises glittered with contempt. "Class is now in session."

44

"FIRST LESSON: MURDERING people to purify the population isn't evolution," Fang explained in his patient teacher voice. "That's genocide."

Chuck squinted at him, obviously weighing Fang's words against what he'd been taught. He wasn't quite ready to challenge Fang, though—not without the support of the other kid. And Renny was looking up at Fang with open adoration, his shotgun leaning against the rock pile.

"And second..." Fang walked slowly around the boys, noting the positions of cacti in his path as he gathered strength to make his move. "If you like to pick on the weak, you should remember that there's always someone stronger than you."

Moving fast, Fang kicked Renny's gun away, then snap-kicked the kid's knees before he could make a move. He spun around, lunging toward Chuck, but the bigger kid had already flipped his weapon to his hip.

"*These* make us strong," he said, curling his lip as he pointed it at Fang. "Freak."

And then he pulled the trigger.

Fang launched himself into a somersault right as he heard the first loud *pop-pop-pop* and saw the dust fly at his feet.

Then, when he grimly expected the next volley of bullets to rip into his flesh, Fang heard Renny squeal and Chuck groan instead.

Turning, he saw a blur of motion: a sneaker driving into Renny's gut, pigtails flying as legs propelled in a wind-mill toward Chuck's red face. All of this was at lightning speed, too—by the time the shells from the first round hit the ground, the acrobatic avenger had both boys on the ground, curled up, gun free, and moaning.

"Star?" Fang said, recognizing the preppy blonde who'd been a member of his mutant gang when he'd broken off from the flock. Star had supernatural speed, sometimes moving too fast to be seen. And even in this stifling heat, she hadn't broken a sweat.

"Think you can handle them now?" she asked. Without waiting for an answer, she sped off.

"As I was saying..." Fang looped the rifle slings around his neck. "There's always going to be someone more skilled than you, more powerful than you. Now, march."

Fang hauled both boys up by their shirt collars and prodded them in the back with a rifle. Ideally he'd love to pick them up and fly around with them until they barfed, but he wasn't up to that. Not in the shape he was in. He would have to improvise.

There was a rough outcropping of rock, maybe about three feet wide, that leaned far over a canyon. It was a little canyon, only a couple of hundred feet deep, but the boys would certainly go splat if they took a misstep.

"Keep going," he said mildly, edging them onto the outcropping.

Frowning, the blond kid turned around to protest, but Fang pointed a rifle at him.

Carefully the boys took tiny sidesteps, holding on to each other. The blood drained from their faces as Fang urged them farther and farther over the canyon.

"So what have we learned, kids?" Fang asked when the boys were only inches from the edge.

"That you're a big jerk," Renny said, though his voice quavered.

Fang laughed, then said, "No. We've learned that what goes around, comes around. We've learned that if you target the weak, you'll be targeted by someone who sees *you* as weak. We've learned that guns are a no-no." With that, Fang unlooped the straps and tossed the rifles over the ledge.

The boys cried out in unison, lunging and grasping at air as the rifles disappeared over the cliff.

"You might as well have killed us!" Chuck said, his bravado failing him. "How are we supposed to protect ourselves without guns? Or hunt?"

Fang almost felt a twinge of guilt for leaving them like this—the boys weren't much older than Gazzy or Angel. The only difference was, they'd bragged about killing dozens of people.

That was enough of a difference for Fang.

"Whatever you do, don't eat the purple flowers," Fang advised, backing away. "They might smell nice, but trust me, that's not the kind of trip you want to take."

"You can't just leave us here!" the kids wailed.

"Sure I can," Fang said, praying he had enough energy for his takeoff.

"We'll get eaten by bears or something!"

"Survival of the fittest," Fang called over his shoulder. "Now *that's* evolution. Class dismissed." With a running jump, he threw himself out over the canyon, snapping his wings out and feeling grateful that even in their sorry state they could still support him. Now he just had to find Star again.

45

STAR WAS ALREADY more than five miles down the winding trail when Fang spotted her. He came to a somewhat clumsy landing right behind her and called her name, but she didn't acknowledge him, and Fang felt anger flare in his chest.

Star had betrayed him, his gang, and the flock, and now *she* was ignoring *him*? Still, at this point, Fang badly needed any tips he could get. From anyone. He kicked up red dust as he trotted to keep up with what, for her, was no doubt a snail's pace.

"I just wanted to say thanks," he said, breathing heavily from the continued strain on his still-mending body.

"Yeah, well, I owed you one," Star said curtly, and kept her gaze fixed straight ahead into the mountains. "Now we're even."

Star had a lot of pride, and that was probably about as close to an apology as Fang was going to get, but now that he was facing the girl who had caused him so much anguish, he couldn't hide his disgust.

"*Even?*" he sneered. Star and her best friend Kate's betrayals had resulted in the death of Maya, Max's clone and another member of Fang's gang. "I would say that you and Kate both are still pretty far from even."

"Save the lecture," Star said, whirling to face him. "I wasn't trying to make up. I just thought it'd be pathetic to watch a former leader get slaughtered by stupid Doomsday kids." She put her hands on her hips and smiled, her tone cutting. "I took pity on you, Fang. That's all it was."

"Well, you haven't changed much," Fang muttered.

Always a delight to be around.

In fact, Star had changed a lot. He'd known her as a rich boarding school priss who always had perfectly applied makeup, but now she was haggard, her cheeks sunken. The girl had always been rail thin, but now she was downright gaunt. Fang knew her metabolism ran as fast as the rest of her, which meant that if he was struggling to eat, she was, too.

Star turned from him, her pigtails swinging behind her, and took off again.

"Hey!" Fang yelled after her. This time, she was almost out of sight by the time he got the word out. "Do you want some food?"

Reappearing in just seconds, Star grabbed the jerky

Fang held out and shoved it hungrily into her mouth. As hard as it was for Fang to watch his precious meal disappear, it was worth it if it would buy him some information.

"Have you seen any of these Horseman things?" he asked while she chewed. "What should I watch out for? What do they look like?"

"Like anyone," Star said around a big bite, suddenly sounding a lot more amicable. "Like you. Like me."

"What do you mean?"

"It depends on what they were before." Star shrugged her slight shoulders. "That's what I learned when Jeb promised me a way out. He tried to inject me with the serum, said it was just going to give me an upgrade."

Blood rushed to Fang's temples, and his whole body tensed.

"Relax, bird breath." Star rolled her eyes, but she was clearly enjoying his discomfort. "You think I'd actually let them do that to me? I told them I didn't need a Remedy, that I was perfect enough, thanks. Then I hightailed it outta that Siberian wasteland faster than you can say 'Ah.'"

Siberia? "So *Jeb's* the Remedy?" Fang felt sick. Once Jeb had been his surrogate father. Once Fang had thought he was capable of love and goodness. He knew better now, but was Jeb really capable of the ultimate act of evil?

"Jeb's the manufacturer," Star corrected. She propped her instep against a boulder and started to stretch, wincing. "I don't know who's pulling the strings at the top."

Fang didn't know whether to be relieved Jeb was just a

pawn or frustrated that the Remedy's identity was still a mystery. Either way, he had to find that lab.

"And this is all going down somewhere in Russia?"

Great. Another thing Angel can hold over us. Fang smiled to himself, though, feeling a surge of love for his bossy little sister.

Star nodded, massaging her knotted calf muscle. "That's what I heard. I heard them call it Himmel."

"Angel has people gathering in Russia already. I don't know what she has planned, but I've got to get there a-sap. Join me?"

Star snapped her head up sharply at the suggestion. "Uh-uh. No way." Fang could see the fear in her usually defiant ice-blue eyes. "Those people don't want to make improvements—they want to replace all humankind with robots. I'm fine on my own."

This time when she ran, she didn't wait for him to catch up. The only evidence that she'd ever been there at all was the dust cloud disappearing over a distant ridge and the jerky wrapper on the ground at his feet.

46

BY MY CALCULATIONS, I was somewhere in the Mojave Desert, and I hadn't seen another person in twenty-seven and a half days.

Of course I was keeping track—what the heck else was there to do?

After my last two encounters with people and what I'd overheard in New Jersey, I chose the harshest routes and flew high in the clouds, avoiding cities for fear of running into prowling raiders.

Then, before I knew it, I didn't really have to try anymore. As far as I could tell, there wasn't anyone else alive. At first it was a relief—didn't have to avoid anyone—and then it became really bleak. And really lonesome.

I resorted to having long, drawn-out arguments with

myself, like, for example, did a lizard or a tarantula have a higher protein content?

(Probably the tarantula.)

If a bird kid screams in an empty desert, does she still make a sound?

(All signs point to yes.)

Yeah, my brain was mostly fried.

So when I saw the human silhouette with a giant wingspan soaring between the distant mountains, I was pretty sure I was hallucinating.

I flew toward it anyway, keeping my eyes trained on the graceful shadow diving and climbing, gliding and dipping. As I got closer, the mirage didn't disappear, but instead multiplied, and I found myself holding my breath.

I knew my flock's flight patterns like I did my own name, and it clearly wasn't Fang, or anyone in the flock.

But the five shapes ahead of me were definitely bird kids, and *man*, could they fly! Their wings were larger than mine, and their movements were so natural, so graceful, that you saw the bird in them before you noticed their human bodies.

I'd planned to approach cautiously, but several of them were already flying close and playfully cutting under my slipstream.

For the first time in months, I didn't feel the weight in my tired wings. I just felt the pure joy of being able to freaking fly with others of my kind, without having them suddenly turn on me. Also, maybe they had food—they looked in good shape, from what I could glimpse.

"You guys are amazing!" I called out. They didn't seem to hear me, though—the wind was probably too gusty.

Taking a risk, I followed them back to their homes, which were...uh, *nests* balancing between mountain ledges. Okay, that was unusual. I dropped down carefully, and several of them turned to stare at me with curiosity.

"Hey! I'm Max. Have you guys seen any other bird kids?" I asked. As more of them landed, I was struck by the way they knelt on the ground, folding their wings behind them. "I'm missing part of my flock. A guy named Fang—he's dark, with dark wings...or a tall blind guy, or a shorter blond boy?"

Then it hit me: They looked like the flock—tall and lean human bodies with wings attached behind the shoulders—but they behaved...differently. As I spoke, they cocked their heads in sharp little movements and made clicking sounds in the back of their throats.

And...they were naked. Not naked as in acres of skin, but naked as in without clothes. These kids were covered with feathers *all over*—thick, downy feathers, everywhere but their heads.

Between my cracked lips and matted hair, I'd been feeling pretty feral, but these kids were straight-up *wild*. They flew like birds because they actually *were* more like birds than humans.

As the possibility of communication dwindled, the giddiness I'd felt at finding another flock seeped away, to be replaced by disappointment. And when I felt someone nuzzling against my shoulder, I jumped.

His light brown hair was curling and tousled, and his bright smile was punctuated by two perfect dimples. He was about my age, with unusually large eyes that were a gorgeous shade of amber. He was adorable. In an avian-mutant kind of way.

"And who are you?"

"Huryu!" he repeated gleefully. "Huryu, Huryu!" He was like a parrot latching on to a new word. So they really didn't talk like people. My disappointment turned into crushing despair with no warning. The first people I'd seen in twenty-seven and a half days...

My throat closed up and my eyes started to sting. I couldn't believe it. Would it kill the universe to cut me a break once in a while? Turning away, I wiped my eyes and wondered what the heck to do now. Then I felt something tugging at my feathers.

I whipped around. "What are you doing?"

"Huryu?" he asked, wide-eyed, and combed his fingers through my hair. Of course he hit snarls immediately, and with a look of concentration, he carefully picked at them, easing them loose, stroking them with his feathers. He was grooming me, making little cooing, chirruping sounds.

Instinctively I wanted to push him away, but I'd been on my own for so long...and he was kind of like me, my flock. With tears running down my face, I sat there and let myself be groomed.

47

THE SUN WENT down, but no one made a fire. Mostly in pairs, sometimes in small groups, these bird kids began curling up in their nests, huddling together for warmth. I made camp a little ways away from them, on flatter ground, feeling desolate and somehow more alone than ever.

I was almost asleep when the velvety sound of sweeping feathers made me look up. It was my number one fan, and lo and behold, he came bearing gifts. He had brought me a seriously large rattlesnake, and as he fluttered down in front of me, he dropped it at my feet.

The snake had only been stunned, and it quickly wound itself into a deadly coil. Its tail rattled in warning— it was wide awake now, and definitely within striking distance.

"Jeezum!" I said, scrambling backward. "What are you doing?"

But he flashed his dimpled grin and picked the snake up by the end of its tail. He swung it overhead and whipped the head against the ground, then proudly presented it to me.

"Huryu!" he said softly, and patted the snake.

"Yeah, I get it..." I said. "Uh, good boy."

Then he held the scaly body up to my lips, nodding eagerly. Did this count as flirting in the animal world?

"Cool. Let's cook it first, though, okay?" After the raw fish, raw seagull, and raw termites, I was desperate to have something warm for once.

The bird kid looked shocked when I struck a flint and made a small fire, then appalled as I skinned and gutted the snake. He clearly thought those were the best parts, because he quickly gobbled them up as soon as I dropped them on the ground.

I skewered the long body on a stick, turning it over the fire, and I had to admit, it wasn't bad and there was plenty of it. If you're wondering, it tasted kind of like chicken.

My new pal ate with sharp little movements, jerking his head forward to peck off a chunk of meat, but he studied me the entire time with those wide eyes.

"What?" I said. "I'm sorry, but I don't speak bird."

Then, from who knows where, he took out a crumpled piece of paper and thrust it at me. And I suddenly understood why he was so drawn to me.

It was a folded, wrinkled page of magazine from about a year ago. I touched the picture with trembling fingertips, tracing over the faces: Nudge and Gazzy hamming it up for the camera, Angel looking sweet and defiant at the same time, Fang standing protectively just behind my shoulder.

"'Maximum Ride and Flock Take On Congress.'" I read the headline aloud, choking up at the memory.

"Maaaaaaax," said the bird kid, my name sounding odd and guttural.

I looked up at him.

"Maximum," I said, pointing a thumb at my chest. "Maximum Ride. But you can just call me Max."

"Maaaax Mum. Maaaaax Mum. Maaaaax Mum," he repeated, and I sighed.

"Okay. Maximum it is."

He touched his own chest. "Huryu."

"Uh... that's not actually a name," I muttered, thinking quickly. "Harry," I said firmly, and touched his chest. *"Harry."*

He reached out and touched my chest and I tried not to scream. His gentle fingers stroked the cloth of my ratty sweatshirt carefully. "Maaaax," he said softly.

I nodded again. "Max." And for some reason I teared up.

48

"GET READY..." Gazzy said, lighting the waxed rope.

Iggy stuck his fingers in his ears.

There was a low, nervous clucking sound, and then a big bang. Feathers rained down, snagging on the pine trees, and when the smoke cleared, three wild turkeys were no longer very wild.

"Most excellent," Gazzy said, beaming, his face covered in black film.

"Well, that's one way to cook a turkey," Iggy laughed.

It was hard not to be giddy. After the miles and miles of mass destruction they'd flown over these past couple of weeks, they'd found the forests of Appalachia somehow untouched. Now they were sitting on the cement platform of an old campsite, chowing down on the first hot meal they'd had in what felt like years.

"Ig, no kidding, this is the best thing I've ever tasted." Juice ran down Gazzy's chin as he devoured the meat. "You should have your own postapocalyptic cooking show or something."

"Oh, totally. 'Tune in next week for *Seasoning the Squirrel, Blowing Up the Bird*,'" Iggy said in an announcer voice. Then he pursed his lips. "I was actually thinking it tastes a little funky."

Gazzy tore off another big hunk, considering. "Maybe you went a little overboard with the rosemary?" he suggested.

Iggy paused with a turkey leg halfway to his mouth. "Rosemary?" he repeated skeptically. "You don't think it might have something to do with the fertilizer you used?"

"Hey, I got a fire going, didn't I?" Gazzy pointed out. "I didn't see any gunpowder or ice packs in that farmer's shed, did you?"

Iggy shrugged. "Well, it's definitely a step up from bugs and rats."

"Are you kidding?" Gazzy said, poking the charred birds with a stick. "This is a regular Thanksgiving feast. Hey, maybe we should say what we're thankful for!"

"I'm thankful I'm not currently eating bugs and rats," Iggy said immediately.

Gazzy nodded. "I'm thankful for the stupidity of wild turkeys."

"Since this is supposed to be Thanksgiving, I'm thankful for the *memory* of garlic mashed potatoes drenched in butter. Or yams with marshmallows." Iggy sighed.

Gazzy's eyes twinkled. "Oh, man. Remember when Nudge wanted us to celebrate Thanksgiving like normal people, and we went all out trying to cook, but the marshmallows caught on fire?"

Iggy chuckled, remembering. "We almost burned down Dr. Martinez's kitchen!"

"And then Ella ate all the burned yams to make Nudge feel better, insisting that she just really liked the smoky flavor?"

At the mention of Ella, Iggy went silent and stopped eating. The lines around his mouth deepened in pain.

"Ig?" Gazzy whispered after a few minutes.

"Hmm?"

"I miss the flock," Gazzy said even more quietly.

Iggy nodded, but his milky, blind eyes were like a concrete wall.

"But Ig?"

"Hmm?"

Gazzy reached a tentative hand out and squeezed Iggy's shoulder. "I'm thankful I've still got you, though. And that we're still alive."

Iggy turned his head in Gazzy's direction, his face softening. "Me too, little bro. Me too."

And just as the moment started to feel a little too heavy, a low, hornlike sound rippled through the air. The fire flared up in response.

"Oh, God!" Iggy scooted away, holding his nose.

Gazzy was giggling like a maniac.

Iggy shook his head in disgust, but he was grinning. "Gasman, I knew I could count on you to keep it real."

"Freeze, scumbags!" a gravelly female voice shouted from the woods.

Iggy and Gazzy leaped to their feet, sending burning pine needles flying.

But they were already surrounded.

49

AT LEAST A dozen heavily armed teenage girls circled Iggy and Gazzy just beyond the trees, holding crossbows.

"What didn't you understand about the word 'freeze'?" asked the leader, a girl with dreadlocks and sharp eyes, stepping closer. When she saw the burn marks on the ground, color rushed to her cheeks. "Did you actually try to blow up our silo?" she barked.

Silo?

"Are you kidding me?" Iggy said as Gazzy gaped at the cement circle they'd assumed was a camping platform.

The boys had been working their way north toward Pennsylvania to try to find the blog commenter and his silo. They never imagined they'd been sitting *right on top of it.*

"You Doomsday guys think you can come here with your cleanup crews, take whatever you want, kill whoever you want?" another girl with dark hair asked shrilly.

"No! We're not—"

Dreadlocks narrowed her eyes. "We play by different rules." She cocked her weapon, and the sound echoed around the circle as all the other girls followed suit, stepping out from behind the branches.

With the flock backing them up, the boys might've had a fighting chance, but with just the two of them, they were seriously outnumbered.

"We're not armed!" Gazzy shrieked, putting his hands up.

"And we're not with Doomsday," Iggy, who had once been hypnotized by the cult, said more calmly. "We're mutants, see?"

He unfurled his pale fifteen-foot wings over his head, and Gazzy did the same. As if that weren't proof enough, they fluttered their feathers.

The leader stared at them, unimpressed. "The Remedy's got plenty of mutants working for him," she noted, and the crossbows stayed trained on Iggy and Gazzy.

"Not us. We came because we have a friend here," Gazzy explained hurriedly. "From the Internet. We had this flock, and not bragging or anything, but we were kind of famous..." He knew he was babbling, but he was desperate to buy some time. "So he went on our website and said we were welcome to visit. He called himself PAtunnelratt? It was an avatar?"

He looked around with raised eyebrows, waiting for recognition, but Dreadlocks' answer was flat and final: "Don't know him."

Iggy pressed. "Are you sure? He said his dad—"

"Must've been somewhere else," she snapped. "The government built fallout shelters all through these mountains in the 1950s. Could be anywhere."

"But—"

Another girl's impatient voice cut in. "There aren't any guys living here, period."

Iggy's eyebrow jumped with interest. "Just girls?"

"Yeah," she said. "Just us."

"Sweeeet." Gazzy exhaled in wonder. From his dopey expression, he seemed to have forgotten about the threat and was convinced they'd landed in heaven. Iggy elbowed him.

The girls sighed in annoyance but seemed to understand that the bird kids didn't pose much of a threat, and they relaxed their grip on their weapons.

"You still owe us for those turkeys," Dreadlocks said, gesturing at the pile of feathers and charred meat. "The forests are almost picked clean of game, and we can't afford to lose them."

Iggy crouched down and ran his hands over their meager supplies. "We don't really have anything to barter. Maybe we can pitch in?"

The leader regarded them coolly. "And what makes you think we need any help?"

"You know, with guy stuff." Gazzy broadened his nine-year-old chest. "I know it can be hard without a man around. Any basic repairs you need done? Heavy lifting?"

Dreadlocks scowled, and her finger hovered over the trigger again, threatening to release the arrow.

"Jackie, don't we have that thing we need done at the *bottom* level?" the dark-haired girl interrupted. "You know." She wiggled her eyebrows at Gazzy and flashed a white, sharklike smile. "Men's work."

The leader frowned in confusion at first, but the other girls around the circle started to laugh. Iggy and the Gasman were definitely not in on it, but Gazzy grinned anyway, happy to have the attention of so many giggling girls at once.

Iggy's expression was more uncertain. Without the benefit of sight, he was more attuned to the subtleties of sound, and he was pretty sure the laughter was at their expense.

Dreadlocked Jackie relaxed as she, too, understood what the dark-haired girl was implying. "Actually, come to think of it," she answered, "there *are* some things we could use some muscle on. Thank God you showed up!"

50

"NICE GOING, DOOFUS," Iggy grumbled.

"I was just trying to be neighborly," Gazzy said, his voice echoing around the small room. "What if they had really needed our help?"

The boys were on their hands and knees, scrubbing crusty cement walls with hard-bristled brushes and heavy-duty chemicals. Iggy sat back on his heels and nodded at the armed guard he heard pacing the scaffolding above them.

"Pro tip, macho man: When someone has a crossbow pointed at your head, they're probably not all that vulnerable."

"I *said* I was sorry!"

The room was at least a hundred feet underground, at

the very bottom of the silo. The dim light made it hard to see—and though that didn't make much difference to Iggy, Gazzy was grateful. He didn't want to know what the walls looked like, or what they were scrubbing.

They could both smell it well enough.

"*'Men's work*,'" Iggy scoffed, shaking his head. "Oh, would Max get a kick out of this. I can almost hear her laughing from across the ocean."

"At least Max never made us clean toilets," Gazzy said, dunking his brush into a rusty metal pail of cleaner.

"We call it the dump tank," the guard called from above them. "We figured since most guys are crap, you two would feel right at home."

"I'm pretty sure that girl with the black hair has a thing for me," Gazzy said wistfully as they worked.

Iggy shook his head. "*That's* what you're thinking about right now? Man, you sure have a one-track mind."

"Hey, she totally wiggled her eyebrows in my direction. I think she was checking out my wings." Gazzy spread his wings proudly in the darkness, as if the girl were watching right now.

But Iggy was skeptical. "She was, like, probably almost twice your age."

"Women dig a younger man. When we get out of here, I'm gonna make some fireworks—you know, romance her the old-fashioned way."

"I'm glad someone has motivation."

Iggy's mind was on something else, though. He was

remembering what the leader, Jackie, had said—that the woods were almost picked clean of food. The guys had thought they'd finally found an untouched paradise among all the wreckage, but it sounded like they wouldn't be able to survive here for long. And neither would these girls.

"Gasman? I've been thinking," Iggy said in a more serious tone. He heard Gazzy stop scrubbing for a second, waiting for him to continue. "Maybe we should join up with the flock again. Somebody needs to stand up to this Remedy dude, and there are obviously some tough survivors left in the world."

As nervous as Iggy had been when they were first surrounded, when he'd learned that this troupe of street-smart survivors was against the Remedy, his spirit had been buoyed with hope.

"If we met up with Angel, and convinced some of these girls to join us..." Iggy trailed off.

"Then we might just stand a chance," Gazzy finished. Iggy couldn't see, but Gazzy's eyes were glistening.

"Let's do it," he said enthusiastically, and nudged Iggy's shoulder. "Let me just go grab my girlfriend, and we can leave for Russia right now!"

They heard a gurgling sound, and then a pipe protruding from the wall started to spit. Fresh sludge surged onto the floor.

"Gross!"

The guard laughed as they scrambled away from the slime. "You missed a spot," she taunted.

"It's a regular comedy hour down here," Iggy muttered, lifting his wet feet in disgust.

Gazzy watched the waste circling down the drain. "What's the point of cleaning this place if it just keeps pumping down?"

Iggy pulled his shirt up over his nose to filter the fresh stink. "There is no point," he said, his voice muffled. "*That's* the point—we're unnecessary."

"Ugh, I just can't take the smell," Gazzy said, gagging.

Iggy chuckled to himself. "Oh, Gasman, I think that aroma's called *karma*."

Gazzy socked Iggy in the arm.

"Wait, I smell something else," Iggy whispered suddenly. "There's someone in here with us."

51

HORSEMAN STEPPED FROM the shadows and clamped a
hand over the Gasman's mouth before he could turn around.

"Don't move," Horseman whispered, keenly aware of
the guard standing overhead. "Stay calm."

But when you've spent your entire life running, someone telling you not to move seems pretty suspicious.

The Gasman bit down on Horseman's fingers so hard
that, even through the gloves, he almost cut through bone.
Horseman cursed, hunching over his wounded hand, and
everything dissolved into quick chaos.

"Get out of here, Iggy!" Gazzy screamed.

Iggy shook his head. "I won't leave—"

"Go!" Gazzy insisted, pulling something from his
pocket. "I'm right behind you!"

"What's going on?" the guard demanded, waving her crossbow. "Who's that down there?"

Iggy heard the snag of the match and dove for the ladder just as Gazzy tossed the small flame into the bucket of chemicals they'd been using for cleaning.

And then the blast drowned out everything.

It made the walls shudder and the floor disappear. It blew Gazzy, Iggy, and Horseman upward. Horseman shot his arm out to catch the ladder, dangling to the side. As smoke billowed up through the shaft, the dangerous mix of chemicals burned his eyes. He squeezed them shut, but the insides of his eyelids felt like they were lined with thorns.

He didn't have time to worry about it, though—just kept his eyes shut and scrambled up the ladder as fast as he could, three rungs at a time. The fire alarm was wailing, and the army of girls was spilling out of the floors he'd been blown past.

"Breach!" they shouted when they saw Horseman on the ladder. "Stop him!"

Two arrows whizzed past his ears, and he heard the warriors climbing after him in fierce pursuit. He hadn't heard the Gasman or Iggy since the explosion.

Horseman's left hand felt nearly crippled, but the chute was too narrow to fly through, so he did the only thing he could do: He climbed as fast as possible.

His eyes still burned, and he tried opening them. Tears poured down his cheeks—everything was blurry and he couldn't see through the smoke. The ladder seemed end-less, but finally, after at least a hundred rungs of agony, Horseman burst out of the silo and blinked painfully in the light. His eyes were still tearing, but a quick glance showed him that the bird kids were nowhere to be seen. He turned quickly to screw down the heavy cement lid over the manhole, ignoring the loud bangs coming from beneath his feet—he'd deal with the group later.

He wiped his eyes with his sleeve and turned over his wrist, where he saw a number of impatient queries on the screen. The letters blurred—had the chemicals perma-nently damaged his vision?—but Horseman knew the gist of his master's concerns. He tapped out a quick message to the Remedy: *"The Gasman is dead. The kid blew himself up."*

Standing on top of the silo, Horseman turned in a slow circle.

Now, where is Iggy?

52

HORSEMAN SAW THE flash out of the corner of his eye—a figure disappearing into the trees like a pale ghost.

"Iggy!" Horseman called, blazing after him on the trail through the pines. "Let's not make this harder than it has to be."

Horseman didn't exactly *enjoy* this part of the job—the kids' fear reminded him too much of how he felt around the doctor—but he knew his body was made for the hunt. His wings were longer, his body stronger, and he had the eyesight of a hawk.

Well, usually. Right now, he felt like he was looking through a milky lens.

But however clouded his vision, Horseman still had Iggy in his sights, and he could cruise as long as he needed to; his lungs were built to outlast Iggy's twofold. It was only a matter of time.

"Iggy!" Horseman shouted again as he wove after him through the underbrush.

"Don't call me that," Iggy yelled over his shoulder. "Only my friends get to call me that."

Iggy was distracted now, and Horseman was gaining on him with each breath. Closing in.

"You don't want to be my friend?" Horseman asked with a smile as he darted forward.

Iggy laughed and veered up sharply, winding toward the clouds.

Horseman grasped at the air in frustration. He'd thought he had him.

He strained his neck to keep track of Iggy's movements above, desperate not to lose him now. Though Iggy was blind, he was a magician in the air and seemed to possess a sixth sense that made him even better at navigation... and almost impossible to track.

Almost, Horseman reminded himself. *Not impossible for you.*

He had to keep Iggy talking, keep him interested enough to stay close.

"Or maybe you meant friends like the Gasman," he taunted. "Did he call you Iggy?"

The movement above stopped.

"You killed him, didn't you?" Iggy's voice cracked

in despair. "Gazzy said he was right behind me, but he's dead, isn't he?"

Iggy's accusing voice seemed to come from a hundred different directions, and Horseman squinted up through the maze of twining branches, trying to locate his prey.

"You've got me all wrong," he said, his voice earnest, persuasive. "Just stop for a minute, and we can talk."

I'll tell you about the doctor and his plans, Horseman thought. *I'll tell you the truth.*

It didn't matter. He knew Iggy would never stop. There was only one way this could end.

Horseman glimpsed movement to his left—far from where he'd been searching. He turned his head to see the swoop of a light-colored wing standing out against the brown bark.

He took off like a bullet.

Following little more than the quiver of branches as they snapped back into place, Horseman plowed through leaves. He snagged his wings on burrs and dodged between whiplike vines. He followed the bird kid doggedly, recklessly, gaining distance, gaining speed. . . .

And when Iggy turned and dipped sharply, Horseman slammed face-first into a thick tree and, almost a hundred feet in the air, momentarily blacked out.

His limp body started to plummet toward the forest floor.

Luckily—or really, unluckily—he slammed to a stop

when his legs fell on either side of a stray branch. Horseman collapsed against the trunk, breathing heavily as waves of pain and nausea rolled through his body.

This mission has not gone as planned, he thought.

He'd hoped to find Gazzy and Iggy alone, and hadn't thought it would be too difficult in the middle of the Appalachian wilderness. But he *certainly* hadn't expected to be trapped underground with a community of rebel girls armed to the teeth when a chemical bomb went off.

Horseman's palms started to sweat as he thought about all the witnesses, and whom they might be reporting to. The news about the Gasman would satisfy the Remedy momentarily, but if he found out the other target was on the loose, there would be serious repercussions.

"If you should fail," the doctor had said, *"it would be my pleasure to send the next Horseman along after you."*

Horseman had to get to Iggy fast, before things spiraled out of his control.

What he needed was a new strategy.

53

HORSEMAN COULDN'T SEE. That was his biggest problem.

Well, he could *see*, but everything was slightly blurry, his depth perception was off, and he was pretty sure he was seeing double. He didn't know if the chemical damage was temporary or permanent, but he had to figure out a way around it.

He'd thought he had Iggy—*twice*—when really, the *blind kid* had better spatial accuracy than he did.

Would no vision actually be better than faulty vision?

At this point, anything was worth a shot. Horseman stripped off his shirt, rolled it over his eyes, and tied the sleeves around his head. The world went completely dark.

Just like it was for Iggy.

Horseman felt instant relief in his eyes. The burning lessened, and the flow of tears subsided.

The rest of his body seemed less sure about his decision. His boots teetered on the branch, and his stomach dropped sharply as he felt the nothingness all around him. Never in his life had he felt so completely vulnerable.

For a moment he grasped wildly at the air, his arms flailing desperately. Then, feeling his fingers touch bark, Horseman hugged himself tight to the trunk of the tree, trying to stop hyperventilating.

Maybe he should've tried this little experiment closer to the ground.

It was a stupid idea. For all he knew, Iggy might actually have been programmed with additional senses, and if not, he'd had his whole life to develop them. Horseman didn't have years; he just had right now.

And if he didn't do this, he wasn't going to have a tomorrow.

Horseman exhaled against the tree. He just had to trust his instincts—they hadn't failed him yet.

Slowly, Horseman edged back out onto the branch, keeping a light touch on the bark to steady himself. He took a long, deep breath, trying to open up some kind of latent third eye.

This time, when he let go, Horseman realized he could still sense the trunk to his left—the solidness of it, the heft.

Now or never, he thought, and he raised his heels, leaned forward, and took off.

He felt removed from his body and highly connected to it at once—almost like he was a pilot maneuvering a small plane instead of controlling his own muscles.

Horseman's muscles were tense as he waited for the moment when he would smash into another tree, but it didn't come. In one panicked moment, he felt branches rake lightly across his bare chest, but he quickly adjusted, and veered away from the tree in his path.

After that, his reflexes became faster each moment, and his other senses started to come alive.

The pores in his skin opened up to take in the information around him. Each time his wings flapped, he felt the air they moved bouncing off the objects around him, telling him how far away they were.

Horseman found it surprisingly easy to measure how high up he was flying. He smelled the tangy sap when he was low, near the exposed trunks. Near the treetops, the pine scent was more intense.

And his ears were attuned to every anomaly in the quiet forest. He heard the groan of trees as they swayed, and detected the distant sound of branches snapping.

Iggy.

Iggy had pulled far ahead of him, but Horseman knew he was faster, and he was no longer handicapped by sight. As he grew more confident and more comfortable, Horseman started to close in on his prey.

Below him and just ahead, he heard a slight whisper as something—maybe wings—brushed through the branches.

Horseman held his breath, folded his wings tight for speed, and shot through the forest. Seemingly striking at nothing, he punched his arm ahead of him and felt the crunch of bone.

Iggy screamed.

54

"ARE YOU KIDDING me?"

I stared at the cliffside nests the bird kids had built, at the bits of string and dried leaves. All of them were empty.

"Are they just out foraging? Why didn't you go, too? Or—they haven't really left, have they?"

Harry cocked his head at me curiously, his handsome face as innocent and blank as usual.

Oh, this is stellar.

He started picking affectionately at my wings again.

"Uh-uh." I shook my head, smoothing my feathers back down. "I have to think."

I watched him scuffing up dirt, relishing a dust bath.

I stopped moving and crossed my arms. "Harry, this has been great, but it's time for me to move on."

"Haaarrryy!" he cawed happily, and my face softened. After years spent on the run, I had a soft spot for strays, and the poor guy couldn't help it if he'd been programmed with the intellectual capabilities of a Tickle Me Elmo.

He stared at me with a dopey, thrilled expression, like I was the most incredible thing he'd ever seen.

At least someone thinks so.

"Okay, look," I said, knowing my words sounded like gibberish to him, as his language did to me. "Let's go find your flock, and then I have to bounce, understand?"

"Maaaax Mummmm," Harry cooed, and nuzzled against my shoulder.

"Right," I said, and pointed. "You lead the way."

We flew west, and again I marveled at Harry's grace in the air. Every part of him was crafted to be as aerodynamic as possible—from the overdeveloped shoulder muscles that made his wings work almost effortlessly, to the incredible core strength that held his whole body parallel to the ground.

I'd always been the top flier in the flock, but now I was aware of my legs dipping slightly below my upper body, causing drag. And while I was gulping air as I pumped my wings to gain speed, with feathers that cut through the air like blades, Harry barely had to flap.

On land we couldn't understand a thing the other said, but in the sky, we spoke the same language. Harry slowed imperceptibly to coast beside me while I studied landmarks, and pulled ahead so I could ride his slipstream through turbulent patches. When I was just starting to notice a twinge of hunger in my stomach, Harry was already diving for prey. For hundreds of miles, we were in perfect synchronization.

Until we reached the Pacific Ocean.

Harry started to turn left, but something made me hang back...I had a weird feeling of retracing Fang's steps—a sense of urgency.

North, my gut insisted.

Harry was cruising so fast, I had to shout over the wind. "Wait up!" I tapped his shoulder and pointed the other way, but with a quick shake of his head, Harry pulled harder to the left.

"I know we're looking for your flock, but I'm looking for someone, too, okay?"

Harry's brow was wrinkled with anxiety.

"What is it?"

"Pfft!" Harry's eyes widened, and the way he flung his fingers open reminded me of one of Gazzy's IEDs.

"A bomb?" I asked, grabbing his wrist. "A bomb went off, to the north?"

My breath caught in my chest as I thought of the charred remains of Tanzania and the watery grave of New York. The giant I'd fought had said the Remedy would punish the whole world, and the voices on the radio had been carrying out that mission.

They wanted no survivors.

"We have to check it out," I decided, and as I started to

turn, Harry shook his head in alarm. Of course the other bird kids would've avoided the place—birds and animals tended to be the first ones to flee during disasters.

I was already headed up the coast, though, scanning the northern landscape for smoke and steeling myself for whatever we might find.

Call me stubborn, but I always listened to my gut.

55

EVERYTHING WAS SO still. So quiet.

As we landed, the wind from our wings moved dust that seemed like it had blanketed the ruins for years, and when I coughed, the sound echoed even in the open, leveled space.

I'd say Seattle was a ghost town, except without the town part. There were just piles and piles of rubble as far as we could see. Exactly like the bombed city in Africa.

All desolation starts to look alike, I guess.

Or maybe I'm just jaded.

"Looks pretty bad, huh?" I said.

"Max Mum..." Harry pleaded.

"Yeah, yeah. We won't stay too long," I said. To be honest, I was ready to split the moment we landed, too. The place was giving me a major case of the heebie-jeebies, but since I'd dragged us here, we had to at least check it out.

We shuffled through the colorless haze, gaping around us like archaeologists digging up a lost city. We walked under archways that stood alone where buildings had fallen, and passed skeletons of cars that still smelled of gas. I saw a hard hat lying in the dirt and reached for it, but it crumbled on contact.

"There's no one," I whispered. No survivors, no bodies. Just ash.

Turns out, almost everything burns, and history is quick to turn to dust. Except for that smooth glint of metal over there . . .

What is that?

I cocked my head to stare at the large, disklike object. For a second, I thought that, on top of everything else, the world was being invaded by aliens.

Then I understood.

So *that* was what had happened to the famous Space Needle. The long white base was nowhere in sight, but somehow the UFO-shaped top had ended up over a mile from the coast. It was half submerged in a pile of debris, like it had skidded onto a dull gray planet.

"Come on!" I said, dragging a less-than-enthusiastic Harry behind me.

The windows that circled the perimeter had been blown out, and we had to climb over the twisted metal dividers to get in. The initial blast must've blown the aerodynamic disc inland before the mushroom cloud incinerated everything else, though. Because inside, apart from the white chairs that were overturned and piled everywhere, the objects in the restaurant were surprisingly intact.

There were even a couple of cracked dishes sitting on a table. And a small, black, rectangular object, just lying there, like it had been forgotten...

I snatched up the phone. *No. It couldn't be.... Impossible.* But true.

It was *on*, and *working*, and four full bars shone in the corner—the thing actually had *service!*

"Do you know what this is?" I laughed, shaking it at Harry.

"Harry!" he squawked, responding to my excitement.

"Communication!"

I held it in my hand, my heart thudding, and then realized that none of the flock had phones. An intact phone with full service, found in a city completely destroyed by a nuclear bomb, and I had no one to call. I did not smirk at the irony.

But if I could get on the Internet...

I tapped the smartphone's screen and a browser opened. I typed in the address of Fang's blog.

Maybe he has logged in.

Maybe he's tried to get a message to me.

Maybe there's something he wants me to know.

Harry peered over my shoulder as I scrolled through the comments. I didn't find a single post from FangMod, but a thread with the subject "DEAD FLOCK" made me stop cold. I clicked to expand, but the stupid thing took forever to load.

"Come on. Come onnn," I muttered, jabbing my finger at the screen.

Flockfan23: *Rumors here that some of the flock have been murdered. My cuz said Angel told her and was crying. Any1 else have info?*

I pictured Angel's tear-streaked face, her blonde eyebrows knitted in grief. I held my breath.

There were half a dozen responses. PAtunnelratt, the commenter we'd been communicating with before, was the first to answer.

PAtunnelratt: *The story around here is Gasman got blown up and one of the H-men grabbed Iggy in the woods. Heard they were looking for my silo, so I'd feel mad guilty if it's true.*

I shook my head. *Lies.* They had to be.

Yeah, the boys had said they were headed to find some green in the US, but Gazzy was a genius with explosives, and Iggy couldn't be caught. I scrolled down for the next comment.

ImMargaretA: *Nudge was drowned in an underground cave on some Pacific island. The dog, too. Skewered with a speargun.*

My mouth went dry and I reread the lines several times, chewing the inside of my cheek. How did she know about the island? How would anyone know where Nudge and Total were? Or that they were alone?

That I'd left them.

Other commenters had already challenged Margaret A.'s sources, but she was defiant.

ImMargaretA: *I'm on the inside. Got it from the Remedy himself. They're taking out the bird kids one by one. Army meeting Fang in Alaska. You'll see.*

My hand was so sweaty the phone almost slipped out.

Alaska.

Was that what had pulled me so urgently west? What had made me turn north? It couldn't be true, could it?

TeeniBikeeni: *No way, not my Fang. He'd never let himself be captured. Please nooo.*

Flockfan23: *What about Max? Has anybody heard anything about Max?*

My eyes were blurring and all I saw was smoke pouring out of an underground hole, the spearguns the fish kids had used, an army of giants waiting in the snow . . .

"*No*," I said aloud, blinking my eyes clear again. I knew none of it was right. It had to be Doomsday kids infiltrating the blog—that was the only explanation. Or other killers who wanted to scare us, to make us think we didn't have a chance.

Still, I couldn't stop staring at the words at the bottom of the small screen.

ImMargaretA: *Maximum Ride is next.*

56

HARRY'S WINGS SHOT out, making me jump.

I let out my breath with a nervous laugh and looked up from those stupid words.

"Okay, okay. I know you're ready to get out of this place." I wanted to toss the phone and the lies I'd read with it, but I knew it might come in handy. Maybe I could throw it at the next person who attacked me. "I guess we've seen enough. Come on, Harry. Let's g—"

Then I saw Harry's eyes staring behind me and realized he hadn't been nudging me to leave. The snap of his wings had been a flight instinct—Harry was *scared*. I turned quickly and glimpsed a flash of white through the windows. Something flitting between concrete pillars.

Something that was trying to ambush me.

No, Maximum Ride isn't going to be next. Not today. Not ever.

"Hey!" I yelled. I stumbled over the chairs and took off after it—whatever it was.

I kicked through pieces of brick and sharp metal and skidded around collapsed buildings as I chased the hint of movement, something small and quick and just beyond my reach. When I lost the trail I took to the sky, searching, searching, and then—

There!

A tiny figure ducked into a hole, and I dropped down nearby. It was the opening to a cellar, but the house above was completely gone, ripped right off the foundation. As I peered down into the darkness, Harry landed softly behind me.

"This is a good idea, right?" I asked him, and though he cocked his head doubtfully, I crept down the stairs, gripping my now-rusty knife tightly.

Part of the room was blocked by beams that had fallen through the ceiling, but the rest of the cellar was clear. At first I thought I'd made a mistake and nothing was there, but then, behind a washing machine, I found her.

"Oh, my God," I whispered. Over the years, I've seen more awful things than anyone should ever have to see. Horrible mutated experiments gone wrong, people injured, killed, tortured, animals mutated by toxic waste...and this poor kid was definitely on the list. The girl was probably around six years old. Even in the low light, I saw that her skin was pink and raw, the flesh bubbled. There were patterns in some places—spots where clothing seams or textures had burned right into her flesh.

How did she survive this?

I blinked hard as I thought of all the people who had been far enough away to avoid being incinerated into ashes, but not far enough to escape unscathed. The burns, the pain...*oh, my God.*

"Hey there," I said, my voice hoarse. "It's okay. You don't have to be afraid."

The girl stared up at me silently, and her strange gaze was unnerving. Her pupils were golden, like a small flashlight permanently shone on them. I wondered if she could see me, or if she was blind, like Iggy.

I just wanted to give this poor kid a hug. I stepped closer, and Harry made a chirpy sound in his throat— some kind of warning.

Glancing at him, I saw that his arms were crossed and his feathers were puffed up, making his wings appear about twice their usual size. Living with his flock high in remote mountain cliffs, Harry probably hadn't had much contact with non-mutants, let alone burned, freaked-out little kids.

"It's okay, Harry," I reassured him. "Look, she's just a little girl."

But when he came closer, the girl ducked her head down, curling into herself. Between the curtains of her dark hair, there were bald patches visible on her scalp and darker burns on the back of her neck.

This is what nuclear war looks like, I thought angrily. I wanted to make someone pay for this girl's unspeakable pain and loss. I wanted to pummel whoever had done this.

The Remedy.

"My phone..." the girl whispered.

That's why she's been spying on us—we stole her phone.

"You can have your phone," I told her, and crouched down to her level. "Are you all by yourself? Where's your mom? Your family?"

The girl was gripping something tightly in her hand. Maybe a memento, or a clue about who she was.

"Whatcha got there?" I asked.

She mumbled something into her fist.

"What's that?" I asked, leaning close to hear her meek voice.

"One Light," she said more loudly, and as she thrust her hands toward my face, a pale green gas spilled from her palm.

In my last flash of consciousness, I realized I'd been trapped.

And there was no way out.

57

THE NEXT DAY started in the absolute worst way possible: I woke up in a cage.

The light in the room felt like an attack. My eyes stung from the gas, and the back of my throat was raw. Moving an inch made my stomach churn with nausea.

"Where..." I mumbled, disoriented, and then heard a low whimper.

Harry was crouched next to me on the metal floor, his wings folded in and his head tucked down. I touched his back. He was shaking all over.

I squinted through the bars of the cage, expecting a dungeon or a lab, maybe—but we were in the middle of a lecture hall. Kids sat in the rows of seats rising up all around us.

Some of them were burned like the girl had been, and some had those weird golden cataracts in their eyes. Others' eyes just looked glazed.

The words came back to me then: *One Light*. That was what the little girl had said right before she'd knocked us out with the gas.

They were Doomsday followers.

Iggy had been brainwashed by the cult once, so I knew how hard it was to get through to them. Still, I had to try.

"Yo, Children of the Corn!" I reached an arm out of the cage and waved. "Snap out of it! Let us out of here and I promise to return your brains in one piece."

"Shh!" A girl in the front row glared at me.

"The Remedy is speaking," another chided.

The name was like a bucket of ice water to the face, and I jerked my head around toward the front of the hall.

As I gripped the bars of our cage and gaped at the small man pacing the platform, the pain and devastation I'd felt in Africa and then New York flooded my heart, and for a second, I couldn't breathe. This was the man who'd destroyed the world, the man who'd killed billions of people.

This was the man I'd been hunting.

As the mastermind of world devastation, he wasn't much to look at. He wore a wrinkled suit and had a scraggly brown beard. His voice in the microphone was shaky and high-pitched, his manner feverish. He was short, balding, and giving some sort of lecture on Napoleon. Images flashed on a huge screen behind him.

"So *you're* the piece of scum known as the Remedy!" I shouted. "You look more like the Problem!"

The man on the stage stopped pacing, startled to hear sounds coming from his zombified audience.

"Napoleon fanatic—go figure. I gotta be honest, I thought you'd be taller."

The Remedy reached up to smooth his thinning hair and walked down the stairs, stopping far short of our cage.

"It can talk," he observed, more to his pupils than to me. "I thought they'd bred that out by now. This mutant is definitely out of date and toward the end of its life span."

The kids in the bleachers chorused their approval, gawking at us like we were zoo animals, and I stood fuming in front of Harry, who probably didn't even know he should be offended right now.

"*It* can even form full sentences," I said, narrowing my eyes. "And *it* is Maximum Ride, in case you want to memorize the name of the mutant who's going to destroy you."

The Remedy crossed his arms over his chest. It was supposed to look threatening, no doubt, but the way his shoulders hunched forward and his head ducked down made him look uncomfortable. Scared, even.

"Considering where you're standing and where I'm standing, I think you might not get that chance, Maxine."

He had actually inched back another foot.

"It's Max*imum*," I sneered. "And keeping the dangerous animals locked up is kind of cheating, isn't it?"

The coward turned away, climbing back onto the stage

to continue his lecture. He clicked open a slide titled "World Domination in a Historical Context."

Context? Context? I have some context for him, all right.

"Did you tie up my family before you killed them?" I yelled after him, my voice shaking with fury. "When you silenced Nudge underwater, did you think she couldn't talk, either? When you blew up Gazzy, did you have to look at his nine-year-old body parts? Or was that too much 'context' for you?"

"Napoleon's downfall was ego," he continued doggedly.

"What about *your* ego? Did you think you wouldn't have to pay?" I shouted more loudly, rattling the cage. "Did you think I'd let you get away with it?"

"You might not get that chance." His words echoed in my head, snagging on the last one: *"Maxine."* Was it just a taunt, meant to infuriate me?

Or did he really not know me?

58

SOMETHING WASN'T ADDING up.

The giant had known me, and he'd said the Remedy had sent him. And the girl in the chat room, ImMargaretA, had claimed the Remedy was specifically hunting the flock. But even if they were both liars, something seemed off about this guy.

I quieted down and watched him carefully—his expressive face and breathless cadence, the way his eyes bulged with urgency.

"It was Goebbels, with his understanding that nothing human could be sacred, and the Hulk, with his appetite for complete and total destruction, who laid the foundation for our current revolution..."

Even I, with my sketchy grasp of history, could tell he

was making no sense, but it didn't matter. He rambled in circles until he had them eating up every word. He was a storyteller, for sure.

But a killer? A megalomaniac bent on world domination? Uh-uh. This guy was a *joke*.

"It's not him," I whispered.

"Max Mum?" Harry said, looking at me.

"These kids all believe him, but I don't. He's not the Remedy."

So why was he pretending to be?

Probably to save his own skin. If what I'd heard was true, the Remedy wanted to wipe the planet completely clean, sparing no survivors. No one was safe...except the Remedy himself.

So this guy had conned some cleanup crews, convinced them he was their revered leader. It probably hadn't been too hard. Doomsday was a cult, after all, made up of vulnerable kids easily duped by smooth talkers.

And the man could *talk*, I'd give him that. He was so desperate to sell his story, it almost made me feel sorry for him.

Almost.

After all, he was still pretending to be the deadliest, most despicable man in the history of the world. And he'd put me in a freaking cage.

"He's not the Remedy!" I yelled. "This man is lying!"

Finally some of the Doomsday kids heard me. I saw heads turning, heard whispers spreading.

"I'm sure some people in this room would beg to differ," the impostor said, flashing a nervous smile at his dead-eyed groupies. "As well as some not-so-fortunate people outside of it."

"Okay, Mr. Remedial, so how'd you do it, then?" I demanded. "Who developed the virus? Who are the Horsemen?"

"There are unsung heroes in every revolution," he answered vaguely, his voice going up an octave. "Loyal soldiers who are tasked with doing the hard work."

"Like the burned kids in this room, whose families you freaking *bombed*?"

"We all have to make sacrifices for the greater good..." His eyes flicked around the room at his disciples.

"One Light," a few voices murmured, and I scoffed.

"Where'd you get the bombs?"

"I—" His face twitched.

"And how come you're here babbling about history to a group of kids instead of, you know, ruling the world? Let me guess—you're a failed actor, right? Or maybe one of those carnival guys—the grifters who are always trying to cheat people out of the big stuffed animals? Whatever you are, you're just a Remedy *fanboy*," I spat. "And that's almost as disgusting as being the mass murderer himself."

Fear flashed behind those eyes. Desperation. The man raced back down the steps and leaned close to my cage this time—almost within reach.

"Do you know why *you're* here?" he hissed, just loud

enough for me to hear. "Because if I make sure my students have someone to sacrifice to their 'One Light' every so often, they think I'm legit."

Pink splotches appeared near his temples, and he was trembling, but his eyes were victorious. "Let me condense it for you, bird girl: As long as *you* die, *I* get to live."

"Faker!" I shouted, swiping at his smug face. "Liar!"

I grabbed a fistful of tweed fabric through the bars of the cage, but he shrugged off the jacket, pivoting out of my grasp. He stumbled away from me with wide, terrified eyes.

"Kill them!" he yelled into the microphone. "Kill the mutants!"

59

THEIR FEET SOUNDED like thunder. Hundreds of kids streamed down from the stands, tripping over one another in their eagerness. They were smiling giddily and chanting, *"One Light! One Light!"*

But dark intentions flashed behind those grins.

Professor Phony wasn't a legitimate dictator, but his followers were the real thing. They were Doomsday kids who idolized the Remedy and had done his dirty work picking off survivors.

Kids who had probably already murdered dozens of people and were now coming at us from all sides.

The reality of the situation set in: We were totally screwed.

Harry was in the corner, with his neck tucked in and

his feathers all puffed out, rocking back and forth, banging his shoulders against the bars in desperation.

"Get in the middle!" I yelled, and yanked him close to me. "Crouch down. Quick!"

Harry and I huddled together as the lynch mob rocked the cage with frenzied bloodlust. For a brief moment, I was grateful for those thick metal bars holding us in—they were also keeping everyone else out. Then the kids started poking knives and sticks through the spaces.

So we'll just die a little slower, then.

All the horrible deaths I'd read about on the blog had been true, and now there would be two more. Even if the Remedy wasn't in this room, he'd gotten to me.

There had never been hope for any of us.

Harry leaned his head back and made a horrible, high-pitched sound, and though I'd only known him for a couple of days, his plaintive cry awoke a fierce maternal instinct in me.

I stood up, sheltering him from the blows like I would my own flock. In my mind I saw flashes of their faces twisted in pain—Fang's anger, Iggy's shock, and Nudge's fear—and though I wanted to break down, I became a stone. I knew I was just delaying the inevitable, but if they wanted Harry, they'd have to go through me first.

The Doomsday kids pressed their hateful faces against the bars, leering as their arms swiped at me with knives and hangers, fingernails and pieces of glass.

At first I fought them. I broke fingers and tried to pry

weapons from fists. I used every self-defense move I'd learned over the years, every honed skill. But I was locked in a box that made me vulnerable on all sides. If I wielded a knife, it was knocked from my hands. If I leaned back from a swinging fist, another ripped out a handful of my hair. They gouged and slashed, tore and pummeled. There were just too many of them.

Like the fake Remedy had said, I'd been brought here to die. My life was going to end like it had started—caged like an animal, being poked and prodded, with absolutely nowhere to run.

I clenched my fists together and stood stronger, prouder, even as my arms ached and I lost all hope. I wasn't going to cry.

"You're all cowards!" I snarled. "At least I didn't give up! At least I didn't—"

Something struck the side of my head and I fell, crumpling to the floor.

When I blinked and looked up, Harry's wings were open, cramming the small space full of feathers.

"Harry, what are you . . . ?" I asked, dazed with pain.

When Harry thrust his wings out through the bars, leaving them completely exposed to the murderous masses, I thought he was giving up. Until he started to flap.

Amazingly, the cage floor shifted below my feet and I tumbled sideways. Some of the Doomsday kids took advantage and beat me harder or gouged at Harry's fluttering wings, but most were staring with open mouths and puzzled looks.

Incredibly, the cage was rising off the ground.

Harry's face turned red, and veins popped out of his neck as he strained. Me, the metal cage, the kids gripping the bottom...Harry's head was tilted forward and he was supporting the full weight of it on his shoulders as his wings flailed outside the bars.

He was that good of a flier.

I scrambled to my feet and joined him, shoving my wings out through the bars, pumping in rhythm with his so we wouldn't collide. After just a few seconds, my strength was already starting to fail me.

But with the added power of my wings, the kids couldn't hold us down anymore. The cage jerked us side to side, rebounding as, one by one, their hands fell away from the floor.

"We're doing it!" I marveled as, untethered, we carried our small prison up and over the stadium seating. The cult members chased after us, shaking their fists and chanting their words of sacrifice, but we'd already flown high into the top of the dome.

We were actually getting away.

60

WE SMASHED THE cage against the ceiling, the impact jolting me down to my toes. Then Harry's face grew even more determined and we rose again. And smashed again. My teeth snapped shut hard and I tasted blood.

"What are you doing?" I yelled. "Harry, stop!"

One last time, still trapped inside our metal box, we crashed smack into the ceiling. One last time the force ricocheted through my body, chattering my teeth and rattling my bones.

The heavy door of the cage sprang open just as the ceiling broke from the impact. Chunks of plaster rained down, we scrambled away as the cage dropped, and then we were bursting through the ceiling into the sky above. A huge clang and some screams of agony told me the cage had landed.

We didn't have to talk—we just flew high, hard, and fast, until the building was out of sight. When I could finally speak without coughing, what came out was laughter. Rolling, uncontrollable giggles that almost sounded like sobs.

Somehow, once again, I'd made it out alive, and I felt so shaken, so insanely grateful, that I had to put the rest of my dark reality aside for the moment and just laugh it out.

Harry looked alarmed at the sounds I was making, so I tried to get my hiccupping snorts under control, and held up my hand for a high five.

"Good job, Harry!" I said. At the sound of his name, that dazzling smile was back, along with his dimples.

I choked out another laugh. "Well, that was a pretty epic escape, huh?" I said.

In response, Harry crowed and soared even higher. I knew exactly how he felt—man, it felt good to be *free* again.

Even this far from the city, you could see the explosion's effects. Many trees were stripped of bark, others look singed, and many of them had simply been broken off right above the ground.

There was still some life, though, scampering through the underbrush, and Harry was already scanning the ground for prey. My stomach rumbled at the idea. We hadn't eaten in almost two days—since the rattlesnake feast Harry had delivered.

Harry screeched like an owl as he swooped low to the

ground, and when I followed suit, my voice came out like a war cry. It felt good to be loud and primal, to hunt our own dinner in the woods, to stretch my wings and know my speed and feel my power.

By the time the sun had completely set, we'd strung more than a dozen rodents up over the fire. For dinner, we had a mix of radiation rat, charred chipmunk, and nuclear squirrel. It was absolutely disgusting.

And absolutely delicious.

"This is just like the old days," I reminisced, tearing into the gamey flesh. "When we were running from the whitecoats, me and the flock—"

I stopped, worried about letting those dark emotions in, but Harry was looking at me with wide, curious eyes, and I *wanted* to talk about my family. I needed to feel like they were still right here.

Or needed to believe they were still *somewhere*.

"Here, look."

I licked squirrel juice off my fingers and grabbed a nearby twig. "Here's me, Maximum," I said, tracing a simple shape in the dirt—a stick figure with two triangles for wings. I added another next to it. And then five more. I even drew Total, but he came out more like a fuzzy sausage with a weird growth on his back.

I told Harry about Nudge's love of fashion, about how Total had adored Akila, and how Iggy was the only one of us who could cook. I described the tree house Dylan had built me and how Fang had pulled me out of the swirling tsunami.

I missed them all desperately, and even if Harry didn't understand, it just felt good to say their names.

"We're a flock of two now," I finished, looking at him. "You and me."

"Flaaaack," Harry echoed wisely.

"Show me your flock, how you grew up." I handed him the stick.

But Harry didn't draw his friends or family. He drew a boy with huge wings and a square box with bars around him. Harry pointed to the boy's frowning face, and then tapped his own chest.

The twinge of protectiveness I'd felt earlier in the Doomsday hall returned. Harry was strong and an exceptional flier, but he was still so vulnerable.

"That was scary today, huh? I'm sorry for not listening to your instincts before," I said quietly. "Don't worry, though. It's all over now."

Harry kept sketching with the stick. Outside the cage, he drew other figures—people with masks over their faces. Scientists, without a doubt.

I noticed that Harry had started shaking again, his down trembling.

"I understand," I said, reaching for Harry's hand. I squeezed it tight, trying to comfort him. "It happened to me, too."

Then suddenly Harry leaned over and planted his lips on mine.

That kiss brought back every sweet memory of

Fang—shy moments from the beginning when a kiss meant the whole world, and then that last night we spent together...

It made me think of Dylan, too, though, and my cheeks burned with confusion.

I pulled back abruptly. My eyes swam with tears—but my chest hurt like I'd been stabbed. The grief threatened to overflow. I rubbed my eyes with the heels of my hands and pressed my lips together.

Get it together.

"Max Mum?" Harry asked.

Harry lacked even the most basic communication skills. How could I explain that I still loved a boy who was dead, and another who had left me?

"Harry..." I started.

"Harry!" he crowed in response. He jerked his head forward again, but I was quicker to move this time.

"No, Harry," I said. Looking at him, I drew an X through the Max stick figure on the ground. I slowly shook my head for emphasis.

"You must never. Do that. Again."

61

ANGEL'S HEAD THROBBED. The visions were coming more and more frequently now, the flashes almost like electric shocks as they assaulted her consciousness.

She saw Nudge's face underwater, her eyes wide open in terror. She heard Gazzy's heart thundering, and then an explosion that drowned out everything else. She felt Iggy's pain as his body was cracked like a whip.

Angel dug her fingernails into her palms. It didn't have to be like this. She'd warned them. Why hadn't they just come with her?

Because of Max. Max was used to running everything, but Angel understood something Max never had about being a leader: She couldn't do everything all by herself.

So when the flock had bailed, she hadn't gone to Russia.

Not yet. Instead, she'd traveled all over the world, working her small, tired body to the bone, gathering survivors one by one for her cause, meeting people who would *listen*.

Now she was back in North America, about to cross what had once been the Canadian border. It was all coming together, just like she'd seen, and Angel had one final, awful task left.

It was the vision she couldn't shake, the one that made her want to smash her head into one of the rusted-out boxcars of the train she was walking past.

Then Angel heard voices.

No, not voices. *Thoughts.*

She concentrated to hear them more clearly, and what she picked up were two boys who were cold, desperate, and afraid. As Angel focused on them, she learned that their names were Matthew and Lucas—Matthew and Lucas Morrissey. Why did those names sound familiar?

It hit Angel like a splash of cold water. Matthew and Lucas Morrissey: They were exceptional microbiologists who had made breakthroughs in the field when they were still in high school. Angel had glimpsed part of a TV special about them, years ago. But lately she'd heard from several different sources about the interesting things the brothers were up to.

Angel gripped the metal handle and slid open the boxcar door.

Two older teenage boys stood shivering inside. One had a slight build; the other was taller, with broad shoulders. But they definitely looked like brothers—their ebony faces had the same high cheekbones and the same wide, haunted eyes.

"One Light," the bigger guy said in his best zombie voice.

The imitation was so bad, Angel actually giggled. "I wonder if the Remedy knows the boy geniuses who burned down his lab are pretending to be on his cleanup crew? Is that the best you can do, *Lucas*?"

Fear came into their eyes.

"Please," begged Lucas. "We were recruited to make an antidote. We thought the lab was helping people, but they were just making more people sick."

Angel already knew this. She looked at his brother, who was maybe two years younger. He had one gangly arm hidden behind his back.

We're dead if she tells anyone, Angel heard him think. *If I swing fast enough...*

"Before you try to split my skull open with that crowbar, Matthew," Angel said, her face darkening, "I know why you ran. I know about Olivia."

Lucas's eyes flashed with anger and pain as he stepped in front of his little brother. "Don't you speak her name."

Poor Olivia, Angel thought sadly. "It's okay. I know you thought you were saving her, giving her a vaccine." Instead, the virus had taken her in two days.

"H-how do you know that?" Matthew stammered.

Angel heard Lucas's mind whirring, imagining ways to

escape. She felt sorry for them even as they were thinking of smothering her. These guys had been on the run for a long, long time.

"Yeah, how do you know us?" Lucas asked uneasily. "Who are you?"

Are you a Horseman? was what he was asking.

"I'm someone who will show you the truth." Closing her eyes, Angel pushed her way into their minds, using her power to direct the information this time, instead of withdrawing it. She made them *see*.

"You can save the sick," Lucas said in wonder.

Angel shook her head. "I'm not a healer, just a messenger. Do you want a chance to start over?" Lucas and Matthew both nodded, their brown eyes looking a bit more hopeful now. "Then I'm the one who will lead you."

She gave everyone she met the same instructions.

"Go to Russia. Get there any way you can. Find Himmel. Bring your weapons."

62

JUST A LITTLE farther, Fang thought.

He sat cross-legged on a salt-crusted boulder that jutted out over the ocean and shoved handfuls of raw salmon into his mouth. The fish was so cold it made his hands ache, but Fang didn't care—it tasted better than anything he could remember eating.

After traveling all the way up the west coast of the United States and Canada, Fang had arrived in the Gulf of Alaska last night. Once he finished his early-morning breakfast, he would head inland. He wished he could stay along the water—so did his stomach—but he knew that route would take extra time.

Time was something Fang just didn't have.

He *had* to get to Russia, and if he wanted to make it to

the Bering Strait anytime soon, he'd have to cut diagonally up through the middle of the state. He figured he could clear it in a couple of hours, cross over to Russia, and then join the flock by the end of the week—assuming Angel had convinced the rest of them to meet there.

The encounter with Star should have shaken him up, but the truth was, he felt calmer than he had in years.

Maybe it was because he finally had some information, some *clue* about what was going on that would help stop the massacres.

Maybe it was the belief that he'd see Max again—if she hadn't been bullheaded, if she had listened to Angel. Not a sure bet. But he hoped.

Or maybe it was Alaska itself. From his rock perch, Fang saw a humpback whale breaching, and every time it twisted its massive body out of the water, his spirit felt a little lighter. Just knowing it was alive, that not everything everywhere had been destroyed. This place seemed so separate from the mess of the rest of the world. It was still so wild. So green.

Fang twisted to look behind him. Green. Not just near the water, but up in the hills, too, and at the tops of the surrounding mountains. Even this far north, spring had come.

The snow had all melted.

So he was going to die one day. So what? That could be years from now, and he had to live his life in the meantime.

Which meant finding the flock so they could get back

to doing what they'd always done: fighting for those who couldn't defend themselves.

This time it just happened to be the whole human race.

He just had to get to Jeb. He and the flock had to stop the damage. Then maybe he could bring Max back here, where the world was still untouched. They could begin again.

Of course, Fang was enough of a cynic to know it was never that easy.

He had no idea if Jeb was the Remedy, or if he had help, and he knew Max was going to be unbelievably pissed at him. She'd look at him with that little smile, but her eyes would flash warnings of imminent violence. She might not take him back this time, not after the way he left her, the morning after—

But he had to try.

Licking his fingers, Fang tossed the fish bones aside. He inhaled the crisp, clean air, snapped open his wings, and took flight.

Little more than an hour later, he was soaring over a mirrored lake that reflected a towering white hunk of rock in the distance—what he assumed must be Mount McKinley. He'd made good time—he just needed to clear Denali, and then he'd take a little break.

But as he neared the mountain, the temperature dropped steadily, despite the greenness everywhere. The wind started to whirl, snow started to fall, and before he knew it, a ferocious blizzard closed in on him.

Fang lowered his head and clenched his teeth as ice particles stung his face. He tried to plow his way though, but the storm jerked him back and forth, tumbled him around and around, until he couldn't see the mountain peak anymore, couldn't see the lake or the trees, couldn't even tell if he was flying toward his destination or away from it. All he saw was white. There was nothing around him that was recognizable.

Until there was.

There, on a now white-topped peak less than a hundred yards away, was something Fang was more than a little familiar with—something with fur, wings, and wolfish features.

Erasers.

With no warning, the wind released its grip, and Fang stopped in midair faster than if he'd hit a brick wall. Even in the extreme cold, he felt feverish, and his palms were slick with sweat. His peripheral vision fell away and it was like he was looking through a long tunnel.

At the end of that tunnel was the exact scene that Angel had put inside his head so many weeks ago. His death scene.

Only right here, right now, it wasn't Fang that the Erasers were tearing apart.

It was Dylan.

63

FANG WAS STRUCK by a sudden realization: He didn't have to die.

Angel had made it seem like his death was inevitable, but maybe she was wrong. He could change his fate and turn around, right now. He could fly away from this place where he was supposed to die.

He had a choice.

At first, Fang didn't move. He hovered there, watching Dylan fight. Fang had never realized how strong Dylan was—each of his punches seemed to land with the force of a sledgehammer, and even against five Erasers, he was holding his own.

When Dylan spotted Fang, the look of shock on his face

was priceless. Despite the gory scene, Fang knew Dylan was having a "Fancy meeting you here" moment.

As Dylan's head was turned, looking at Fang, a clawed hand sliced four parallel cuts across his cheek, but Dylan didn't flinch. "Good to see you!" he shouted. "Now get out of here, Fang! This isn't your fight!"

In that moment Fang realized what a coward he was being and shook himself into action. If Fate was coming to get him, he would look it in the face.

Besides, they were only Erasers. He'd taken them many times before.

Fang surged toward the fight, and two of the wolfmen broke away from Dylan to meet him in the air. Fang smiled menacingly—up here, he had the advantage. Sheer bulk made Erasers strong and dangerous, but they were clumsy fighters and even slower fliers.

"Ready to be reunited with your old pal, Ari?" Fang growled. The Erasers didn't seem to hear him. And to his surprise, they zipped after him expertly and turned on a dime. They definitely didn't have the awkward, grafted-on wings he'd seen in the past.

Their skill was a shock, too. With two against one, Fang was on the defensive from the start, blocking blows and spinning away from deadly jaws. Fang had fought dozens of Erasers in his lifetime, sometimes four or five at a time, but these weren't like any he'd encountered before. They were stronger, faster, better.

Still, something about them seemed familiar. Maybe

it was the way they fought—it was almost like looking in a mirror. They anticipated Fang's moves and knew all of his tricks. They threw everything back at him with double the force. Fang *knew* he was a fierce fighter, yet he couldn't seem to land a single hit.

What was wrong with him?

"They're Horsemen!" Dylan warned from the peak below. He was only fighting two attackers now; the third lay off to the side in a fetal position. At least Dylan was making headway.

"What are you talking about?" Fang shouted as he dodged a roundhouse kick.

"They're...enhanced. Upgraded."

Star's words came back to Fang. "*Jeb promised me a way out,*" she'd said. "*An upgrade.*"

Fang didn't know anything about these so-called Horsemen. If they weren't Erasers, he had no idea what he was up against.

They were a pack, but they didn't seem to care about protecting each other. As Fang watched, the one who had the strongest grip on Dylan grabbed the second Horseman by the scruff of the neck. He smashed their heads together, and both Dylan and the unfortunate Horseman crumpled to the ground.

With Dylan out of the picture, the other Horseman joined the attack on Fang, and if fighting two was difficult, fighting three was almost impossible. Fang couldn't dodge the blows anymore—there was always someone behind him now, kicking him forward toward the other brutes or tearing into his legs.

One wrenched Fang's arms backward while another grabbed the sides of his face and slammed his head down against its knee. Fang's forehead split, and blood from the gash streamed into his eyes, temporarily blinding him.

Then a hairy fist connected with his jaw and spun his head to the side so hard he swore his brain shook inside his skull. It felt like he had hunks of gravel in his mouth, and when he spat a blood-streaked loogie into the face of the guy who'd hit him, Fang saw two of his teeth fly out with it.

He looked down at Dylan's sprawled body, not knowing if he was alive or dead, and felt utter desperation.

This wasn't like with the Cryenas. Fang was exhausted, and no part of him felt invincible. He felt every scratch and bite, every broken bone. Every part of him hurt.

"You know it's useless to fight, Fang," a voice called from below. "This is your fate. It's always been your fate."

He glanced down to see the man standing on the cliff.

Was he hallucinating, or was it...

64

JEB.

It was you all along, Fang thought. *You destroyed everything.*

This was the confrontation he'd been waiting for, and the sight of his nemesis sent a surge of adrenaline through him, giving his muscles an extra kick. He wrenched away from his attackers and raced toward the ground, concentrating the last of his speed and power on one goal: tearing out Jeb's throat.

But he just wasn't fast enough. He wasn't powerful enough.

Fang was so close, only *inches* from that smiling mug, when the Horsemen caught him, slamming him to the ground at Jeb's feet.

Fang roared in frustration as he wrestled against them. There were two on his back now, pinning his arms beneath him, and one kneeling in front of him, its fists raining down on Fang's head.

"You can't beat them," Jeb said, calmly looking down on the bloody scene. "You're a part of them, Fang. You're what makes them strong. *Stronger.*"

"Stronger than what?" Fang slurred through swollen lips. Another punch landed with a *thwack*, and he felt like his eye sockets were caving in.

"They're not quite invincible," Jeb observed as the Horsemen pummeled Fang. "Not yet. But with the next generation, or the one after, we'll get there—we'll engineer the species that cannot die."

Between blows, Fang squinted at the Horsemen, thinking about the familiarity he'd felt. Jeb had trained the flock in martial arts—that explained why they fought just like Fang. There was something else, though. The way they moved, appeared out of nowhere like shadows...

"You should be proud, Fang. You're going to have a huge impact on the world for generations to come."

Fang stopped struggling just for a second and looked up at Jeb with an expression of utter horror. Finally, he understood what Jeb was getting at.

When they had kidnapped Fang and run all those tests, when they'd taken his blood, it was to create something else. Something unspeakable.

They'd used his DNA.

"You bastard," Fang spat. "You had no right."

And in the midst of that brief distraction, Fang felt a sudden, excruciating rip, and one of the Horsemen tossed a strange object to the ground.

It landed next to him with a heavy sound of finality, and Fang stared at the dark, feathered mass for several seconds, unable to make the connection to his own throbbing pain.

Gritting his teeth, he gathered his energy and bucked the beast off his back. With an arm finally free, Fang was able to reach over his right shoulder. He touched wetness. A nub of jagged bone.

Nothing else.

Fang's skin felt clammy and cold. He started to shake all over.

My wing, he thought vaguely as he went into shock. *They took my wing.*

Fang saw Angel's face. Tears were streaming down her cheeks, but she was smiling at him. His heart broke in that moment—he knew what it meant.

"No," he murmured. "Please."

It's almost over, Angel soothed him. *Just let go.*

65

ANGEL CURLED HER body tighter into the nook of the fir tree, where one of the branches met the trunk, and wept.

She held her throbbing head in her hands, her fair hair twisting around her fingers as she gripped it. The images in her head played on a loop now, but they were often just glimpses, like small snippets of film. Close-ups of yellow eyes narrowing, yellow teeth flashing. Fists clenching, feathers falling. Snow stained dark with blood.

Angel wasn't sure if what she was seeing was in the past or the future, and it was so hard sometimes to know what to do.

It was even harder to wait for the answer.

Angel had been waiting a long time. As the migraines

had worsened, she'd sought out the quietest place she could find. Far north, in the middle of nowhere. She'd crawled inside this tree days ago, and the branches had grown heavy with snow, forming a cocoon around her small body.

She chewed a piece of bark to stave off her hunger, working the soggy wood methodically between her teeth. There wasn't much else to eat—in this deep cold, most of the animals had gone into hibernation. Like the bears and the squirrels, Angel just wanted to sleep until things got a little easier.

Her mind wouldn't let her rest, though. Her temples were electrified with each pulse of her blood as horrible scenes flashed behind her eyes, again and again.

Trust in yourself, she tried to remember. *Nothing else matters.*

But she was exhausted and hopeless, and sometimes she fantasized about smashing her forehead into the trunk of the tree, hitting it over and over until her skull caved and the pain stopped...

Angel.

It was a voice inside her head—a *male* voice, and Angel sat up.

She'd been Max's voice, projecting her own thoughts to Max, trying to help her when she was struggling. Angel had never had anyone to guide her like that, but for a second, she thought that had changed.

Come on, Angel, where are you?

No. This wasn't a voice. She was hearing someone's thoughts—someone nearby.

Someone who knew her.

Angel separated the branches and looked out into a world coated in white. She blinked against the harsh brightness of the snow, feeling like a siren was screaming in her skull.

There. She saw a figure coming out of the blizzard, a fuzzy outline slowly taking shape.

Angel watched the heavy boots sinking in the snow. The broad shoulders looking a little stooped. The powerful wings sagging low behind him. It was something out of a dream—a dream she knew well.

Angel tensed. She had prepared herself for this moment for so long, steeled herself against it, but she was still surprised to feel the icy tears running down her face.

She saw how strong he was, how powerful, and knew her intuition had been right: He would always be the one to prevail.

"It's you," Angel whispered as the figure stopped in front of her. "I knew you'd come."

66

HORSEMAN PEERED THROUGH the branches of the fir tree and looked Angel in the eye. Her lashes were icy webs—she'd been crying—but unlike the others, Angel stared back at him with a wounded look of acceptance.

Of *course* she'd known. Angel had a different sort of power.

More power, even, than the Remedy, who had planned out the future he wanted. Angel *saw* that future. She knew the outcome of today, and all the days after that.

But could she change it?

Horseman was silent as they regarded each other warily. She was probably reading his mind, anyway. He curled his toes inside his boots, willing himself not to turn away from her relentless blue gaze.

For the first time in a long time, Horseman felt his vulnerability. His reflexes, his superior programming, none of it mattered. Angel was the only one in the world who was ready for whatever happened next, and he found himself waiting for her cue.

Sensing this, Angel swung her legs over the branch and jumped down from the tree, landing almost silently in the deep snow. She stood in front of him, tall for her age and malnourished, and for a moment neither of them moved.

Horseman eyed Angel's white wings, almost disappearing in the all-white surroundings. Her skin was so pale it seemed translucent, and from the purplish circles under her eyes, he could tell she hadn't been sleeping. She looked so frail.

Horseman knew better, though. He would not underestimate her.

Angel was studying him, too, and the tension seemed to mount with the falling snow. Could she see the blood on his dark coat? Did she wonder whose it was?

He caught her eyeing his scabbed knuckles, and then the scratches on his wrist, snaking toward the touch screen embedded there. She finally spoke.

"Is it done?" This time, the smallness, the meekness, was gone from Angel's voice.

Horseman paused and nodded. "Fang is dead," he said, and knelt at her feet.

Book Three
WITNESS

67

"NOOO!" I WOKE up gasping, and the word came out strangled as I inhaled.

I couldn't get enough air and I was having heart palpitations like I'd just run a marathon.

I thought I might throw up.

I couldn't remember the details of the nightmare, but I knew I'd been falling. It wasn't one of those falling-off-the-couch dreams, either—I had been falling for miles.

I'd been having that kind of dream a lot lately, but this time, I couldn't shake the sense that something was very, very wrong. Blinking, I reoriented myself—me, check. Harry, check. Woods probably somewhere around the Washington-Canada border, check. Sanity? Maybe a bit iffy.

Maximum Ride is next.

I held my breath, certain I heard the rustle of branches or shoes shuffling through the fallen pine needles not too far away.

"Did you hear something?" I whispered, and elbowed Harry next to me, but his only response was making twittering noises in his sleep.

So much for his evolved reflexes.

I listened again, trying not to breathe, but the only thing I heard was the hoot of an owl somewhere in the distance. Okay, maybe I was being paranoid. The adrenaline had kicked my senses into overdrive. I just needed to calm down and try to get back to sleep.

But it had gotten so cold. It felt rooted deep in my body, and I was shivering too much to relax. Since Harry was asleep anyway, I scooched closer to him, trying to get warm. His wings folded forward to encircle me, and for a moment I almost convinced myself that they were Fang's wings, guarding me from whatever might come.

My breath started to slow . . .

Suddenly my face hit the dirt as Harry yanked his wing out from under my cheek. When I scrambled to my knees, he was already hovering in the air, alert. The kid had my back after all, and I would have smiled in appreciation if I hadn't been so concerned with what had set him off: a figure materializing out of the trees.

A guy.

With wings.

Seeing the outline of feathers, Harry relaxed a little, but the sight made my pulse race faster.

I thought of the way my gut had been telling me to come this way all along.

The way I'd been so sick with worry I'd barely been able to eat.

I knew I would find him.

But...

"Dylan?"

"Hey, Max," he answered, as if he'd just run to the store and was back now. I'd thought he was *dead* all this time.

"Max Mum?" Harry asked uncertainly.

Dylan looked past Harry to where I was still sitting on the ground, but all I could do was blink back at him dumbly. After my silence lasted a beat too long, Dylan asked, "Aren't you happy to see me?"

"Yeah. I just. I thought," I said haltingly, still out of sorts. "For a second you looked like... Fang."

Dylan's entire posture stiffened, but his face seemed to crumple, his gaze falling to the ground.

Nice one, jerkface. Real sensitive.

"I'm sorry," I blurted, starting to recover from the shock. "I mean *yes, of course!*" I scrambled to my feet and ran to him. "I am *really* happy to see you, Dylan."

Now I was a grinning idiot, so freaking relieved that he was safe. When he folded me into a hug, I loved the way he squeezed me a little too tight, held on a little too long. I sighed against him, but I was confused by the way my heart was leaping like a frog on speed when just a minute ago I'd wanted so desperately to see Fang.

I had to pull back.

"Everybody thought you were dead!" I said. I was gripping the sides of his arms, and his muscles were bigger than I remembered, more solid. His hair was changed, too—cropped close to his skull—and his eyes, which had always been so clear and bright, looked strangely cloudy.

"Why do you look so different?" I asked, my gaze traveling down from his black coat to his heavy combat boots. "And why are you dressed like you're in a biker gang? You even have gloves—so much more prepared for this weather than me."

Rather than answer me, Dylan turned behind him, and a smaller figure stepped forward.

"Oh, my God! *Angel!*" My heart lit as it always did when I saw her. I rushed to her, saying, "I was on my way to join you! I can't believe you're here, too!"

But Angel wasn't smiling, and the expression on her face stopped me in my tracks. Something wasn't right.

"What's wrong? Why are you looking at me like that?" I frowned.

Angel pressed her lips together, like she was trying to hold something in tight. "Max..."

That cold feeling returned, flooding my whole body, and my voice rose shrilly.

"What's wrong?"

68

THEN ANGEL RAN to me, crashing into me, almost bowling me over.

"Oh, Max!" she cried. She wrapped her arms around my waist and buried her face in my shirt as her too-thin body shook against me.

I rubbed her back, smoothed her hair. I was so relieved to be holding her like this, so grateful to have my littlest girl back with me that I didn't want to speak. I didn't want to ruin that one happiness.

But I had to know.

"They're dead, aren't they?" My voice was flat, certain. "The rest of the flock is dead. Fang, Nudge, Iggy, Total..."

Angel pulled back from me, her eyes red.

"No." She wiped her nose with her palm and shook her head. "Nudge is okay. Iggy. They're not all—"

"I saw on the blog. They said Gazzy..." My voice cracked and I swallowed. "I guess if you screw around with explosives for long enough, that's what happens."

"It's not true," Dylan said, stepping forward. "The deaths were faked. The kids are fine."

"You don't have to lie to me," I said bitterly. "I can handle it."

But Dylan had always been one of the most honest people I'd known—he was often a little *too* truthful about his feelings—and I saw he was serious now.

"*I* faked their deaths," he clarified.

"You wha—" I stared at him incredulously. I thought about the misery I'd felt reading those words, the wrenching uncertainty of the past few days. I narrowed my eyes, and my voice was razor sharp. "Why would you do that?"

Dylan sighed and shook his head. "I had to convince the Remedy I'd killed them, so he wouldn't send the other Horsemen."

I looked at him sidelong, confused at first. And then I understood, and my eyes flew open.

"The *other* Horsemen?" I repeated. I stepped closer to him, already balling my fists. "*You're* one of the Horsemen?"

"Not exactly..."

Dylan built a fire, and over the next hour, he explained what had happened when he'd left us—how he'd been trying to find the water jugs by the lake and had gotten disoriented.

"I guess it was the toxic gases from the volcano. I just kept stumbling around, retracing my steps. My shoe got stuck between rocks, and when I yanked my foot free, the shoe was completely charred. I knew I had to get out of there, but by then the smoke was so thick I could barely see, and my ears were still fuzzy from the blast. So when I heard someone shout my name, I thought it was one of you."

The knot in my stomach tightened.

"When I turned," Dylan went on, "a metal pipe smashed into my face. I fell forward onto my knees, and then someone stabbed my neck with a syringe."

"Who was it?" I prodded.

Dylan shook his head. "Never got a look. Next thing I know, I'm in an underground lab surrounded by cages."

Harry's eyes widened—"cage" was a word he understood.

"What did they do to you?" I asked.

"I found out later they call it *upgrading*." Dylan shut his eyes for a second, his jaw tightening. "When it was over, I did feel different—stronger." Unconsciously he flexed his fingers, and I remembered how he'd felt so much more muscular.

He looked at me. "But the complete reprogramming didn't take. I was still me, but I was supposed to be somebody else. The only clue I had to go on was a note in my hand."

He took a piece of folded paper from his pocket and

held it out to me. "'One True Way,'" I read. "Sounds like some Doomsday nonsense."

Dylan nodded. "I thought the same thing, but when I walked out of the lab, I saw that the streets all had names like that—Right Path, Just Causeway. One True Way was an address, not a slogan."

"How did you just walk out of the lab?" I asked.

"I don't know—one day the door was open. I went through it, expecting to be captured at any second, but I just kept going. Then it was up a bunch of stairs, and I was on a street."

"Where? What city?" I pressed.

Dylan shook his head. "I don't know. I didn't recognize it. And when I got to the address on True Way, Dr. Gunther-Hagen was waiting for me."

"Wait, Hans is *alive*?" I perked up. The last we'd seen of the German geneticist was in the fiery blaze of a plane crash over a year ago. We'd all assumed he was dead.

Dylan glanced at Angel, and she gave a slight nod. He turned back to me and rested his hands on my shoulders. His face was serious.

"Max, Dr. Gunther-Hagen is the Remedy."

69

"WHAT?!" I WAS on my feet, my mouth hanging open.

"I wasn't sure what to make of him at first," Dylan continued. "I tried to keep quiet, feel him out. But after a lecture on how the only solution to the ecological crisis was completely eliminating human impact, he asked me to kill the rest of the flock."

"You have to be kidding me. Häagen-Dazs? Last I heard, he wanted me to start reproducing! Now we have to be eliminated?"

Dylan and Angel both nodded somberly. The three of us shared the unspoken knowledge that Dylan had been designed to be my mate, my perfect partner.

"Well, nothing should surprise me, at this point," I said. "And yet I'm surprised." Needing a minute, I stalked around the woods, trying to figure this out. Dylan was one of the Horsemen. Angel had arranged to have him pretend to kill the rest of the flock—convincingly, I might add. Now Dr. G-H had turned out not only to be alive, but to be the biggest honcho in all of honchodom.

I thought back to what Dr. Hans had said about Fang's special DNA. How ambitious the doctor had been. How he had millions in grant money at his disposal.

Dr. Gunther-Hagen might have been a philanthropist, an environmentalist, and a brilliant scientist. But he was also a rich, manipulative extremist with a God complex— never a good combo.

I'd never liked him.

"He's the force I've seen building for so long," Angel said when I got back. "He is plague, and war, and famine, and death."

"What you mean is, he's a total asshat," I said bluntly. "And we could've stopped him sooner."

Then I got angry. Nail-spittingly angry. I was furious at everything Dr. G-H had done, and I wanted someone to pay. *Right now.*

"So, let me get this straight," I said to Dylan. "This mass murderer was right in front of you, asking you to join his murder team and kill your friends, and instead of taking him out right then, you *accepted* the mission? And you just *left* him there?"

Dylan looked at me like I'd slapped him, and color rushed to his cheeks as if I really had.

"If I had killed the Remedy then, I would have been dead myself a second later. He has guards everywhere. But by pretending to follow his orders, I've been able to save the flock, gather information, and help Angel in her plan. Is that not good enough for you?"

"Why didn't you come get me?" I pressed. "I could've helped you."

"You were halfway around the world!"

"So was everyone else!" I yelled.

As Harry crouched on the other side of the fire, his head jerked back and forth between Dylan and me.

"I told you, the doctor was sending reinforcements, the other Horsemen!" Dylan threw up his hands in exasperation. "I had to get to everyone first and convince him you were all dead. Or you really would be!"

"But you—" I started again, but realized I was running out of objections.

It was possible Dylan had actually done a really good, selfless thing.

Maybe you should stop berating him, Angel's voice said inside my head as she cocked an eyebrow. I glared at her, knowing she was right.

When I looked back at Dylan, into those aqua eyes that I'd missed so much, the fight drained right out of me.

"You did it all on your own?" I asked more calmly. "You risked your life to save the rest of the flock?"

"You guys are my family." Dylan shrugged, humble as ever. "It's what any of you would've done."

269

My heart melted right then, and I nodded.

Yeah, it is. Time to eat crow. So to speak.

"C'mere, Boy Wonder." I yanked Dylan toward me for the tightest hug, squeezing those pumped-up biceps until he understood how thankful I was—for what he'd done, and that he was still alive.

That he really was part of our family.

"So everyone's safe, then?" I said, once the hugfest was over. "Where's the flock? Are they close? I can't wait to have us all back together again."

Dylan winced and looked at Angel.

"What is it?" I asked.

Something was very wrong.

70

"*ALMOST* EVERYONE'S SAFE." Angel spoke carefully.

I frowned. "Is someone hurt? What happened? Is it Nudge? Total?"

"It's Fang," Dylan said softly, not looking at me.

"Yeah? What about him?"

"He's . . . dead, Max."

You'd think those words would've laid me out, but they didn't.

Because they simply didn't make sense. I had once thought Angel was dead. It had been bad. I had *feared* that Dylan was dead, since we'd left the island. I had *worried* about each person in my flock, worried until it ate away at my insides and destroyed my sleep. But I'd never, ever imagined that Fang would actually ever be dead.

Ever.

Not until I was dead, too.

"I don't understand," I said stiffly. "There must be some mistake."

Tell me it was a mistake. Tell me the reports of Fang's death have been greatly exaggerated.

Tell me.

"I knew it was gonna happen." Angel's voice sounded like it was underwater. "I've known it forever, and now it's real."

Real. Dead. Fang, my Fang, was no longer in this world. The world was still turning somehow, but without Fang.

My body seemed to understand the words before my head did. Just like this morning, I couldn't get enough oxygen, and my heart and lungs were working double-triple-overtime. This time, my heart was physically breaking.

"Why do you think that?" My voice was remote.

Dylan hesitated. "It was the Horsemen—upgraded Erasers."

"No. Take it back," I choked out.

Make this feeling stop.

"Take what—" Dylan started to ask, but I grabbed him by the collar of his jacket and slammed him against a tree, pressing my forearm tight against his throat.

"Max!" Angel gasped.

"Take it back!" I repeated in a shrill, maniacal voice I didn't recognize.

Dylan looked back at me helplessly, his beautiful eyes full of anguish.

"Say he's not dead!" I roared, and shook Dylan harder.

Stop it, Max! Angel said. She had weaseled her way inside my head, and I felt my fists unclenching despite what I was telling them to do. *Let. Him. Go.*

My arms fell to my sides, Dylan fell to the ground, and then I dropped to my knees, crying so hard I couldn't breathe.

71

I SAT ALONE in the dark, leaning against the trunk of a tree, pressing my face into my knees. My eyes were bleary from exhaustion and tears, but I wouldn't lie down. I couldn't go to sleep.

Thirty feet away, Angel, Dylan, and Harry still sat around the glowing coals, talking quietly. Well, not Harry. They'd left me alone after I had broken down. I'd cried so hard I'd thrown up, retching into the pine needles, and then I'd cried some more.

I felt their helplessness, their shared pain, but they had no idea. No one had ever possibly felt this bad before. Not like this. When Harry had tried to pat my shoulder, I had punched him. My squalling grief had shut Angel out of my head completely. Finally I'd crawled off into the darkness, stopping only when I ran into a tree. My exhausted brain didn't know what else to do, so I had curled up in front of the tree.

They hadn't come after me. They were probably afraid I was going to freak out again, get violent. Or that I'd make that horrible, wrenching sound of pain again, sobs that shook not just my body, but the earth, the trees, the sky. They were afraid that next time, I wouldn't stop.

I was all cried out, though.

And as I slowly came back to my senses, I saw how stupid it was to cry over something that was so obviously not true.

This was Fang we were talking about. The Fang who had once fought five Erasers at once and had come out with only a bloody nose. Fang had healed from a bullet wound in two days. He could slip invisibly between shadows and fly with the speed of a fighter jet and was one step ahead in a fight, always. He had almost died once, when Dr. Gunther-Hagen had almost completely drained his blood and replaced it with chemicals, but with a shot of adrenaline, Fang was back up in no time. He had survived a fiery apocalypse and pulled me from the grip of a tsunami.

The kid had invincible DNA, for crying out loud. He couldn't just *die*.

And if he wasn't dead, which he wasn't, that meant I needed to find him.

I looked over at the group gathered around the fire. It

looked so warm over there, so cozy. For a second, I ached to be with the family I had missed for so long.

I couldn't see their faces from here, and their words were only murmurs. If I got closer, I'd have to look into their sad eyes, and I'd want to scratch them out. If I heard the lies spilling from their mouths, I'd want to plug them with a fist.

They were right to leave me alone. They were right to be afraid.

I didn't think I would ever forgive them for a lie like this.

Not true not true not true, I shouted inside my head like a mantra, trying to drown out their voices.

72

ANGEL WALKED TOWARD me, and I sat up a bit.

"I'm so sorry, Max."

"I'm okay," I said, without looking up.

"Harry's pretty cool, huh?" she said after a minute. "His thoughts are so funny. All jumbled and excited. Like a little kid's."

"Mmm."

You just can't stay out of anyone's head, can you?

If Angel heard my thought, she didn't respond. She just stood silent, a silhouette backlit by the fire, watching me. Her gaze was gentle, but I knew those icy blue eyes could turn cold and ruthless. I remembered that she and her cherubic face had betrayed me again and again. I reminded myself that Angel would do anything to get what she wanted—even put a voice inside my head to challenge my decisions.

She was lying this time, too. She had to be.

"Do you have something to say?" I asked finally, looking up.

Just tell me what all this is about. Tell me the truth.

Angel sighed. "I don't have all the answers, Max. I just know we have to get to Russia. I think everything has been building to this. We really need to leave soon, to go meet up with the other kids."

"Okay."

"Yeah?" Angel's eyebrows lifted in surprise. "That's great! Me and Dylan had a pretty rough day flying through a blizzard, though. We should get a few hours of sleep first." She laid her hand on my back. "You could use some rest, too, Max. We can head out in the morning."

I stood up and began to pack. "Take Harry along with you guys, okay? He needs to be with other bird kids, and there's something I need to do alone."

Angel glared at me, her mouth twisting into an angry knot. "I thought you'd learned your lesson, Max. I thought that was why you came after us. But you're just going to walk away from your flock? Again?"

When I didn't answer, she batted the bedding out of my hands.

"So when it's finally time to do what you're meant to do, you're running from your destiny? I have news for you, Max: You don't have a choice."

Annnd, after approximately one hour of sweetness, Angel the Tyrant was back.

I rolled my eyes. "Don't be such a drama queen. I'll catch up with the flock. There's just a place I need to stop by first."

"The only place we need to go is Russia. All of us."

I didn't respond. She knew I was headed to Alaska.

"There's no point." Angel trailed me to my small pile of clothes. "I told you, he's *dead*."

"Stop it. Stop saying that." I wrenched my hand away from her and closed my eyes, blocking out the words.

It's a lie it's a lie it's a—

"It's *true*. I don't know how to make you believe it."

I clamped my teeth together and started tossing dried food in a bag.

That's why I'm going to Alaska. To see for myself.

"There's nothing to see, Max. Fang faced his fate." She paused and then said more loudly, "He wasn't a coward."

I glared daggers at her smug little face.

"Did you see him die?" I challenged. "You weren't there, were you?"

"I told you, I've seen Fang die a thousand times!" Angel's shout was half sob. "It doesn't matter if I was there, because I can't get the nightmare out of my head."

"If you weren't there, then you don't know." I turned away from her, scooping up the sleep sack from where it had fallen. "Not for sure."

"I was there."

Dylan was still crouched by the cooling embers. His face was in profile as he leaned forward, hands clasped over his knees, and his voice was so soft I wasn't sure I'd heard right at first.

"What?" I managed to squeak, and he turned his head.

"I said I was there. I saw it."

73

I HAD TO go, had to leave now.

"Max..." Dylan said, walking over.

It took everything in me not to run. I grabbed a handful of clothes and busied myself with layering for the cold flight ahead.

"*Max*, look at me. Please."

I pulled my sweatshirt over my head slowly, losing myself in the fabric. When Dylan tugged it down, I started to turn away, but he held my shoulders firm, forcing me to face him.

"I was there." He sighed heavily. "To warn him. To fake his death like I did with the others. But I guess the Remedy didn't think I could handle Fang, and he sent reinforcements."

"And you didn't help him?" My voice sounded small,

weak. I blinked hard, but my sore eyes burned with salt. "You didn't save him?"

"I tried!" Dylan pressed his palm against the trunk of a tree and shook his head. "There were too many of them, and I lost consciousness..."

"You blacked out?" I focused on that last scrap of hope—the final possibility that could mean it was all a big mistake. "So you didn't see him die, either."

It's a lie a lie a lie.

"I saw the Horsemen tear into him."

That's when it all started to feel real again, and the tears began to leak everywhere.

"Max Mum!" Harry's feathers were all puffed up again, and he was glaring at Dylan.

"I'm fine, Harry." I was blubbering, but I held my hand up to tell him to stay where he was.

Dylan lowered his voice and knelt down next to me. "I know this is hard for you," he said gently. "I know you still don't trust Angel, and as for me..." My heart clenched and I looked up just as he glanced away. "Well, I have no idea what you think of me anymore.

"But you know I wouldn't lie to you." His gaze was steady, and he took both of my hands in his. "Fang's not coming back, Max. Not ever. I even sent the video to the Remedy as proof. It was the first time I reported a death that wasn't a lie."

My whole body stiffened.

"What do you mean, the video?" I asked, and Dylan winced. "Tell me."

"They put a tech chip in my arm to communicate," he explained reluctantly, and pulled up his sleeve to reveal a small screen. "I was recording to sell the doctor on what I thought would be a faked death, like all the others, but then..."

"Play it for me."

Dylan's eyebrows shot up. "What? Max, no. Trust me, you don't want to see that." When I didn't look away, Dylan started to pace. "Look, maybe *I* don't want to see it again, either, okay? When I woke up and saw him lying there, all..."

Dylan took a deep breath and raked his fingers through his hair as if trying to pull the image out. He looked back at me with an expression of utter horror, but I tugged at his arm desperately.

"I'll never believe it," I pleaded. "I'll never let it go. I just need to know, Dylan. To move on."

Dylan pressed his lips together in disapproval, shaking his head. He pushed a button on his wrist.

The picture was grainy and chaotic, and dark forms swooped in and out of the frame, massive Erasers who kept landing hard hits. I heard Dylan's voice pleading, and then Fang's voice, and then Dylan's moan, just as a set of ugly wolf jaws seemed to come right at the screen, blurring the video for a second.

"This is where I blacked out," Dylan said.

But the camera kept rolling. Now that Dylan wasn't jerking all around, it was actually a lot clearer than before.

At first you only saw fat, white snowflakes, with the mountainous skyline stretching far into the background. I watched those snowflakes for several long seconds, feeling anything but calm as the quiet rang in my ears.

Then, a voice offscreen. A man's voice was calling up to Fang, taunting him. A voice I recognized.

"What the hell was Jeb doing there?" I jumped to my feet, shouting at Dylan.

But before he answered, we saw action on the video screen. Fang crashed into the image with three giant Erasers snarling on his back. Fang was more beat-up than I'd ever seen him. His lips and eyes were so swollen and bloodied that his face was almost unrecognizable, and the huge wolves were still going to town, biting into his flesh and pummeling his skull one after the other.

"Why isn't he fighting back?" I demanded, watching as Fang raked his nails along the ground, trying to crawl free.

"He was," Dylan answered. "But they're not just Erasers. They're Horsemen."

My hands covered my mouth and half my face so that just my eyes were peeking out. I watched as a steel-toed boot connected with Fang's torso, and I felt my own body shudder as I heard his ribs crack. I didn't know how much more I could take of this, when, mercifully, they tumbled out of view.

Jeb was on the edge of the screen, though. We heard the grunts of the fighters, and he was crouched next to them like a patient referee waiting to call the match. Then, even though I couldn't see what happened, I heard Fang scream in agony.

The sound made my eyes fill with tears and my blood run cold. I was shaking all over.

But Fang and the Horsemen rolled into view again, and I exhaled with relief. This time, Fang had his arms locked around the three hulking bodies, grabbing fistfuls of fur and straining necks—whatever he could grasp. He seemed so confident, I thought he'd gotten some advantage, channeled a new power.

But then he started to roll.

"What is he doing?" I whimpered. "Oh, God, what is he doing?"

Despite his obviously weakened state, Fang's will was unstoppable. He dragged the frantic Horsemen toward the edge . . . and then they were offscreen again.

Afterward, I held my breath as I waited for Fang to stumble back in front of the camera, listening desperately for the sound of his ragged breathing.

There were only snowflakes, though—and silence.

The silence seemed to go on forever.

Dylan started to turn off the video, but then I spotted Jeb, awkwardly dragging something toward the edge.

"Wait!" I squeezed Dylan's arm. "What *is* that?"

It was black and oddly shaped, textured and smooth at once.

"Stop it," I said abruptly. I felt bile rising in my throat as I remembered the screams. "That's enough."

It was way more than enough.

It was Fang's bloody, mangled wing.

"He took the rest of them out with him," Dylan said reverently. "The best assassins the Remedy had. He was brave, Max. To the very end. I thought you might want this," he added. "To remember."

Dylan held out a feather, about a foot long, beautifully black and shiny.

If you've ever loved someone like I did, if they made you crazy and happy and exasperated and elated and if you wanted to hold them and shake them and sometimes kick them and if, after all that, they were like part of your family and part of your soul . . .

Imagine seeing that feather. Imagine what that felt like.

It made it real.

It wasn't just a punch to the gut; it was a rip, too—like someone had torn all the hope and love, plus all the muscle and bone, right out of my body. I had nothing left to stand on.

I'd fallen to my knees before I'd even felt them buckle, and the nausea finally overcame everything else.

"I'm sorry, Max!" Dylan cried miserably as I retched again and again into the dirt. "I'm so sorry."

74

I AWOKE FEELING cold again. But this time, the cold felt heavy in my gut, and it didn't go away.

Angel led us. Harry and Dylan formed the V, and I hung back, riding the slipstream and letting them carry me for thousands of miles. We flew up along the west coast of Canada and over Alaska, and I didn't look down once. Didn't want to see the flattened cities and charred forests. Didn't want to see the landscape as bleak as my mind.

I don't deal with death well, you might have noticed. I don't really deal at all—I go on autopilot. The flight to Russia felt like one long hallucination, and I didn't eat, or talk, or cry.

It seemed like I barely breathed.

I do know that as we flew over Alaska, we were pelted with a blizzard so fierce it almost knocked Harry from the air. The cold made Dylan's teeth chatter and Angel's breath come in gasps, but I hardly felt any of it.

My thoughts were as blank as the snow.

Numb.

The Bering Strait was less than a hundred miles across, but the slate-colored water looked like an endless dark hole, trying to suck me down.

Once, I stopped flying completely, letting my body hang limp for a second too long. I folded my wings in and started to drop, imagining myself plunging into the freezing water, having it hit me like concrete at that speed. A fast death.

But then I saw angry clouds in the distance and jerked back up. I was sure I'd glimpsed Fang's stormy eyes, and thought I saw his face just beyond the horizon. The wind whispered to me: *Not yet. Not yet.*

"Cut it out, Angel," I mumbled. "Get out of my head."

She didn't look back, though. It was Fang's voice, gravelly and insistent, that urged me on, reminding me why I was still here, and what I needed to do.

So I kept moving forward, mile by mile, and the cold feeling inside me started to heat up into rage and harden into resolve: I would get to the Remedy, whatever it took.

And I'd kill him myself.

I'd expected the Remedy's den of death to be as wrecked as the rest of the world, but when the water became land again, the gray, barren coast of Russia turned to lush, green forests. Mountains were untouched by ash, and rivers still flowed blue. After all the devastation I'd seen, it should've given me hope.

But I was in no state to embrace such a positive emotion, so naturally, it just fueled my fury. He didn't deserve this. *I* didn't deserve it.

Not yet.

We were flying over a forest of tightly packed trees when I noticed Dylan scanning the ground. I broke formation and flew up next to him.

"Where is he?" I didn't have to clarify who I meant.

"Underground. A place called *Himmel.*" Dylan pronounced the last word with an accent.

"Himmel?"

"Heaven," Dylan explained. "It's German."

My mouth tightened into a hard line and I wondered what the German word for hell was. I was going to show Dr. Gunther-Hagen that everything has an opposite.

"Okay, let's go," I said grimly.

"Wait, Max." Angel reached for my arm. "We have to join the others at the camp first." She smiled faintly. "It's just another few miles."

Reluctantly I nodded, figuring "the others" were the rest of the flock, but when a clearing opened up in the woods, I saw rows and rows of makeshift tents made out of everything imaginable, from plastic tarps to blankets to flowered bedsheets. Between them, *thousands* of people went about their business. After seeing hardly anyone for so long, it really was a sight to behold.

"Where did they all come from?" I asked in awe, and Angel shrugged.

"All over."

I had seriously underestimated her. And for once, that was a good thing.

"Look." She pointed. "There's the rest of the flock."

I hadn't let myself believe I'd see them again. Not fully. I'd already lost something so huge, having hope seemed like being a sucker asking to get burned.

But the sight of their faces cut through my shield, and I was shaking so hard I could barely steer myself to a landing. I hadn't lost it all. Nudge, Iggy, Gazzy. Even Total—they were all here, waiting for me.

Alive.

75

THE FIRST POOR soul in my path of suffocating love was Nudge, and I tackled her, knocking her to the grass.

"Agh!" she said as I almost crushed her with the force of my embrace. Strangers stared at the bird girl acting like a lunatic attacker, but I didn't care as long as I never had to let my little sister go again. Finally, I pulled her to her feet.

"Oh, Nudgelet," I said with a shaky breath, "I'm so glad you're okay." Nudge's eyes glistened.

"I missed you, too, Max." The bite on her cheek had healed into a gnarly scar, but her brilliant smile made you hardly notice it.

"Don't I get a hello?" Iggy asked from behind me.

"C'mere." I yanked him into a fierce bear hug, squeezing

tightly until he started coughing. Then I held him at arm's length, looking him over.

"You scared the crap out of me!" I shouted, jabbing him in the chest.

"Whoa, take it easy!" Iggy put his hands up defensively.

"I thought you were dead!" I shoved him. "Do you have any idea what that does to a person? Do you?"

"It's not my fault! Dylan spread the rumor!" Iggy protested, but now he was laughing as he blocked my jabs. "Besides," he said, flashing a wry grin, "how much more do you love me now that I'm not dead?"

I rolled my eyes and mussed his shaggy blond hair in exasperation, but the truth? *A lot more.* Or at least I was a lot more appreciative of my weird, lovely little flock than I ever had been.

I hugged Gazzy and Total, too, my face muscles constantly quivering between sobs and smiles. It was definitely an emotional reunion, to say the least.

"How did they say *I* died?" Gazzy asked eagerly.

"You got blown up."

"Cooool." His eyes lit with morbid delight, and when I pursed my lips, unamused, he cackled like a maniac. "And also totally bogus you would believe that, Max. Do you have any idea how much I know about combustible materials and the rate of conflagration?"

"No, I don't," I said, trying not to imagine all the times Gazzy's experiments had come close to blowing us all up in our sleep. "And for that I'm incredibly grateful."

"Well, jokes aside, I'm incredibly grateful to be alive," Iggy said. He clapped Dylan on the back and pulled him in for a hug. "Seriously, man, I don't know how you pulled that off, but thank you."

"It wasn't a big deal." Dylan blushed.

"Not a big deal?" Nudge echoed in disbelief. "I almost died of shock! I could've done without waking up to Total slobbering on my face, but you saved all of our lives, Dylan!"

Dylan smiled, but his eyes flicked to mine and Angel's and his smile faded.

He didn't save all our lives. He didn't save Fang.

"An act of heroism to rival any of the classic demigods," Total was gushing. "Achilles..."

Suddenly my chest hurt and my throat ached. "Okay," I said, and coughed. "So what's the deal with the kids at the camp? Why are we here?"

76

"I TOLD YOU. We're here to fight a war," Angel said. She looked out across the crowded field. "And that's why we brought an army."

I watched Angel's face, trying to figure out what was different about her. She seemed removed from the group, somehow. Apart.

"Gasman and I just got here a couple of days ago," Iggy said. "But Nudge has been chatting everyone up for the last week, pulling together their stories."

"We're pretty sure the Remedy detonated nuclear warheads on every continent," Nudge reported. "Maybe close to a hundred."

"That's insane," I said in horror.

"No, what's insane is that there're over four thousand

left, stockpiled here in Russia," Gazzy said. "And this wackjob has full access."

I thought of the flattened cities I'd seen. The caved-in homes, mangled bodies, burned flesh. Then I imagined one man, alone in a room, pushing a button to make that happen.

Then pushing it again. And again.

A hundred times.

"It's time to end this," I said through gritted teeth. "Now."

"Supplies are low anyway," Iggy agreed.

I glanced at the dense forest around us, at the still-green leaves and undeveloped land. There had to be a ton of wild game nearby.

"We know how to hunt," I reminded him. "And Harry here is stellar. Harry—"

"Harry!" He'd been hanging off to the side, but now he crowed his name on cue, and Nudge's face lit up.

Gotta be the dimples. Every time.

"We can definitely use him," Iggy said. "But a lot of these other mutants are city kids, and they have no idea how to feed themselves."

"They're not all mutants, either," Gazzy said. "Like the girls we brought from the silo—they're human, but they're super hard-core." He beamed. I raised a suggestive eyebrow, and Gazzy snickered, always the lady-killer. "There's also a lot of lab escapees, like the bug boys over there."

I followed his gaze to where a bunch of small, athletic

kids were kicking around a ball of newspaper tied with rope in place of a soccer ball. They almost didn't look like mutants at all, except for the hard brown shell that started on their upper arms and went down their backs. There was a paler kid with them who seemed familiar.

"Is that..."

"Holden from Fang's gang?" Iggy said. "Yeah, that's the Starfish. They actually have contests over who has the weirder epidermis." He chuckled. "Kate and Ratchet are here, too, somewhere."

"Kate?" I jerked my head around to stare at Angel. "The traitor?"

"I found her and Ratchet in San Francisco, in an abandoned mall," Angel explained. "They were emaciated, living off whatever hadn't rotted in the food court. Almost everyone else within a thousand miles had died of the H8E virus, but since they were immune, they'd set up a clinic and were transfusing their own blood to save other kids."

Well, what little martyrs.

"But she still *betrayed* Fang," I repeated, emphasizing each word with my open palm. "She and Star sold him out to Jeb."

It had meant the death of my clone, Maya, and the dissolution of Fang's gang.

"Trust me, Kate regrets that," Angel said. "That's why she's here—to fix what she did. And we're going to need her strength against the Remedy's forces."

Dylan nodded in agreement, and I remembered what

he'd told me about the Horsemen, how they were almost superhuman. Kate might have lightning reflexes and be able to punch with the force of a wrecking ball, but she could never "fix" what she'd done.

"Speaking of Fang's gang," Total said curiously, twitching his furry ears. "Where is our dark, brooding brother?"

"Yeah, I thought Fang was coming with you guys," Iggy said. "Dylan told us—"

"Fang is dead," Angel answered bluntly.

The words were still like knives, slicing up my heart.

"Yeah, right." Gazzy started to laugh but then saw the looks on our faces, and his expression morphed into horror. "What do you mean, he's *dead*?"

"He was killed by Horsemen," Dylan said, clenching his fist. "I tried to stop it, but there were just too many of them."

The words tore through the flock like a hurricane. It hurt to see them realize that nothing would ever be the same.

Nudge's face crumpled and she buried her face in Dylan's shoulder as her body shook with sobs. Total flopped on the ground, wailing. Tears ran down Gazzy's cheeks and he sat abruptly, ripping at blades of grass. Angel rubbed his back, trying to comfort her big brother.

Iggy walked off to the side and blindly stared into the woods, his body incredibly still, his face a mask I couldn't read. Just like after Ella.

Only I stood alone, my eyes dry. I wouldn't revisit that grief—not yet. At that point I felt only pure, distilled anger, a seemingly bottomless well of fury.

At Angel, for saying it would happen. At Dylan, for making it true. At myself, for letting him go.

And at Fang, most of all, for leaving. For dying.

How could I ever, ever forgive him for that?

So when Total suggested we say some words for Fang, when Gazzy said we would fight the battle in his name, and when Nudge wanted to hold a candlelit vigil, I bit down hard on my tongue to keep from screaming.

I didn't want to tell stories or share memories. I didn't know if I could even say his name.

With the taste of blood in my mouth, I shoved my hands in my pockets and turned away.

"Max?" Nudge called after me, a quaver in her voice.

"I'm sorry, I can't," I said as I walked away from my family. I trudged deeper into the camp, ducking under clotheslines and trying to lose myself in the sea of strangers.

"I just can't."

77

THE NEXT DAY, the camp buzzed with nervous energy as everyone prepared for battle.

Iggy and Gazzy had rigged up a catapult out of fallen trees, and Holden was shouting directions about angle placement and velocity. All around me, kids were trying to psych each other up, banging their weapons together like they'd seen in movies, even though no one knew what we were up against.

Most of us didn't, anyway.

Angel was the one who'd gathered us here, and of course she was nowhere in sight. And Dylan was the one person who'd actually seen the underground layout, and so far, he'd told us nothing.

We were here. It was time. What were we waiting for?

Restless, I wandered through the muddy rows of the camp, veering right to avoid a damp-eyed prayer circle Nudge was leading, complete with candles. I ground my teeth.

"Not into that praying crap, either, huh?"

Startled, I turned to see Ratchet lying on a tarp, doing sit-ups.

"We're gonna win or we're gonna lose. Personally, I think we're gonna lose. But either way, praying to some yahoo isn't going to change anything."

"Where's Kate?" I asked.

"Over with the baby general." Ratchet nodded past me without breaking rhythm.

About a hundred yards away, near the edge of the woods, Angel was talking to Kate and Dylan.

"If they wanna whisper secrets," Ratchet said, taking a breath, "maybe they shouldn't be so loud about it."

I could barely see their expressions from here, let alone hear their voices, but with his extraordinary senses, not much got past Ratchet.

"What secrets?"

Ratchet did several more sit-ups, his trademark aviator glasses reflecting back at me with each one. Finally, he stopped and wiped his forehead with his sleeve.

"Maybe you should go find out for yourself."

When I approached, Angel seemed completely different than I'd ever seen her. Her voice was still the same, soft and young, but her tone was one of unmistakable authority.

Sitting on a stump with her legs tucked under her, she looked like a child empress, consulting with her trusted advisors.

Which apparently didn't include me.

As I approached, they stopped talking abruptly. Dylan coughed and shifted uneasily, and Kate flashed me a wide fake smile.

"Getting chummy in the cool kids' club?" I asked.

"Hmm?" Angel said distractedly. "What is it, Max?"

"Sorry to break up this little party, but is someone going to explain what the heck is going on? Shouldn't we be casing the entrances? Or at least organizing the giant mass of people you convinced to meet here?"

"Dylan and Kate have been working out a strategy of attack," Angel said, standing. "And I was about to make an address on the field that should answer some of your questions."

"All I need," I said coldly, "is a face to smash my fist against."

78

ALL EYES WERE on Angel now. Yet, hovering a hundred feet above the field, facing her makeshift army, she felt about as powerful as a sparrow.

Her wings ached from constant traveling. Like all bird kids, she was naturally skinny, but her weight had dropped dangerously from the stress. And after so many sleepless nights, she was almost delirious. Everything had been building to this, though—this was the most important moment in her life. Angel gathered her strength.

"Thank you for coming," she began.

But her small, quivery voice was swallowed up by wind, and the kids below frowned uncertainly, fidgeted, whispered to one another. They stared up at the pale little girl who had led them here, her white wings keeping her aloft. They waited.

Angel took a deep breath to steady herself and smelled the ash drifting in on the wind. It was now or never.

We have kids here from all over the world, she continued. This time, her lips moved, but she didn't shout. She wanted them to hear every word, *really* hear her, so she spoke inside their minds.

Some of you came because you were starving. Some because you were homeless. Some because you wanted to fight . . .

Angel glanced at the silo girls standing near Gazzy, ammunition draped across their chests.

. . . And others came because you were afraid.

She nodded at Lucas and Matthew Morrissey.

But I know all of you want to understand what happened. You want to know the truth.

She saw Max's face twitch, her eyes narrow. Angel nodded.

Let me show you.

Angel stilled her body until her feathers were barely moving. She relaxed her breathing and closed her eyes. She let the connection open up.

Her brain flooded with thoughts from thousands of other minds—worries, doubts, judgments, memories—all blurring together until the din was like a swarm of locusts buzzing inside her skull, furious and deafening.

Then she took her own vision, her own terrible knowledge, and she pushed it into that space. She made them *see*.

Angel showed them the round, perfect globe as only astronauts had seen it, blue and naked and seeming to glow.

She showed them the enormous asteroid and its fiery tail, roaring through the darkness, pulled like a magnet. Closer, closer.

The smaller pieces breaking off as it entered the earth's atmosphere, scattering throughout the Pacific.

The many shooting stars that got brighter and brighter until it felt like your eyelids were peeled back, unable to shut out their light.

The moment the biggest chunk hit on the western coast of Morocco, there was too much to see at once, too much to know. The images flashed faster and faster, like a flip-book of drawings:

The main meteor, almost a mile wide, smashing against the earth, creating a new, gigantic crater where Morocco had once been.

The ring of fire that circled the massive crater, burning for months.

The jolt after the impact that rippled though the water within moments, churning into tsunamis.

Angel showed them the blinding flash that North Africans saw just before their bones vaporized in the heat. The mile-high tidal wave of water arcing over New York and most of the East Coast of the United States, Venezuela, and Spain just before it sucked everything back to sea. She showed them forests from Eastern Europe to the western US that burst into flame all at once as hot ash pelted down.

And the shudder of shock waves racing underfoot around the globe, toppling cities, causing a domino effect of volcanoes to erupt with devastating results.

Angel showed them everything she could, and when she was done, she opened her eyes with a gasp, severing the connection.

Angel saw Nudge right below her, tears spilling down her cheeks. Many others were weeping, too. Just as Angel had.

Angel didn't show them what had happened days and weeks after—the death and famine, the raids. They already knew all about that. There was just one more thing they didn't know.

The Remedy did this, she told them. *This, and much more. He dropped bombs, unleashed a virus. He tried to wipe all traces of humans off the earth.*

The field of people was silent. They looked up at her with damp, desperate eyes, asking her what to do.

We have to fight, she answered.

Angel winced as a bolt of pain shot through her temples and a vision flashed behind her eyes—a split-second glimpse of this same field, littered with the wounded and the dead. She knew she was leading many of these kids to their deaths, but she had no choice.

The world doesn't have very many people left, but it has us. You've survived. But is just surviving enough?

"No!" a few eager kids shouted, but others still looked uncertain.

The Remedy drops bombs and builds superhuman androids

305

to do his dirty work, but he's never gone to battle, Angel said, her words gaining force. *The Remedy stole our planet, murdered our families, and destroyed our homes, but he's never seen our faces. Are you going to let him walk away?*

"NO!" the crowd roared in unison.

Angel fluttered down until she was just a few feet off the ground. She wanted to see the dirt on their faces. She wanted to be able to meet their eyes. All she had was these kids, and all they had was her, and whatever they'd grabbed from the rubble. Her fighters were armed with barbecue forks, baseball bats, broken crutches, lengths of rusted rebar, pitchforks, tree limbs, junior archery sets... their bravery humbled her.

"The Remedy thinks he has won," she said aloud, her voice strident and clear. "But he can't see the future. *I can.* And I swear, if you follow me, we will see him fall."

Right there, Kate fell to her knees in the dirt, her dark hair hanging as she bowed her head. Beside her, Ratchet knelt as well. One by one the others followed, until over a thousand kids were kneeling before Angel, ready to serve.

79

ALL I'D WANTED was to fight the Remedy. But as the troops were finally moving out, I was pushing backward against the tide of bodies, searching for blonde hair and white feathers.

I needed to talk to her first.

"Angel!" I yelled, elbowing my way through. "Ange!" I grabbed her hand and turned her around to face me. "What *was* that?" I demanded. I could still see the imprint of the explosion behind my eyelids, a sudden camera flash. I felt the heat, as real as if it were flaying my own skin. "Tell me what that was."

In the middle of all this chaos, with people bumping past us and shouting directions, Angel had the stillness of a monk.

"You know what it was, Max. The day the sky caught fire—it was Armageddon."

"But that doesn't tell me anything!" I said, more frustrated than ever. Everyone was acting like Angel had given all the answers, but all I had were more questions. "How do you know it was the Remedy? And what about the bombs, and the Horsemen?" I was shaking her now. "How do you know what you saw is even real?"

"Because I *know*!" Angel shouted, wrenching free of my grasp. "Because I saw it, just like I saw Fang's death—*before* it happened!" She looked up at me with watery blue eyes, and in that moment, I finally saw Angel for what she really was.

Not just a psychic or a mind reader. A *prophet*.

She was also a seven-year-old who'd been carrying around the most terrible secret in the world, all by herself. I noticed the ragged cuts around her fingernails where she'd torn the skin away, the dark circles around her eyes, and realized how much I had failed her.

"Oh, honey," I said. When I put my hands lightly on the outsides of her arms, she tensed. "Why didn't you tell me?"

"Because," she said, her small bow lips quivering, "you never wanted to listen."

"Of course I—" An image of Fang's face flashed in my mind, and I winced.

Fair enough.

"I'm listening now," I said gently.

We walked to the edge of the clearing, away from the

rest of the kids, and Angel sat back down on the stump and pulled her knees up to her chest.

"The visions started after they altered my eyes at the school."

My chest tightened, remembering that awful time after Paris. We'd all believed Angel was dead for weeks before finding her in one of Jeb's corrupt labs.

"At first I thought I was blind, like Iggy. But then I realized I could actually see *more*—stuff that hadn't happened yet. I kept seeing these flashes, and it was so scary, Max," she said, resting her chin on her knees to look up at me. "I could never see the whole picture, and I didn't know if it would be this year or in five years or a hundred years."

"Did anyone else know about all this? The meteor and bombs and apocalypse?" I asked, still trying to figure out where the Remedy fit into all this.

"The scientists did, and the world leaders," Angel said. "I didn't find that out until the day it hit, when I heard Dr. Martinez's thoughts."

"But my mom was worried about the H8E virus," I said. I remembered her telling Fang and me about the plague the Apocalypticas had developed, how we should all be safe from it, on the island. "She didn't mention the meteor."

"That's because the Russians had planned to blast it apart with nuclear weapons. *'They were going to nuke it'*— that's what Dr. Martinez kept thinking the day the sky caught fire. *'I thought Russia was going to nuke it.'*"

"But somehow Dr. G-H got control of the nukes first?"

Angel nodded.

"He just...let it...hit us," she said, looking up at me in bewilderment, and I'm sure my face was a mirror of shocked, sickened horror. Angel started to weep, and I hugged her close to me. "I swear I didn't know about the Remedy, Max." She cried harder, her tears soaking my neck. "I just knew we had to get to Russia."

"I know, sweetie," I whispered, smoothing her hair. "I'm so sorry I didn't listen."

"I'm sorry, too," she hiccupped. "And I wasn't trying to hurt Fang by showing him his fall. I just didn't know what else to do."

I couldn't think of Fang without feeling the cold grip of nausea in my gut, and I stiffened. Angel felt the shift and pulled away from me, wiping her face.

"We should go. I said I would lead those kids."

My little prophet.

"You really were great up there earlier, Angel. A true leader."

"I know," Angel said matter-of-factly, and I laughed. "What?" She smiled. "I told you I know stuff. You taught me a lot, though, Max."

"Oh yeah?" I cocked an eyebrow. "Like what?"

"Like how you never stop fighting for the right ending. Even after the apocalypse."

That's my girl. I snapped open my wings, and Angel did the same.

"Let's show Dr. God what hell feels like."

80

ONCE AGAIN, ANGEL hovered above her army. The icy wind cut through her thin clothes and whipped against her cheeks, but Angel faced it unblinkingly. This time, she was officially their leader, the general leading them to war.

And, for some of them, to death.

We will win, though, Angel told herself, though her visions had never shown her the final outcome. *We have to.*

As they shivered in haphazard lines awaiting Angel's command, she studied the layout of the battlefield below. Years of living with Max on the run had taught her to look for vulnerabilities, and she saw that geography was in their favor, at least. The main entrance to the underground city known as Himmel was in a clearing, so they had unobstructed access, and though Dylan had warned her about vents in the surrounding ground, the surrounding woods provided a natural barrier against escape. From her vantage point in the sky, Angel saw beyond the trees as well—to endless miles of flat Siberian wilderness.

The Remedy might have an advanced security system, but he was still underground. There was nowhere for him to run.

"Prepare the catapult!" she yelled down to Gazzy and Iggy. She watched as they started to load the homemade smoke bombs.

Himmel's entrance didn't look like much from above. From the ground it appeared like the mouth of a cave, but the outcropping was hidden by the wiry grasses that covered the rest of the countryside. From up here, apart from a small mound in the earth, you'd barely know it was there.

"*FIRE!*" Angel commanded.

Gazzy launched the grenades one after the other, but apart from the sound of the egg-like objects singing toward Himmel's narrow mouth, the field was silent. The air felt full of static, it was so pregnant with anticipation.

Then, as the bombs started to release their gases, Angel heard a barrage of new thoughts, all at once.

Not the thoughts of her own army, but of the army below—the one she hadn't been sure was there.

They were there, all right, and Angel realized with alarm that there were more than she'd ever anticipated. There were many thousands of fighters in the Remedy's army. More than they could ever take on.

"*HOLD!*" Angel shouted a little hysterically at her ranks. But the events had already been set in motion, and thick clouds of smoke began billowing out of the hole. The angry, panicked thoughts of the Remedy's army buzzed louder, louder. "Hold..."

The survivors and the mutants on the field twitched uncomfortably in response to Angel's reaction. They didn't hear the deafening thoughts, couldn't fathom how many soldiers there were; they saw only an empty field.

Her friends had no clue what was about to happen.

They waited, watching the smoke-filled hole.

They tensed, readying themselves for what was to come.

"*CHARGE!*" Angel screamed the moment she saw the outline of bodies through the smoke.

As her fighters surged forward, the Remedy's troops started to emerge, but the entrance to Himmel was so narrow it formed a bottleneck. Only a few of the Remedy's soldiers could get out at a time, she realized.

There was still a chance they could hold them off!

The billowing smoke blocked her view, but right before the armies clashed into each other, Angel saw her troops hesitate, just for a moment.

What are you doing? She sent the question telepathically to Kate, their strongest fighter, who was on the front lines. *What's wrong?*

"*They're kids, Angel,*" Kate answered her. "*Just little kids.*"

Angel's heart broke, but the rest of her shook with fury. They'd been mentally, if not physically, prepared for the Remedy's superhuman Horsemen or his armed Russian guards. Using children to fight his war was way more despicable.

They were fighting, though. They were Doomsday soldiers, brainwashed to hate humans and mutants alike. Angel watched more and more of them pushing past her soldiers, weapons held in fierce grips, eyes lusting for blood. If her survivors didn't push back, they'd all be killed.

Luckily, the flock, at least, had dealt with these kids before. Nudge let out a terrifying battle cry and launched herself forward in a roundoff backflip, her feet catching two machete-wielding warriors midair. The rest of the troops followed, battling the Remedy's child army in hand-to-hand combat.

Angel worked on breaking into the minds of the Doomsday fighters, but she knew from past experience that the cult mind was extremely difficult to crack into— the One Light had an incredibly powerful hold on them.

Still, she burrowed into their minds, hammering at the boundaries of their psyches, her head throbbing as she worked to free them before too many had to die. In a trancelike state herself, Angel was concentrating so hard on battling back the warped thoughts that she almost didn't hear Dylan's desperate cry.

"*THE VENTS!*" he was screaming at full volume now. "*ANGEL, THE VENTS!*"

As dozens of Horsemen burst up through unseen vents in the field, Angel shook in despair. These Horsemen were elite models, robots whose actions were completely controlled by the Remedy, so she couldn't read their thoughts.

But she knew their power.

"*Ratchet! Kate! Dylan!*" she summoned them telepathically, her voice tinged with real fear for the first time. "*Get to Max!*"

Even if they didn't win this battle, even if she couldn't save these kids, Angel knew, as she'd always known, that Max was their only chance at saving the world.

81

THE GROUND UNDER me shook violently. Like everyone else on the front lines, I couldn't see anything through the smoke, but it sounded like the world was breaking open.

Our whole army was bunched in a tight cluster in the center of the field. It was obvious we were in an extremely vulnerable position, but we had to hold back the ranks upon ranks of Doomsday psychos who kept pushing out of the entryway.

Right now, I was in a hair-pulling battle with a surprisingly vicious pigtailed eight-year-old and standing on an older boy's windpipe as I tried to pry his fingers off his homemade scythe. I thought that was more important than worrying about an earthquake...until I realized it wasn't an earthquake.

It was another army, shooting up out of holes in the ground all around us.

An army of M-Geeks.

At least that's what I thought they were. They sure looked like the flying robots that had annoyed us since the days of Mr. Chu—right down to the weapons grafted onto their arms in place of hands.

RAT-A-TAT-TAT! came the sound of machine-gun fire.

The field became a tangle of chaos and panic. I knew how to fight these villains, though. I'd done it before.

Leaving behind the Doomsday kids I'd pinned, I shot into the air. I flew erratically, hearing the pop of bullets and trying to find a clear view of one of the robots.

"Watch it!" Ratchet smashed into my side, knocking me off balance.

"Hey!" I scowled. "You watch it!"

"You were about to fly into the path of a bullet," Ratchet explained testily. Only someone with crazy heightened senses like his could've seen that. "You're welcome."

Looking down, I saw that most of our army was scattering for cover, but Holden and the bug boys were running full speed toward the M-Geeks. Bullets ricocheted off the armored mutants, and though Holden should've been full of holes, his elastic cells regenerated at such a high frequency that they barely slowed him down.

Closer to me, Gazzy teetered on the shoulders of another M-Geek, determinedly slamming a big rock on its head. But the head didn't split like an orange as before—they'd evolved. Instead, the gloved hand reached for Gazzy, grabbed him by his messy blond hair, and slammed him forward onto the ground, where Harry was already mewling in pain. The robot pointed his gun arm, execution style, at my wounded friends.

I got ready to dive.

Time for a reunion, Geeky.

But before I could drop, Dylan shot past me. He reached the M-Geek first, tearing him off Gazzy and smashing the armored face until the metal actually dented.

I started to look for another M-Geek, but I saw we had bigger problems to worry about.

Beyond the bodies fighting on the field around me, I saw something else charging out of the forest. My mouth hung slack.

It was a parade of enemies past come back to haunt me. Some had the snarling, wolfish snouts of Erasers. Some were cyborg Flyboys. Others looked like something entirely new: droids made of metal or giants whose hands could easily snap bodies in half.

I spotted a huge man with a slick bald head and cruel eyes—a carbon copy of the giant I'd met in Africa, who'd told me his buddies would be back to rip me apart. I narrowed my eyes.

This one's mine.

Dropping fast, I snap-kicked the backs of his knees, and when the big oaf buckled, I jumped up and jammed my fingers into his eyes, following with a quick uppercut to the chin.

Now I'd made him mad.

Roaring with pain and anger, he lunged toward me. Suddenly a powerful kick exploded against his left side—right to the kidney—and the giant collapsed in agony.

Kate.

"What are you doing?" I groaned, clenching my fists.

"Helping," Kate grunted as she heaved the whimpering giant up onto her shoulders. The giant had to outweigh Kate by about three hundred pounds, but she lifted him over her head as if he were a toy. She spun around and hurled him across the field, where he crashed against a tree and slid to the ground.

"I don't need help," I insisted.

This was a battle. A battle in which, with the Horsemen and the Doomsday kids together, we were vastly outnumbered. Kids were injured all around us, putting their lives on the line, and I should be pulling my weight, fighting alongside them. I *wanted* to fight, more than anything.

But no one would freaking let me!

I felt a dull blade trying to hack into the back of my thigh and whipped around just as I felt it scratch my skin. It was a Doomsday kid with fierce eyes, and I grinned. At last!

I drew my arm back for a sucker punch, but right then there was a head-shattering noise that made my ears feel like they were bleeding and my brain feel like it was liquidating. I gritted my teeth, working through the pain of the audio assault, but I noticed the Doomsday kids weren't faring so well. Not just the kid in front of me, but all across the field, they were blinking in confusion, and their weapons clattered to the ground.

The sound was breaking their hypnosis.

A tornado-like blur whirled across the field. When it finally stopped spinning, the sound cut out, and Star, the last member of Fang's gang, stood there smirking. "I remembered I had some unfinished business," she explained with a shrug.

With the Doomsdayers no longer a threat, I realized we might just have a chance at winning this thing. I looked around, quickly taking stock. The Horsemen had been unfazed by Star's brain-melting noise. Our kids were ganging up on them now, but even against ten of our soldiers, the new mutants were fierce, clearly made to be killing machines.

My heart beat faster as I scanned the muddied mess for my flock.

There were Nudge and Total, getting their revenge against a Cryena with the help of the silo girls.

Iggy, Ratchet, and Star were using their collective supersenses to make a metal mutant shake all over, until sparks shot out of its fingertips.

I inhaled the distinctive stink of greasy canine fur. An Eraser on steroids was making a beeline for me, and I took to the air and assumed an offensive stance. My muscles quivered with readiness, waiting for the ballet of an aerial fight stacked way against me.

That didn't happen, though, because Dylan slammed

into the Eraser first, *again*, getting between us and snapping its jaw with a well-aimed kick.

"You can't take on everyone!" I yelled angrily as Boy Wonder finished off Teen Wolf. "I have dibs on that Eraser over there," I said, pointing. *"OKAY?!"*

"Max, wait!" Dylan grabbed for my arm. "You can't fight right now—don't be stupid."

My eyes almost bugged out of my head. If there was ever a time that I was going to actually rip someone's head off, it was then. I was many things, but I was *not* stupid.

"Wh-what I mean is," Dylan stuttered, seeing the rage in my eyes, "now that the Doomsday kids are down, the entrance is clear." He pointed, and I saw it was true. "I think our soldiers can handle the rest of the Horsemen.... So do you want to meet the Remedy, or not?"

I didn't hesitate. "Now you're talking."

82

NOT THAT FINDING the Remedy was so easy. Underground, I followed Dylan through the dank tunnels filled with stale air, and I was pretty sure we were going in circles.

"It didn't look like this before," Dylan explained. "It was a huge city, with skyscrapers and neon lights."

"Uh-huh. And what is this, the subway station?" In every direction, all I saw were damp, sloped walls lit by faint tracking lights.

"I mean they were three-D projections," Dylan said irritably. "And my eyesight isn't so great after Gazzy's explosion in the silo, okay? Here. I think this is the door to the lab."

"I got this," I assured him. "You take the mansion."

Dylan didn't want to split up, but we needed to cover as much ground as possible. There was no way I was letting the Remedy slip through my fingers.

Still, as my footsteps echoed down the hall, I started to feel uneasy. The air was getting colder with every step, but even if it had been a hundred degrees down there, the place would've given me chills.

I didn't know if there would be a bunch more newly created Horsemen to attack me or a blast of gas to knock me out, but everything about this place felt wrong.

When I pulled open the single door at the end of the hallway, I understood why.

It was an exact replica of the lab I'd grown up in. The same large dog crates lining the walls. The same gurneys covered with crinkly paper sheets. The test tubes and scalpels. The same acrid, chemical smell of disinfectant.

A whitecoat was there, his back to me, and my stomach clenched as I flashed back to the years spent being poked and dissected on a table like this, sweating with fever as various drugs worked their way through my system, vomiting from exhaustion as they put us through test after test.

My breath was coming in shallow little bursts, and I was trying very hard not to completely give in to a panic attack as I crept forward.

"Hello, Max," the whitecoat said, and I stopped in my tracks, the hair rising on the back of my neck as the last piece of this little nostalgic puzzle snapped into place. The man turned around, and when he pulled the blue mask down from his face, he was smiling.

"Jeb," I said, shaking my head in disgust. "I wondered how you fit into all of this. I should've known it had to do with your passion for cloning your pathetic little wolfboy son, *ad infinitum*."

Jeb looked pained, and he took off his surgical glasses and massaged his eyelids. "Max, when Ari died, I was devastated. I just wanted to bring him back, the way he was."

"A murderous sociopath with staggering daddy issues?"

Jeb leaned against the counter and crossed his arms, sighing heavily in that way parents do when they want to apologize without apologizing and instead skirt responsibility entirely.

"The point is, we're past that now. Through a number of groundbreaking experiments, Dr. Gunther-Hagen helped me see my error—that it was the *humanity* of the mutants that was holding us back. The essential flaw that, if eliminated, would allow for a controlled population of indestructible guardians."

Well, if *that* wasn't a euphemism, I didn't know what was.

"I hate to break it to you, but your murder-bots up there can die, just like everybody else."

"They're still a little buggy—Dylan in particular didn't take well to the change—but with renewed supplies of *DNA immortalis*, we get closer every time. Closer to perfect."

What?

I glanced around at the trays of test tubes. They were full of clear liquid, with what looked like cotton balls floating in them.

DNA immortalis—where have I heard that before?

Then I remembered an image I'd wanted to forget forever, of a body at the bottom of a cliff. Alarm bells started screaming inside my head.

"You made the Horsemen by splicing Fang's genes?" I gaped at Jeb in horror as he shifted uncomfortably.

They killed Fang by using his own strength against him.

"Well, I don't see any of your Horsemen now. You're all alone in here."

"I know it's difficult to understand," Jeb said quickly.

"Yes, it is," I said as I walked toward Jeb. He flinched back against the counter, sending a tray of shiny medical instruments clattering to the floor. "Help me understand, Jeb."

"It was never just work for me, Max," he pleaded. "It was personal. I always wanted you kids to thrive, and thanks to Fang, now you truly can."

"That won't be happening." I grabbed Jeb by the throat. He sputtered, clawing at my hands, but I was a hybrid and he wasn't, and I was much stronger than he was. I squeezed tighter around his neck, concentrating on my fury. "I don't want a Horseman bot with Fang's DNA. I want Fang. And you *killed him!*"

Jeb's face reddened, his eyes losing focus. His blood

vessels darkened into purple webs, and I knew I couldn't do it.

I hated Jeb more than anyone else. But I had loved him once, too, before all the betrayal. He had been like my father once upon a time, and he had saved me from a lab like this one and given me a home. Me and the flock. He'd taught me how to survive and made me feel important, and smart, and loved. For a while.

"There's something wrong with you," I said, releasing my grip. Deep sobs were welling up in me, but I was too well trained as a fighter to give in to them. "There's something seriously wrong with you."

Jeb took a gasping inhale, then hunched over, wracked with violent coughs as he tried to suck in air. For a second, I almost felt bad for him.

Just for a second, though.

The next moment, I felt a white-hot jolt in my side. My teeth ground down hard and every muscle in my body clenched as an electric force pulsed waves of pain through my body.

"Certain safety precautions are required when dealing with large mammals in a lab setting," Jeb explained.

When he withdrew the Taser, I crumpled to the floor.

My legs dangled as Jeb gathered me into his arms. I wasn't paralyzed—I still had a bit of feeling in my arms— but I couldn't get enough control of my floppy limbs to bash his head in.

"You're out of date, Max," Jeb said, strapping me onto a

gurney. My right hand twitched with a bit more purpose this time, my knuckles curling into a claw, but Jeb batted it away with ease as he tapped for a vein.

"Time for an upgrade." He sat on the stool, flicked his fingers against the syringe, and leaned close, ready to drive it home.

No! my mind shrieked. *Stop!*

"Some of us do just fine the way we are," a prep school voice laced with steel said from the doorway.

83

I REMEMBER THE events that followed as if they were in slow motion, but I know it all must've happened in an instant:

Jeb looked to his left, and I tried to move my fingers again.

My arm snapped forward like it was spring-loaded.

I plunged the syringe, which I now somehow held, into Jeb's thigh.

The room sounded like a storm of clanging metal as Star spun forward and smashed into my gurney, but Jeb's bewildered eyes never left mine.

Right up to the point when Kate snapped his neck.

My head still lolled to the side, but my eyes flicked between the two girls from Fang's gang, and the man who had been my dad, sprawled lifeless on the floor.

Did that really just happen?

"Angel said you needed help," Kate said, tucking a strand of hair behind her ear. She seemed as shocked as I was that Jeb was dead.

I nodded. Angel had heard my thoughts. I had needed help. He would have turned me into a monster.

But as I stared into Jeb's stunned face, twisted awkwardly toward me, I didn't feel relief.

I was horrified by his crimes, but I still felt an awful loss and disappointment. I know it sounds stupid, after so many years and betrayal after betrayal, but I'd still, somehow, kept hoping he'd go back to being the old Jeb one day. Now he didn't have any more chances to prove himself or to change for the better. In the end, he had died an evil man.

And that was devastating.

My body started to shake—from the release of panic or tears, I wasn't sure—and Kate, who had such power inside her she could break a man's bones with one hand, began to undo my straps with the utmost gentleness.

"I should have done something sooner," Star said.

I shifted slightly on the paper-covered bed to look at her.

"When I first found out what that maniac was doing, I should've stood up to him," Star went on.

"You were scared," Kate said. She propped me up with sturdy arms. "We all were."

Star started to pick her way through the shards of glass,

sharp tools, and overturned carts her tornado had created in the lab, but stopped right before the door.

"Fang didn't deserve that," she whispered, not looking at me.

No, he didn't, and I hadn't forgiven Star for what she'd done.

But Fang would have. He would have been proud of her for coming now, and she should know that.

"Hero," I mumbled, pointing at her. It was the best I could manage with drool still leaking from my mouth.

Star laughed harshly, and she finally faced me, her eyes glistening. "Yeah, well, we're all just trying to save the world, right? Isn't that what you flock kids keep yammering about? Let's finish this, already."

84

LET'S FINISH IT, I repeated as I stumbled down the hallway a few minutes later. Kate and Star had stayed to guard the lab, but I didn't need them now. Though my body was still weak from the Taser, as my systems rebooted, the surge of adrenaline made me feel almost high. It was time to meet the Remedy.

But when I turned into the tunnel, something grabbed my arm and I almost jumped out of my skin.

"One Light," a boy with large bloodshot eyes and open sores on his face gasped at me. I felt a stab of pity for him, though he was clawing at me murderously while choking on his own coughs.

The H8E virus, I thought, wrenching myself away from his grasp. I wondered how many of the other Doomsday kids on the battlefield were infected. My mom had said bird kids and mutants were immune, but if the Remedy was now poisoning his own, it couldn't be a good sign.

As I ran from the sick boy, I realized how vulnerable I was here, alone, limping through an underground, closed space that we knew contained nuclear weapons. I crept more carefully, sticking to what I thought was the main passage, but I had no map, and all these dark, damp passageways looked exactly the same.

I thought I heard a squeak behind me—maybe a Horseman, or another infected kid—but when I listened, I only heard my heart thundering in my ears.

"Max!" Dylan whispered directly behind me in the dark, and I almost screamed bloody murder. "Shh!" he said, clamping a hand over my mouth.

Naturally, I bit his hand.

"Are you serious?" I demanded. "Who *does* that to a person?" Then I noticed he was alone. "Where's Gunther-Hagen?" I demanded. "You said you knew exactly where his lair was."

"It's been evacuated. I tore the place apart, but the guards—" He eyed my puffy eyes and wobbly legs and stopped mid-sentence. "What happened to you?"

That question was completely overwhelming.

Well, Jeb was creating a master race using Fang's DNA, I got Tased and nearly Horsemanized, the Deceitful Duo showed up to save the day, and now it feels wrong to hate them, even though I still do. Kind of.

"Jeb is dead," I said, drastically simplifying things, and Dylan looked shocked. "What were you saying about guards?"

Dylan shook his head, then said, "The Remedy's Russian guards..."

He turned, and the *RAT-A-TAT-TAT* of machine-gun fire exploded inside the tunnel.

"They followed me!" Dylan yelled, dragging me down a side passageway.

I followed him down winding tunnel after winding tunnel, deeper and deeper into the maze. We passed more sick kids and the smell of death grew stronger, but the echo of military boots thundered after us.

Then Dylan stopped abruptly in front of a black door that looked exactly like all the other black doors. He traced his hand along the front of it.

"What are you doing?" I said, a little hysterically. I heard the thick-tongued shouts of the guards just behind us, and I flat-out *refused* to die before I found the Remedy.

There was a *beep* as the door "read" Dylan, and then the door swung open. "Come on!" he said, yanking me inside just as we started to see the flash-fire of bullets ricocheting off the walls. "We'll be safe in here."

"Where are we going?" I asked, but he had already punched a button on the wall, and I realized we were in a rickety elevator.

"Somewhere safe. Just promise not to judge me, okay?"

I gave him a quizzical look, but he just shook his head and sighed.

When the elevator stopped, we stepped into some kind of alternate universe. There were pink silk pillows, mirrored walls, colorful tapestries, and enough perfume to make my lungs seize.

The place was the stuff of my nightmares, basically.

And in the center of an overstuffed chair big enough for two, a gorgeous girl put down her computer and stood up. She was tall and slim and, unlike me, had bathed within the last month and didn't have blood and gore all over her. I suddenly felt like a horrible, bedraggled rat that was barely human, much less female.

"You came back." The girl's large, heavily lashed eyes filled with joy and she came over to Dylan, closer and closer until, to my shock, she curled against him, nuzzling his neck. "Oh, baby, you really came back."

My eyebrows rose into my hairline as I looked at Dylan over the top of her head.

Consider yourself judged.

85

I HADN'T KNOWN Dylan could *get* uncomfortable. I'd seen tons of girls throw themselves at him, and he'd always charmingly bantered with them while deflecting their advances. Right now, he was frozen in place, looking like he'd rather go back to the battlefield and resume being bludgeoned by Horsemen.

"Can you hang on just a minute?" he asked Princess Doe Eyes, prying her off him. He pulled me to the side.

"Don't look at me like that," he hissed. "I didn't want her, but Dr. Gunther-Hagen made her as a new match for me." He dropped his eyes. "To replace you."

I glanced back at the girl, noting her lack of battle scars, her smooth, soft, clean—everything, the whole cozy room, which even contained a bed.

"Gosh," I said dryly. "She's awesome. Can I get back to killing the Remedy now? You know, the crusher of hopes, murderer of billions, destroyer of the world?"

"But we're safe here," Dylan sputtered. "And I'm not, I mean, she's not—"

"Baby, I was so worried about you," the girl crooned, and flipped silken hair over a slim shoulder. Then her beautiful eyes seemed to notice me for the first time. "Is this a...friend, sweetie?"

"Yes," he said, taking her hands in his. She blinked up at him with so much naked adoration, I thought I might vomit.

"I'm going," I announced, and walked back to the elevator. Right now, certain death seemed preferable. I jabbed the elevator button.

"Listen, I know this is hard to understand right now," Dylan told Stepford Girl quickly. "You think we're supposed to be together, because that's what you've been told. But we're not."

This poor girl had been created with one purpose, and Dylan had to tell her it wasn't going to work out. He was being so gentle with her, though, so kind. The way I'd never been with him.

Don't turn around, I thought guiltily. *Just keep staring at this elevator door.*

"But we were made to be together," she insisted sweetly. "I've done everything you wanted, tried to become everything you wanted. I know you like to read, so I've been reading. Since you wanted me to have a name, I took it from this book."

I glanced over my shoulder at the cover. It was *The Handmaid's Tale*, by Margaret Atwood.

Margaret A. ImMargaretA. The commenter with "inside info" on Fang's blog.

"*You're* ImMargaretA?" I asked, turning to gape at her.

Her eyes widened and darted to Dylan nervously, and then she smiled at both of us, blinking like she had no freaking idea what I was talking about.

"You posted on the blog," I said testily. "You described the deaths of my flock. *Remember?*"

Margaret's face flushed. "The doctor let me follow all Horseman's adventures," she chirped happily, but I saw the anger behind her eyes when she looked at me—like I was spilling a secret we shared. "So I would know when he would come back to me."

When she looked back at Dylan, she turned on the charm, but now I saw something else beneath her adoration: fear.

She still thought he was a real Horseman, I realized. And she was terrified.

On the blog, she wasn't trying to spread false information; she'd only repeated what she had been told was true. She'd really been trying to warn us about the Remedy. About Dylan.

And I'd just sold her out.

"It's okay," I assured her. "Just take us to the doctor."

But she wasn't having it.

"The doctor is busy," Margaret A. answered, glaring at me, and then turned back to Dylan with a coy smile. "You must be tired, baby," she cooed. "Come sit down."

"I can't be with you," Dylan blurted, seeming oblivious to her act. "I love...someone else."

My chest tightened, but Margaret had finally had enough.

"You can't be with me?" she snapped, her sugary voice hardening into something more real—something strong. "Well, guess what? Maybe I never wanted to end up with a contract killer, pieced together part by part, my identity wiped clean. But if I have to be a living doll to avoid getting gassed with H8E or blown to pieces in a nuclear blast, I can play along. *Okay?*"

She fixed Dylan with in icy stare, but her eyes were filling with tears.

"Margaret, listen to me," I said in a low whisper. "You don't have to pretend anymore. We're going to get you out of here."

"There's no way out," she said miserably. "He just keeps moving farther down."

"Down where?" I pressed.

Margaret A. glanced at the mirror, and I met her eyes. Crocodile tears started to roll down her sculpted cheeks, and she broke my gaze. But then, in the mirror, I saw what she'd really been looking at—an imperfection, some kind of seam.

A *door*.

86

DYLAN PUSHED THROUGH the mirrored door to find a winding metal staircase that reached down what looked like several hundred feet into darkness. It was so narrow, there was no question that only one of us could fit at a time.

Max protested, of course, but Dylan insisted on going first. Even aside from Angel's warnings about protecting Max, Gunther-Hagen was Dylan's maker, and he needed to face him alone.

"Don't fall off," Margaret warned him.

That warning seemed obvious, but the staircase was so narrow it hugged Dylan's hips, and as he descended into what felt like the center of the earth, it shuddered and creaked under his weight, threatening to pitch him into the abyss beneath him. He thought he could hear crea-tures in water splashing somewhere far below, hissing and snapping their jaws.

But when he finally reached the bottom, the staircase ended on solid ground—a street. Dylan blinked up at a door, confused. It looked exactly like the door to the mansion where he'd first found the doctor. The streets were holo-graphic projections, Dylan knew, but the reproduction was incredible.

The odd sense of déjà vu continued as his boots echoed across the marbled tile and he approached the grand ballroom and saw Dr. Gunther-Hagen sitting in his office chair, just as he'd left him. Alone.

However, this time, hundreds of screens lined the walls—world maps, weather reports, graphs of ash trajec-tory, and recordings from his Horsemen.

"A10103," the doctor said, swiveling to greet him.

"Actually, it's just Dylan." He removed his worn leather gloves and tossed them to the floor between them.

"How disappointing," the doctor said, but he was grin-ning with satisfaction, and it made Dylan's skin crawl.

"I am not the monster you think I am, Dylan. I only wanted to make you stronger," he said earnestly. "Look around. You can have the life you want. You don't even realize you're fighting against your own kind."

Dylan laughed aloud, and the harsh sound echoed up into the frescoes. He saw nothing of himself reflected in this egomaniacal man who had created him. Once, this had been the person Dylan knew best. But he'd become more and more unrecognizable, and now Dylan felt that he had nothing in common with him.

Absolutely nothing.

"You failed," Dylan announced, leaning menacingly over the doctor. "Jeb is dead, and so are the other Horsemen." Dylan tapped the screen on his wrist, and the bloody battle replayed on-screen. "You did make me stronger. Stronger than all of them—I'm the only one left."

"Not only you." Dr. Gunther-Hagen lifted the sleeve of his white coat, revealing a screen on his wrist that matched Dylan's. "I injected myself with the serum, of course." The doctor's eyes glittered. "My creations shouldn't be the only ones with a chance at eternal life. You and I are left together, son. Something tells me you didn't completely overcome your programming, hmm?" He pursed his lips.

Had he? Dylan dropped his eyes. This was what the doctor had done to him—made him question, made him doubt. Dylan had struggled with his origin from the beginning, trying to determine how much was really him and how much was . . . everything else. He hadn't become a mindless killer, but apart from that, did he really have any control at all?

Dylan heard footsteps echoing through the entryway and looked at his maker.

"No." Dylan shook his head sadly. "I just did what you *first* programmed me to do: I couldn't stop loving Maximum Ride."

"You thought you'd won, didn't you?" Max looked at the doctor from the doorway, her eyes like skewers.

"Oh, I have won, child." Gunther-Hagen sank back in his office chair, unperturbed. "I was just telling Dylan about our coming eternal life."

"He injected himself with Fang's DNA," Dylan explained.

"Is that so?" Max shook her head sadly at the doctor, but she was smiling. "Jeb told me the serum wasn't quite there yet. You might've been trying to live forever, but I'm afraid forever's going to stop a little shorter than you'd planned.

"And, bummer for you, there's been a change in power, so things are probably going to get a little rough from here on out. There's no way you're getting out of here, Häagen-Dazs. We have you completely surrounded."

"The last of the world's righteous survivors, all in one place?" For the first time, Dylan noticed that the doctor was tapping his fingertips carefully against the screen at his wrist. "How convenient."

Dylan! Max! There's a bomb! Angel's voice rang through his head.

"Where is it?" Max growled, her body rigid with caution, her face muscles twitching in fury.

Dr. Gunther-Hagen opened his pristine white lab coat and started to unbutton his expensive collared shirt, fixing them with his icy, amused gaze.

But when the shirt fell open, there was a mass of wires

and steel canisters where his chest should have been. The doctor wasn't *rigged* to the bomb.

He *was* the bomb.

"Jeb was kind enough to hook me up to the last reactor…" The doctor swirled slowly around in his office chair, his voice trailing off. "It's a pity you've killed him—how will you disable it now?"

"I guess we'll just have to kill you," Max snapped.

"Oh, I hope so," Gunther-Hagen said, still smiling. "If I die, the bomb engages, and your little army goes down with me."

87

I THOUGHT OF what Angel had said before the battle. *The Remedy thinks he's won. But he can't see the future.* I can.

We will see him fall.

There was nowhere for him to fall, though. We were already at the bottom of the earth.

"We have to get him out of here," I told Dylan as quietly as I could. "I'll fly him as high as I can, and you start getting people underground."

"Max, no, let me do it. He wouldn't blow me up."

But I was the one who was supposed to save the world. Angel had said that all along. Everything I'd survived so far had been building to this moment. It was the last chance I was going to get.

"He's mine," I said, and my tone left no room for argument. "Let's go, Hansy."

Dr. G-H gave a philosophical shrug and got up, as if he was indulging my silly whim. Pushing him toward the door, I grabbed the collar of his white coat, balling the fabric in my fist. As I started to drag him up the eleventy million steps of the medieval staircase, Gunther-Hagen kept that supercilious grin plastered to his face.

"I guess there's a way out after all," he said smugly.

He didn't set off the bomb while we climbed, nor when we went out Margaret's door and through the dark passageways. Out on the bloodstained battlefield, the Remedy stood still when I hooked my arms around him and took off, my wings carrying us high over where Gazzy and Iggy were leading the other kids in rounding up the prisoners.

"I've so missed the great outdoors," the doctor said. He closed his eyes, seeming to blissfully savor the wind on his face, despite the air, which was becoming more and more ash laden.

Now that I had him in my hands, I didn't want him to enjoy a single second of his life. He was brilliant and could have helped humanity so much. But he'd thought the only solution was to wipe people off the earth.

"No," I said, shaking him. "You don't get to close your eyes, Häagen-Dazs. Look at all those people down there." I pointed to the kids below, the ones who were helping the wounded, the ones who were carrying their dead comrades off the field. "You killed their families, their friends.

You destroyed their homes, but they're survivors. They're free, because you failed. *Look!*"

Gunther-Hagen craned his neck to look at me. "You want me to stay and watch their expressions as the reactor detonates, is that it? I agree, it would be most entertaining to watch."

I ground my teeth together and shot upward, flying high into the atmosphere and east over the ocean, until I was sure the kids would be safe.

"Now I'm the one who'll be making threats." I hooked one arm beneath his neck and gave a little yank. He coughed, his hands reaching for my arm. "So you'd better start talking."

"Ask me anything you'd like, Maximum," Gunther-Hagen said, evidently enjoying this. "I know once you hear my reasoning..."

"Don't count on it. Now, how did you plan it?" I demanded. "And who helped you?"

If any of those scumbags were still alive, we'd deal with them as well.

Dr. Gunther-Hagen pressed his lips together into an ironic smile. "The fates aligned, you might say. I barely had to plan at all...Dr. Martinez did most of the work for me."

I blinked hard at that. "I was with my mom the day of the explosion," I snapped. "She was trying to protect everyone she could."

"Oh, her work with me started much earlier than that. You'll remember her involvement in Angel's modification, I'm sure."

My gaze faltered.

"Jeb knew about Angel's gift, but it was Dr. Martinez who founded the Psychic Initiative," Dr. G-H continued. "She said Angel was just a child—a powerful child who didn't know how to manage her power. That capable, responsible adults needed to take over, so we could learn about the risks of the future." His voice had a dark edge to it. Though I was the one gripping his throat, it felt like he was moving toward checkmate. "All I had to do was fund it."

"My mom was just trying to save the planet!" I said defensively.

"Oh, I assure you, Maximum, so am I. We just had different ideas about how to go about it. Dr. Martinez wanted to alert the world powers about the asteroid and blow it out of the sky with nuclear missiles. But I persuaded her that we should handle things more privately." The corners of his eyes wrinkled with amusement. "So as to prevent panic."

"So instead you unleashed a deadly plague to kill ninety-nine percent of the world, let the asteroid destroy even more people, then nuked all the cities for good measure," I said.

I remembered the pictures we'd scrolled through on the computer. The images of people sobbing, people praying, people running even when they had nowhere to go.

I didn't know how he could live with himself. But then, he wouldn't have to much longer.

88

THE ICY WIND whipped through my tangled hair and tugged at my aching arms, and I almost dropped the psychopath to his death right then. But I wasn't done yet.

Find. Truth.

Dr. Gunther-Hagen was shaking his head. "The virus wasn't my work, I'm afraid. The Apocalypticas left us that little gift, and they leaked it all on their own."

So my mom was right about that.

"I don't think they imagined such initial success. A hundred dead in a couple of days, millions within a week, and by the end of the month, a quarter of the world." The doctor spoke breathlessly, his eyes lighting up. "It was extraordinarily impressive."

"*Impressive?*" My mouth gaped. "Is that what you call murdering billions of people?"

I loosened my grip on his neck, and the doctor slipped down a few inches. His face blanched a light shade of green, but when he answered me, his tone was still measured.

"Let me remind you, child, I did the honorable thing: I developed a vaccine."

"You can buy a lot with a vaccine when the population is in the grips of a global pandemic." I narrowed my eyes. "Like...a bunch of nuclear bombs, for example."

"Actually, those were a gift. My staff had the technology to accurately target the asteroid, after all. With your mother's political connections, the Russians were easily persuaded to hand over the stockpile if it finally meant some good PR for them."

He betrayed her—along with the rest of the world.

"Why develop the vaccine, then?" I pressed. "What was it worth?"

"I do love an eager pupil." The doctor smirked. "It bought me a name."

"A name?" I repeated.

"When the virus was released and so much of the population was infected, you can imagine how much media attention the discovery of a vaccine received."

Yeah, I could. I pictured his face covering the newspapers, his smile flashing out of televisions. *They probably called him a freaking hero.* The thought made me so furious I couldn't speak. I glared at him, daring him to continue.

"After the asteroid hit, suddenly everyone wanted another quick remedy. They looked to me again, of course. Who else could they trust more?"

"So you're saying you were able to push the world into a dictatorial state through *branding*?" I said in disbelief.

"A remedy gave them permission to look away," he explained. "It assured them that someone was capable of eliminating their problems. And I have."

"How can you call yourself a doctor?" I asked in disgust. "Didn't you, like, take some kind of oath saying, 'I will not unleash death and destruction on my patients and all of modern society'?"

"The earth is my primary patient," the doctor reasoned calmly. "And the ecosystem will recover much better with fewer people to compromise it."

"Right, because radioactive debris is *super* healthy for the planet!" I sneered. "Wait, you didn't really think this little confession was gonna save you, did you?" I loosened my grip a bit more.

He flinched, instinctively grasping at air, and I smiled faintly as I pulled him back. Gunther-Hagen's eyes hardened, and his fingers locked around my wrists. "You still don't understand. I don't need to be saved. *Humans* aren't supposed to be saved. My work will live on. My legacy—"

I cut him off. "Your legacy is dead. Jeb is dead. He'll never make another Horseman."

"Dylan is my legacy," the doctor countered. "A truly evolved specimen, despite some remaining glitches. He and the female mate I created for him will help repopulate the earth with a genetically ideal species. *You* were never worthy of him."

The thing was... that last part was completely true.

My expression must have faltered, because the doctor smiled. "You're really very ordinary, you know, Maximum Ride," he said sympathetically. "Weak. And soon, you and your kind will die out, just like your boyfriend did."

He tapped the screen on his wrist. I couldn't see the image, but I could hear that it was the video Dylan had shown me. Even above the howling wind, I heard Fang's screams.

Too. Far.

"Nothing's dying out, you disgusting supremacist," I snapped. My arms quivered with rage as I held him in front of me. I felt the heat rushing to my cheeks as I said the words:

"I'm *pregnant.*"

89

THE CONFESSION HUNG in the air between us, and I instantly wished I could snatch it back. I hadn't told anyone—until that moment, I hadn't fully admitted it to myself. But I couldn't hide from it now. Saying it aloud made it real.

More than that—from the doctor's expression, I knew it had *power.*

"It can't be," the doctor whispered, his face twisting in horror. "Fang is dead."

I remembered when the doctor had kidnapped Fang. He'd told Dylan that Fang had to die because his invincible DNA posed too high a risk. I'd wondered why they didn't kill him that day, and realized the doctor was too power-hungry to destroy the key to immortality.

Wordlessly, I switched my grip to one hand and unzipped my hoodie with the other. The wind whipped open the fabric, and Gunther-Hagen's gaze traveled down to where the T-shirt underneath pulled taut against my stomach, revealing the smallest hint of a curve.

"It's over," he murmured.

"Oh, it's just beginning," I said.

And that's when he pressed the screen on his arm again. "Reactor, *engage*," he commanded.

I inhaled sharply, wincing as I waited for the explosion in the distance, praying that Dylan had managed to save as many kids as he could.

But there was no explosion, no far-off mushroom cloud that spelled death and destruction.

There was no beeping, either, or suggestion of a count-down, and I saw from Dr. G-H's fury that it hadn't worked. There was something wrong with the signal.

I didn't know what had happened any more than Gunther-Hagen did, but I thought of Nudge's hacking abilities, and Angel's mind-reading, and Gazzy's bomb knowledge, and I knew my flock had probably just saved my life for the thousandth time.

"What's the matter, Hans? Is your final plan not working? I guess it doesn't matter if you die now, after all." My tone was biting, but my brain was flooded with such a surge of relief I felt like I was about to pass out.

I guess that's why I was so unprepared for what happened next.

The old man lunged forward, gouging at my stomach with a silver pen. "That child is the virus that will plague the whole world!" Gunther-Hagen shrieked. "And I am the Remedy!"

"You've killed enough people already," I snarled at him. "You *don't* get to kill Fang's child."

Then, with all my strength, I flung him away from me, into the empty sky.

For a fraction of a second, he hung in the air, his white coat billowing around him, his eyes snapped open in surprise, his mouth frozen in a perfect O.

Then he fell.

I fluttered my wings, watching as the Remedy, the supreme terrorist of the world, plunged to the ground. I thought of Fang, how he must have grabbed at the air in the same panicked way.

Just before the body hit, I crossed my arms over my stomach and turned away.

90

EVERYTHING SEEMS STARKER in the daylight, doesn't it? It's easier to see all that you've lost, and all that you've gambled, and how hard it's going to be to get back to where you started.

We never did have a victory celebration. After all the bombs and burned homes, no one was very excited about fireworks. And with blood still staining the field around us, no one could really imagine partying.

Not here, anyway. Not now.

Instead, for the past week, crews had worked on burying the dead and cleaning up the tent city. Others questioned captives and explored Himmel's labyrinth of tunnels.

I had started hauling food up from the vast storage

supplies of Himmel. I needed to do something with my hands—organize supplies and make plans for shelter, or plant some of the seedlings we'd found in the giant greenhouse. I needed to focus on the future.

But everything is so stark in the daylight.

I felt the faintest, mostly healed scratches on my stomach chafing against my shirt. Now that I'd said a certain two words aloud, the future was feeling like a pretty scary place.

I patted my belly button, feeling the swell that was growing a tiny bit bigger every day. I pressed my knuckles against the small curve, kneading in, but it always rebounded.

I really hoped this wasn't going to be a great big egg to lay. How could I possibly sit still on it for nine months?

"What are you doing?" Angel asked from behind me.

I dropped my hand from my stomach and tried to clear my thoughts.

"Sorting supplies for distribution." I tossed one of the frozen meals to her. "Dr. G-H sure loved him some TV dinners."

"You have to put them back." Angel was already messing with the piles I'd made. "Right now. The plants, too." She nodded at the bean plants sprouting in the plastic containers. "They won't survive out here in the cold, and we have to eat what we can in the forest before it's gone."

"What do you mean, 'gone'? The woods are full of wild game. We'll have lots of time to build shelters and get set up out here before winter."

"Try nuclear winter." Angel squinted at the hazy sky. "Do you see how thick the dust is getting? The asteroid and all the bombs sent tons of stuff into the air, and that cloud is coming our way. It'll totally block out the sun."

She looked at the thousands of makeshift tents strewn around us. "Tomorrow we'll get organized, try to contact any other survivors. We'll probably have to go underground in less than a month."

"You want to live in the Remedy's city?" My body recoiled instinctively at the thought of those claustrophobic tunnels, and I shook my head. "I can deal with the cold."

"Not cold like this," the little prophet insisted. She pinched the top of a bright green bean sprout. "They'll grow fine in artificial light."

Could I, though? I thought of the small life taking shape inside me, never seeing the sun, and I started to shake.

Just focus on stacking supplies, I thought, gripping the packaged food so tightly I was crushing the boxes.

You don't have to hide it from me, Angel's voice said in my mind. *I already know.*

My eyes flew to hers.

Angel smiled. "Why do you think I made Dylan and Kate stay glued to your side during the battle?" she said with a smirk.

I was confused about so many things—including whether I wanted to strangle Angel or hug her.

"I'm not ready to be a mom," I whispered. "I don't know what to do."

I'd fought super-mutants and defeated dictators, but this was so far out of the realm of things I could handle, I was asking a seven-year-old for parenting advice.

"Yeah, you do." Angel smiled, bumping my shoulder. "You mothered us, didn't you?"

I remembered the flock's food fights at breakfast. My utter hatred of school. The way Nudge had to remind me to brush *my* teeth.

Not really.

Angel giggled and snuggled against me. I smoothed her pale curls away from her forehead like I had since our days in dog crates.

"I never got to tell Fang," I said after a minute, my voice flat with defeat.

That was partly why I had been tracking him so desperately. I'd needed his help to find the Remedy, but I'd also had something urgent to tell him.

"Excuse me, ladies."

I looked up to see Dylan standing in front of us—I'd been so wrapped up in talking to Angel that I hadn't even noticed him coming.

"Hey," I said, my face burning. I pictured the day that Dylan found out about the baby and just wanted to curl up.

"Max, can you come with me?" he asked. "I need to show you something."

91

ANGEL LOOKED AT Dylan, her head tilted to one side. She frowned, but he met her gaze evenly.

"It'll just take a minute," Dylan said.

"Sure," I said, standing up. I gave Angel a "we'll finish talking later" look and she nodded solemnly at me. Dylan and I set off, and I couldn't help smiling when I saw Iggy demonstrating a homemade wrist rocket to Margaret A.

Dylan saw her, too, and gave me a rueful smile.

"So where are we going?" I asked.

"Remedy's lair."

My head whipped around and I stared at him. "What? What for?"

"I need to show you something," Dylan said again, and I felt the slightest twinge of fear. Now that I was paying attention, he seemed kind of different. I'd hardly seen him for the past week—sometimes in the evening around a fire, he'd show up, looking exhausted. Almost haunted.

Again and again, Dylan had proven his loyalty to me and the flock, but the whole world had spun out of control and I couldn't help wondering if being one of the Horsemen had changed him forever in ways I couldn't imagine.

Or maybe I could imagine them. Maybe that was what the hint of fear was about.

"I am not going down that billion steps again," I said lightly. "My legs are still aching from that."

Dylan gave me an almost sad, distant smile and shook his head.

All around us, kids were working to build us a better future. I took comfort in the fact that there seemed to be people everywhere—no place felt deserted or lonely. Still, when Dylan led me inside Himmel and through the tunnels, I felt myself going on guard. And when he stopped in front of Jeb's old lab, I hesitated and looked up at him.

"What are we doing here, Dylan?" I asked softly.

Again that slightly sad smile. "I have...a present for you. I think."

Okay, that sounded ominous. I took a breath and felt my muscles tense. I really didn't want to go back into that place. Looking up into Dylan's crystalline aqua eyes, I searched them to read his intent. But I couldn't.

He pushed open the door to the lab and gestured to me to go in. The last kids we'd seen had been a couple of minutes ago—out of screaming range. Pressing my lips together, I stepped in, praying that someone had gotten rid of Jeb's body.

The lab had been cleaned up. Everything broken was gone, everything left was neatly arranged and labeled. I looked around in surprise.

"Who did this?" I asked.

"I did," Dylan said. "I've been working in here."

My eyebrows knitted together. "Doing what?"

"In a way, continuing my father's work."

I stared at him, unconsciously moving away and glancing around for possible weapons. "Dylan, come on," I said, keeping my tone even. "What are you talking about?"

"This." Dylan turned and went through a door on the other side of the lab. I instantly sprang over and grabbed a scalpel, though what I would do with it, I had no idea... Dylan was much stronger than me now. Hiding the scalpel behind my back, I waited, and in just a minute Dylan came back—pushing a hospital bed.

Someone was lying on that bed, covered by a sheet.

I saw just a bit of black hair spilling out from beneath the white cloth and almost screamed. My breath came shallowly as I stared at the bed, and then at Dylan.

"What...what in the world have you been doing?" My voice was high and squeaky. "Wh-who...who is that?"

"You know who it is," Dylan said softly, and pulled back the sheet. "It's Fang."

And...that was when my pregnant self fainted like a schoolgirl, right onto the floor.

92

OR I WOULD have hit the floor, if Dylan hadn't had enhanced reflexes and superhuman strength. My eyes fluttered open just seconds later to see him looking down at me in concern.

He was holding me in his arms as if I weighed nothing, and now he gently lowered my feet to the floor. I grabbed hold of a lab table to steady myself and felt anger rising in me.

"I know what you're trying to do," I practically spat. "You know how I feel about clones. Your so-called dad was nuttier than a fruitcake, and you know it! Why would you do this? Why would you make a fake Fang?"

Dylan held up his hands, then pushed them through

his dark blond hair in frustration, seeming to hold his head for a second. His jaw twitched and his teeth clamped together. Suddenly I realized I had dropped the scalpel when I fainted. Dylan must have seen it, must have known I'd picked it up as a weapon.

"Max," he said tightly. "Everything I've ever done has been for you. It's not like I'm a hero—we both know I was programmed to want to...be with you, above anyone else." His eyes met mine. "You know how I feel, and how I would feel about you no matter what, whether I was programmed to love you or not."

My cheeks heated and I swallowed, not knowing what to say. *Why is he telling me this?*

"I love you," he said steadily. "I always have, and I always will. You know that."

I looked away, not wanting him to humble himself this way.

"And I know you love Fang," he went on more softly. "You always have, and you always will."

Now I felt really bad.

"I—" I started, but he held up his hand to stop me.

"It's not anyone's fault. It's just how it is," he said, and I felt a hormonal tear come to my eyes. "Once I hoped—I hoped maybe Fang was your first love, and I...I would be your last."

"I'm sorry," I whispered, feeling an ache in my throat that might never go away.

"It's not your fault," he said again, gently. "This hasn't turned out the way I hoped, but then, what has? The world hasn't turned out the way we hoped, either, right?"

I nodded, praying I wouldn't start blubbering.

Dylan swallowed again and glanced at the hospital bed. "I pretended to kill the flock, so they would be safe. I had less control over what happened to Fang. The Horsemen were there—Jeb and the doctor were trying out a new upgrade—and there was only so much I could do. You saw how Fang dragged them all over the cliff with him. You saw how one of them...took off Fang's wing." The last words ended in a whisper.

I nodded and wiped away a single tear, feeling like the most ancient fifteen-year-old in the world. What was left of it.

"I...waited until everyone was gone, and then...I flew down into the canyon."

My eyes widened. No. I knew Fang was dead. Angel knew Fang was dead—she had felt it.

Dylan shrugged. "The doctor had labs all over the place. I found Fang at the bottom of the canyon, just as he was about to die. In fact, he might have actually been dead. At any rate, by the time I got him to one of the doctor's labs, he *was* dead."

My eyes narrowed. "Okay. And the point is..."

"The doctor had done all kinds of experiments. You can guess," said Dylan, looking disturbed by the memories.

"But he had the means to put beings into stasis, to hold them until he was ready for them, or whatever."

I refused to have hope, refused to even think about it. "For God's sake, Dylan. What are we doing here? Just— tell me."

Dylan gestured to the bed. "That's Fang. And...I can make him live."

93

"WHAT…." WORDS FAILED me. That happened very rarely.

"Actually, it's up to you," Dylan said. "This is Fang, and he's in stasis. His body healed itself, mostly, but his wing…well, it was gone. I've given him a new wing. It's artificial but looks and feels just like the real thing. He'll be able to fly."

My head was spinning, and actually, the room was, too, a little bit. Abruptly I sat down on a lab stool, gripping the nearby table even harder. I just couldn't take it in.

"What are you saying?" My words were barely audible.

"Experiments and artificial…parts. I know you hate it, hated everything that Jeb and the doctor did," Dylan said. "And here I am, doing the same thing. But—I did it for you. Because I love you. I did it because this was Fang, and you love him. So I'm giving you a choice: Do you want me to complete the process? Or would it be better to let him go, the way he should have? Would you still want him, with an artificial wing?"

My eyes felt as big as moons as I stared at Dylan. "Is he a cyborg?" My mouth moved but hardly any sound came out.

"No. It's like a person having an artificial leg," Dylan said.

"He would be alive? And—and normal?"

Dylan nodded slowly. "Flesh and blood and brooding silences, the whole lot."

"I would want him," I said. "I would want him, wings or no wings, arms or no arms, eyes or no eyes . . ."

For a long moment, Dylan looked steadily at me.

"Dylan—I'm going to have Fang's baby." That was hard—it was like a light went out in Dylan's eyes. I felt terrible, seeing that this was the final blow, the thing Dylan would never be able to pretend away.

"Congratulations," he said quietly, his voice cracking. Then he coughed and nodded. "Okay, let's do this."

It was like being in a sci-fi movie, watching Dylan wheel in equipment, flip big switches, instruments jumping. He put diodes all over Fang's still form. I was horrified by my decision, but I knew that even if Fang were a zombie, I would want him, and I would take care of him and protect him for the rest of my life.

Finally Dylan double-checked everything and nodded

again. He came to me, and on his face were a calm acceptance and a sweet honesty that I would remember for the
rest of my life.

"I love you," he said.

"I know. I love you, too, but not—"

"I know. It's okay. I just—want you to forgive me."

"For what?"

Dylan didn't answer, just took my face in his hands, so
gently, and kissed my forehead. "Good-bye, my love."

"Good-bye? What do you mean—"

And before I could move, Dylan grabbed a knot of
wires in one hand and flicked the last switch. The lights
in the room blinked on and off, there was a horrible buzzing, crackling sound, and I saw Dylan's body spasming as
thousands of volts of electricity surged through him. . . .

And into Fang.

On the hospital bed, Fang's body arced once, then fell
back. In the flickering lights I saw one of his hands twitch,
his fingers curl. Dylan slumped to the floor, his eyes wide
and still, his face slack except for the slightest smile on
his lips. He was dead. He had killed himself so that Fang
would live. He had killed himself for me.

I began to scream, and was still screaming a minute
later when Kate and Holden burst into the room.

Epilogue

HER STORY

One

I'LL BET WHEN you cracked open my first book, you didn't know you'd signed up for New World History 101, huh?

Or Her-story, if we're getting technical.

It's hard to document exactly how it happened—hard to do it right—but there needs to be a record, so we don't end up here again, repeating the same mistakes. So someone can see the warning signs, and take a stand.

So you can save the world, if it ever needs saving again. And I'm betting it will.

Right now, all I can do is tell my own truth.

Fang was really alive.

Kate found an envelope addressed to me, from Dylan. It said: "I knew you would choose him, and I accept that. If I can't live with you, then please believe I'm happy to die for you, my love. Forever yours, Dylan."

I cried for like three days over that, over Dylan's unbelievable sacrifice—for me.

Fang was confused at first, having lost months of his life, and had to train his body to work again after being in stasis for so long. But, being Fang, he was soon himself again, and even got used to his new wing faster than I'd expected. It wasn't long before we were taking one of the last outside flights we could take, before the nuclear winter really hit and we'd have to go underground.

And Dylan was really dead. It took years for me to make peace with that, to not feel guilty, to know he had chosen to do that, and that I hadn't killed him. But it wasn't easy. And...I missed him. I missed his smile, his dependability, his sweetness and honesty. I would always miss him. There would always be a Dylan-shaped hole in my heart. But I was thankful every single freaking day that I didn't have a Fang-shaped hole in my heart. 'Cause I wasn't sure I'd survive that.

Anyway, it was on that last flight that I gave Fang the big news.

"A what?" he said, staring at me.

"A baby," I repeated.

He forgot to fly and started dropping out of the sky. I just waited for him, and he soon joined me again.

"Like, a *baby*?"

"I believe that's what they're called, yes," I said primly.

"Are you sure?" he asked, and I rolled my eyes.

"It's kicking me," I said. "From the *inside*."

As you know, Fang is fairly expressionless. But the look on his face when he finally got that he was going to be a dad was...pure exhilaration. The most joy I'd ever seen on anyone. It filled me with a warm glow that kept me going, long after we had to move underground.

But living like a termite (ugh, don't remind me) was harder than I'd imagined it could be. It felt like being buried alive. Some of the illusion technology kept functioning and projected city streets or starry skies, but every time I tried to fly, I crashed into the low ceilings.

When you're a claustrophobic bird kid, an underground compound really is the definition of hell. No matter what blissed-out German word you choose to name it.

Our only window to the outside world was a tiny camera that poked aboveground. We watched the screen for months as rain started to fall, and then snow. Then the temperature dropped and the ice came, and all we saw out of the lens were thick, blue-white crystals.

"Trust me," Angel said. "Not yet."

Not yet.

So we lived like moles, navigating tunnels in near darkness, turning pale in artificially lit rooms. Once I ended up in Dylan's former room by mistake. Several kids had moved in there; it was big enough, and none of its belongings reminded me of Dylan. But still, I saw his face silhouetted against the silk wallpaper, imagined him sleeping on the round waterbed that now held two smaller mutants. My heart ached for him, and all he had wanted, and all he had done for me. It probably always would, and that seems fitting, somehow.

We all dreamed of the sun and breathing fresh air.

It wasn't all bad, though. In the room I shared with Fang, I swore through a much-too-long childbirth and may have punched Fang and ripped a pillow in half, but I ended up with a wrinkled, utterly perfect nugget of joy as a souvenir.

A baby girl. With wings.

I wish I could have taken a picture of Fang holding his daughter, just to capture that expression of wonder and terror on his face. And while she learned to wail and projectile vomit and say "No" to everything I asked (*karma*), we made some pretty amazing progress in other ways.

Star used her talent for making annoying high-pitched sounds to shock the rest of the Doomsday prisoners back to their senses.

Our little seedlings grew into a thriving plant nursery, which meant never having to eat a freezer-burned Salisbury steak again. And, okay, it also meant avoiding extinction as a species.

The Morrissey brothers, Matthew and Lucas, had worked on developing the original vaccine for the H8E virus, and were able to replicate it in the lab using splices of Fang's DNA. Jeb was right—Fang really would have a huge impact on generations to come. Because though the virus was endemic in most of the world, now everyone, mutant or man, would be protected when we returned to the surface.

And one day, after almost four years, we did exactly that.

A sliver of sun peeked through the camera lens, and the ash was finally starting to clear. And when, after days of staring at a clear blue sky, Angel finally nodded *yes*, there was no better feeling than leaving behind our earthworm existence to emerge, blinking, into the light, and become birds again.

Even if the world wasn't exactly as we'd left it.

Though the sun was shining again, the Russian wilderness was still completely encased in ice. The trees in the surrounding forest looked more like stooped snow people, and the cold was bone-breaking. We could not survive there.

For months more, we all made plans. Everyone who could fly had the best chance of getting far enough south. Others carefully gathered provisions so they could attempt overland journeys—we still had hopes that more people had survived.

Finally the day came when the original six of our flock, plus Fang's and my daughter, and Total, of course, and fifteen other bird kids left the home that had kept us alive through the devastation that people came to call Earth 2.

As we flew south, we found that ash and ice had buried cities and hidden landmarks. It was hard to tell where we were, but we knew the blue-white shimmer stretched over a whole lot of the planet.

Until it gave way to just ash.

The sky was clear, but the earth's surface was now gray. And when we flew near the impact site of the biggest crater, the drifting ash had formed dunelike waves that were a hundred, sometimes two hundred feet high.

I don't know how to even explain how massive this meteor was.

It left a crater so wide that we could barely see across it. When we stood at its edge, we were looking into a hole that went down for almost a mile.

It was the literal expression of "awesome"—every one of us was struck speechless with shock, wonder, and reverence at the extreme power of nature.

Finally, Total managed to articulate what all of us were feeling.

"How is it remotely possible that we survived this?" he asked, and we all chuckled, breaking the tension.

"The human spirit," Angel said with a good-natured shrug. "Turns out it's actually pretty tough to kill."

"And the canine spirit," Total said quickly, and we all agreed.

"Mama, what are we going to do now?" my daughter asked, ever curious.

I squeezed her hand and smiled.

"We're going to begin again."

We're living in the Southern Hemisphere now, somewhere in what used to be Peru. The rain forest shriveled up along with everything else, so I'll have to wait awhile to build another tree house, but plants are starting to grow back, bit by bit. I come out to this hillside every afternoon and sit cross-legged among the Incan ruins, where the boulders are still standing, even after the end of the world. I take my feather pen—an old memento—and I write with ink made from ash and stone.

I try to record the past.

Right now, I exhale and lean back against a five-hundred-year-old stone wall, relishing the feel of the sun on my face again. I study this page, and the many pages before it, and wonder if someone will read these words in another five hundred years.

I trace the silky black feather pen across my skin, down my cheek, and close my eyes, remembering.

Two

FANG FOLLOWS MY gaze across the rocky slope to watch our girl playing with her flock family, and his face softens. It seems crazy that she's already almost five now—almost as old as Angel was when she was first kidnapped by Erasers, what seems like several lifetimes ago.

The whole flock is helping to raise her, with Total insisting on French lessons and Nudge making sure she doesn't look like a cave girl (even though we pretty much live in caves). But it's only Fang who spends as much time with her as I do, Fang who patiently teaches the fascinating facts his photographic brain remembers from all those fat books I shunned in school. Fang, because he's her father.

"Watch!" she yells when she sees us looking her way.

"Mama, watch me!" Her light brown eyes widen as she tears down the hill on long, gangly legs.

It's always surprising to see those eyes looking back at me. They narrow at the first sign of danger, and confidently hold my gaze when she knows she's right. When I tell her "No," they are defiant, and when I cuddle her, they melt like honey. They take in everything, all the time.

They're my eyes.

She looks like Fang in almost every other way. When she takes off after Star's blur of speed, her wings trail behind her, the same color as her silky hair—a deep blue-black. Just before she crashes into Harry, he flings her a few dozen feet up in the air. Kate and Harry toss her between them, back and forth, and her wing muscles slide along her back and make her wings flutter. They're still growing, but her primary feathers are all in now, and strong.

When she lands, her mouth twists into a familiar lopsided smirk, asking the same question it always does: *Is it time yet, Mama?*

I turn to the love of my life. My first love, and my last love. The love I accepted a dear friend's sacrifice for. "Do you think...?"

Fang nods before I finish the question.

"You don't think we're rushing it?"

"It's time." He grins good-naturedly. "Like I've been saying for a week."

"Phoenix!" I shout across the hilltop. "Ready for a lesson?"

Her face is maniacal with glee as she races Gazzy—now a tall, lanky fourteen-year-old—back up the slope.

When she was born, the name seemed to suit her—my little Phoenix, helping us all rise from the ashes. She's Fifi to Total and Nudge, Ninja Nix to the boys. But I'll let her pick her own name when she's ready, of course.

Just as I once chose *Maximum Ride*.

Three

"TAKE YOUR CUES from the wind, watch for smaller birds in your path," I repeat for the hundredth time. "And absolutely no dive-bombs without me!"

"Never, ever," Phoenix repeats, and then proceeds to walk on her hands near the rocky edge. Gazzy cackles and tumbles forward, matching her trick for trick. While the rest of the flock hoots and hollers, cheering them on, naturally, I'm over here inventing new swear words and trying not to swallow my bottom lip.

Can you tell I'm way more nervous about my girl's first flight than she is?

"Would you relax?" Iggy scolds me. "Did you forget how easy flying is? Besides, the kid's got invincible DNA, so this should be no biggie. *Ooof!*" he groans as I elbow him in the ribs.

Next to me, Fang chuckles as he watches his daughter give poor, protesting Total a very undignified belly rub. It's hard to remember that there was once a Fang who rarely laughed or smiled. Tiny Phoenix has completely changed him. She's changed all of us.

My fear grows as she picks her way to the edge of the cliff and looks down. I know she's tough. I make sure she gets up again every time she falls down, and I tell her she can do anything.

Even when life throws you a flaming curveball almost big enough to kick the earth out of orbit. Learn how to do what's right, because it takes a lot more guts.

If there's one thing my baby's got, it's guts.

The flock crowds around Phoenix before the group flight, giving pointers.

"Think about using all your senses at once," Ratchet says. "Remember what I taught you, baby girl—*be* the ninja."

"Flap as fast as you can, little Fifi," Total warns. "It's important to gain altitude fast when your wings are so small."

"But don't think about anything!" Nudge chimes in. "That'll ruin it."

Phoenix nods solemnly, eyes wide. You can see her mentally calculating as her eyes flit from face to face.

We face the sprawled green landscape of the rain forest. The sun is a huge eye hanging in front of us, warming our skin. The sky is endless.

One by one, the rest of the flock members take off, their powerful wings pulling them higher and higher into the air. Our V is longer these days as our flock grows, but Angel flies at the center, steering us into the wind, and there are still three spaces at the end, waiting for us to join them.

Phoenix nudges her little feet toward the edge. She takes a breath, and for the first time, when she looks up at me, I see a bit of fear in her eyes. "What if I can't remember it all?"

"Just do what feels right, sweetie," I coach, firmly suppressing my worry.

"You know I would never let you fall," Fang whispers to her with his crooked smile, putting a lump in my throat. "Your mom and I will always be there to catch you."

It's scary at first, but I believe we've all got it in us to soar. Look at me. Like the Remedy once said, I'm really pretty ordinary—just a normal girl slash bird kid slash recombinant life-form who wanted to save the world.

It could've been any of us. Aren't we all just along for the ride?

"Ready?" I ask, squeezing my daughter's hand, while Fang reaches for the other.

"Ready!" Phoenix echoes.

"Now *jump!*"

Also by James Patterson

ALEX CROSS NOVELS

Along Came a Spider • Kiss the Girls • Jack and Jill • Cat and Mouse •
Pop Goes the Weasel • Roses are Red • Violets are Blue • Four Blind Mice •
The Big Bad Wolf • London Bridges • Mary, Mary • Cross • Double Cross •
Cross Country • Alex Cross's Trial (*with Richard DiLallo*) • I, Alex Cross •
Cross Fire • Kill Alex Cross • Merry Christmas, Alex Cross • Alex Cross,
Run • Cross My Heart • Hope to Die

THE WOMEN'S MURDER CLUB SERIES

1st to Die • 2nd Chance (*with Andrew Gross*) • 3rd Degree (*with Andrew
Gross*) • 4th of July (*with Maxine Paetro*) • The 5th Horseman (*with Maxine
Paetro*) • The 6th Target (*with Maxine Paetro*) • 7th Heaven (*with Maxine
Paetro*) • 8th Confession (*with Maxine Paetro*) • 9th Judgement (*with Maxine
Paetro*) • 10th Anniversary (*with Maxine Paetro*) • 11th Hour (*with Maxine
Paetro*) • 12th of Never (*with Maxine Paetro*) • Unlucky 13 (*with Maxine
Paetro*) • 14th Deadly Sin (*with Maxine Paetro*)

DETECTIVE MICHAEL BENNETT SERIES

Step on a Crack (*with Michael Ledwidge*) • Run for Your Life (*with Michael
Ledwidge*) • Worst Case (*with Michael Ledwidge*) • Tick Tock (*with Michael
Ledwidge*) • I, Michael Bennett (*with Michael Ledwidge*) • Gone (*with
Michael Ledwidge*) • Burn (*with Michael Ledwidge*) • Alert (*with Michael
Ledwidge, to be published July 2015*)

PRIVATE NOVELS

Private (*with Maxine Paetro*) • Private London (*with Mark Pearson*) •
Private Games (*with Mark Sullivan*) • Private: No. 1 Suspect (*with Maxine
Paetro*) • Private Berlin (*with Mark Sullivan*) • Private Down Under (*with
Michael White*) • Private L.A. (*with Mark Sullivan*) • Private India (*with
Ashwin Sanghi*) • Private Vegas (*with Maxine Paetro*) • Private Sydney (*with
Kathryn Fox, to be published August 2015*)

NYPD RED SERIES

NYPD Red (*with Marshall Karp*) • NYPD Red 2 (*with
Marshall Karp*) • NYPD Red 3 (*with Marshall Karp*)

STAND-ALONE THRILLERS

Sail (*with Howard Roughan*) • Swimsuit (*with Maxine Paetro*) •
Don't Blink (*with Howard Roughan*) • Postcard Killers (*with Liza
Marklund*) • Toys (*with Neil McMahon*) • Now You See Her (*with Michael
Ledwidge*) • Kill Me If You Can (*with Marshall Karp*) • Guilty Wives (*with
David Ellis*) • Zoo (*with Michael Ledwidge*) • Second Honeymoon (*with
Howard Roughan*) • Mistress (*with David Ellis*) • Invisible (*with David
Ellis*) • The Thomas Berryman Number • Truth or Die (*with Howard
Roughan, to be published June 2015*) • Murder House (*with David Ellis,
to be published September 2015*)

NON-FICTION

Torn Apart (*with Hal and Cory Friedman*) •
The Murder of King Tut (*with Martin Dugard*)

ROMANCE

Sundays at Tiffany's (*with Gabrielle Charbonnet*) • The Christmas
Wedding (*with Richard DiLallo*) • First Love (*with Emily Raymond*)

OTHER TITLES

Miracle at Augusta (*with Peter de Jonge*)

FAMILY OF PAGE-TURNERS

MIDDLE SCHOOL BOOKS

The Worst Years of My Life (*with Chris Tebbetts*) • Get Me Out of
Here! (*with Chris Tebbetts*) • My Brother Is a Big, Fat Liar (*with Lisa
Papademetriou*) • How I Survived Bullies, Broccoli, and Snake Hill (*with
Chris Tebbetts*) • Ultimate Showdown (*with Julia Bergen*) • Save Rafe! (*with
Chris Tebbetts*) • Just My Rotten Luck (*with Chris Tebbetts, to be published
October 2015*)

I FUNNY SERIES

I Funny (*with Chris Grabenstein*) •
I Even Funnier (*with Chris Grabenstein*) •
I Totally Funniest (*with Chris Grabenstein*)

TREASURE HUNTERS SERIES

Treasure Hunters (*with Chris Grabenstein*) •
Danger Down the Nile (*with Chris Grabenstein*)

HOUSE OF ROBOTS

House of Robots (*with Chris Grabenstein*)

KENNY WRIGHT

Kenny Wright: Superhero (*with Chris Tebbetts*)

HOMEROOM DIARIES

Homeroom Diaries (*with Lisa Papademetriou*)

CONFESSIONS SERIES

Confessions of a Murder Suspect (*with Maxine Paetro*) •
The Private School Murders (*with Maxine Paetro*) •
The Paris Mysteries (*with Maxine Paetro*)

WITCH & WIZARD SERIES

Witch & Wizard (*with Gabrielle Charbonnet*) • The Gift (*with Ned Rust*) •
The Fire (*with Jill Dembowski*) • The Kiss (*with Jill Dembowski*) •
The Lost (*with Emily Raymond*)

DANIEL X SERIES

The Dangerous Days of Daniel X (*with Michael Ledwidge*) • Watch the
Skies (*with Ned Rust*) • Demons and Druids (*with Adam Sadler*) •
Game Over (*with Ned Rust*) • Armageddon (*with Chris Grabenstein*)

GRAPHIC NOVELS

Daniel X: Alien Hunter (*with Leopoldo Gout*) •
Maximum Ride: Manga Vols. 1–8 (*with NaRae Lee*)

For more information about James Patterson's novels, visit
www.jamespatterson.co.uk

Or become a fan on Facebook